Big Game CEO

Ozmioz Mak

iUniverse, Inc.
New York   Bloomington

Big Game CEO

Copyright © 2010 Ozmioz Mak

All rights reserved. No part of this book may be used or reproduced by any means, graphic, electronic, or mechanical, including photocopying, recording, taping or by any information storage retrieval system without the written permission of the publisher except in the case of brief quotations embodied in critical articles and reviews.

This is a work of fiction. All of the characters, names, incidents, organizations, and dialogue in this novel are either the products of the author's imagination or are used fictitiously.

iUniverse books may be ordered through booksellers or by contacting:

iUniverse
1663 Liberty Drive
Bloomington, IN 47403
www.iuniverse.com
1-800-Authors (1-800-288-4677)

Because of the dynamic nature of the Internet, any Web addresses or links contained in this book may have changed since publication and may no longer be valid. The views expressed in this work are solely those of the author and do not necessarily reflect the views of the publisher, and the publisher hereby disclaims any responsibility for them.

ISBN: 978-1-4502-0610-5 (pbk)
ISBN: 978-1-4502-0612-9 (cloth)
ISBN: 978-1-4502-0611-2 (ebook)

Printed in the United States of America

iUniverse rev. date: 3/4/10

Contents

Chapter 1: The Fathers 1
Chapter 2: The Sons 43
Chapter 3: The Anarchist 82
Chapter 4: The Ayn Rand Society 100
Chapter 5: The Rose of Scranton 110
Chapter 6: The Tasmanian Producers Festival 119
Chapter 7: The Last Lecture 129
Chapter 8: The Road Trip 141
Chapter 9: The Glory Seekers 148
Chapter 10: The War Seekers 160
Chapter 11: The FBI 175
Chapter 12: The Money Seekers 179
Chapter 13: The Revenge of Ellsworth Toohey 194
Chapter 14: The Power of Love? 210

Zombies, vampires, and werewolves are merely symbols for the dark side of our subconscious. We are scared of the dark because it's real. And there is nothing darker than the depths of an adolescent's soul as he tries to become a man.

— Ozmioz Mak

Chapter 1: The Fathers

Joe and Archie Roark struggle as they carry the buck carcass up the stairs. It has been aging in the basement of Joe's lodge for seven days. With a loud grunt they toss it onto the stainless steel counter of the center island in Joe's kitchen. After taking a deep breath Joe looks over at his older, taller brother, and says, "I just had a brainstorm. This spring the theme for my Literature of the Western World Class will be '*What does it mean to be a man in the modern world?*' The kids will love it."

With his standard alpha-male grin Archie replies, "Those teeny-bopper feminists at your community college will be all over you with that theme."

"You're clueless old man. First off, the culture wars are so 1990s. Second off, there are no culture wars at a community college. Besides, I bet more girls sign up for the course than boys."

Archie replies, "That goes without saying. It's an English course. So what books are you going to cover?"

Joe hesitates. He looks up at the 12"x12" wood beams that support the ceiling of his great room. He then looks out the large picture window overlooking Lake Giles. He answers, "I was thinking Tom Wolfe's *Bonfire of the Vanities*, Fitzgerald's *The Great Gatsby*, Sun Tzu's *The Art of War*, Twain's *Roughing It*, Shakespeare's *Hamlet*, Any Rand's *The Fountainhead*, Jack Schaefer's *Shane*, Hemingway's *A Farewell to Arms*, Dickens's *A Tale of Two Cities*, Herman Melville's *Moby-Dick*,

Salinger's *Catcher in the Rye*, Hawthorne's *The Scarlet Letter*, Steinbeck's *The Grapes of Wrath*, Nietzsche's *Thus Spoke Zarathustra*, Camus's *The Stranger*, and Voltaire's *Candide*."

"That's one hell of a reading list!"

"I like to make sure my students aren't wasting their time drinking their youth away."

"Pull Nietzsche from the reading list. It is too trendy."

"No it's not."

"Yes it is. Besides, do you think community college students have the patience to read Nietzsche? Hell, I didn't have the patience."

"I know, you only read Cliffs Notes."

"It got me through college. I'm sure your students only read Cliffs Notes."

"You really are living in the dark ages. They don't even know what Cliffs Notes are. They all use Wikipedia."

"Students are cheap. There's a shock."

"The more things change, the more they stay the same."

Charlie, the middle brother, walks in from the garage with a large roll of plastic, a reciprocating saw, and a massive 7 ¾" stainless steel Bowie Knife. Without saying a word he unrolls the plastic. Working in perfect unison the three brothers spread the plastic out on one side of the kitchen island. They tilt the buck carcass to the right, reposition the plastic, tilt the buck carcass to the left, pull the plastic under the buck carcass, and with one quick pull Charlie and Archie center the plastic under the buck. With their subtle hand signals and eye gestures guiding their movements it is clear they've butchered a buck many times before.

Charlie quietly cleans his hands at the kitchen sink with soap and water. Using pure grain alcohol he cleans the reciprocating saw and knife. Charlie asks, "Joe, so what was the temperature again?"

Joe replies, "I got ice this year. It never got over 45 degrees."

Holding the knife firmly, and walking slowly around the buck, Charlie smirks, "I don't want a repeat of last year. I can't stand sour meat."

Joe answers, "I'm never going to hear the end of it. Just because we had unseasonable hot weather."

Chapter 1: The Fathers

Charlie says, "You should have gotten ice last year. There is nothing better than perfectly aged deer steaks for Thanksgiving." Joe begins to say something but Charlie points at the fatal arrow wound, runs his hand along the spine, and cuts Joe off, "The boys have come a long way. They did a great job with the field dressing. They didn't cut through any of the ribs, and they skinned the deer without pulling off any of the flesh."

Archie says, "They're starting to think they are better outdoors men than us."

Charlie replies, "They're young. They think youth is more important than experience." Taking the reciprocating saw, Charlie quickly cuts the carcass into left and right halves. Archie and Joe hold plastic near the saw blade to make sure blood doesn't splatter on the walls or floor of Joe's recently built lodge. After making the cut, Charlie says, "The old timers use a hacksaw. What a waste of time."

Joe dries each half of the buck carcass with a slightly damp cloth. Charlie removes the rump and rear legs with the Bowie Knife. He sharpens the knife then quickly cuts perfect 1" thick steaks. Next he slices off a large portion for a pot roast. Joe wraps each piece of meat in butcher paper and writes down the type of cut with a black marker. Archie positions the carcass for the next step.

Charlie removes the loin, which runs down the sides of the deer's spine. He says, "I like to slice the loin into three or four thinner pieces. It makes for better cooking." Charlie then proceeds to the chest area, removing several cuts, including two more pot roasts. He then removes the ribs and says, "I like to leave the ribs as a full rack. They grill up better."

Archie says, "Let's have the ribs tonight."

Charlie says, "Call Jimmy and Nick. We can get a poker game going after the barbeque."

Archie washes his hands, pulls out his cell phone, and walks over to the mudroom to make the calls. Joe stops his job of wrapping the cuts of meat, washes his hands, and takes Archie's position holding the front legs. After sharpening the knife again, Charlie continues making cuts - smaller steaks from the front legs, and then removing the meat from the neck and chest area.

Joe says, "I can already taste the venison chili."

Charlie says, "This buck has more good meat than I was expecting."

Just then Charlie's son Danny walks into the room and says, "The one Bobby got is even bigger."

Joe says, "I didn't know Bobby got one."

Danny says, "This morning from 350 feet."

Charlie says, "There is no way he killed a buck from 350 feet. The best professional archers in the world can't kill from that distance."

Danny replies, "He had a little help from the elevation. We were standing at the edge of a cliff and shooting down at a 45 degree angle."

Charlie says, "It's a little unethical to shoot from that distance. The last thing you want to do is leave a wounded animal in the woods."

Danny says, "You should see the kill wound. Right through the eye."

Joe says, "Right through the eye from 350 feet. Jesus."

Danny says, "We didn't even have to track it. It went about 25 yards before collapsing. With our new bows we could take down a buck from 600 feet."

Charlie asks his son, "When did you get new bows?"

Danny answers, "A few weeks ago."

Charlie says, "I didn't know you were working."

"Bobby's been getting us jobs waiting tables at these exclusive events. The pay is good."

Joe decides to change the subject knowing that it is a sore point with Charlie about his son's lack of career choices, "So Danny, what kind of compound bow did you get?"

Danny says, "Wait a second." He steps onto the deck and returns holding the compound bow in front of him like a fine piece of art. "All three of us bought one of these, the latest in the IceMan series from Diamond."

Joe says, "It's beautiful."

Danny replies, "Just like a supermodel, beautiful and deadly. Single cam technology, precision machined aluminum risers, and noise dampening InVelvet coating. This bow doesn't make a sound. The buck falls dead, and the deer standing next to him doesn't even know what happened."

Chapter 1: The Fathers

Joe says, "What's the arrow speed?"

Danny answers, "Spec sheet says 300 feet per second. I made some adjustments. We had the radar gun out last night doing speed contests. We were all above 320. Howie won with 337 feet per second."

Joe says, "That's almost 30% the speed of sound."

As he finishes his last cut of meat from the carcass, Charlie looks up at his 19 year-old son, Danny, then over to his 51 year-old younger brother, Joe, and says, "I suddenly feel old."

Dan proudly stands there, overly self-confident. He flashes a nothing in the world can stop me smile. Holding up the IceMan with his left hand, and slightly drawing the bow with a pretend arrow with his right, Danny squints a little, as if he is about to take down something big. He confidently says, "And the best part of the IceMan is no sound. With a rifle you don't get a second chance. With the IceMan you can strike twice before your prey knows what's going on. After the first shot they have no idea where you're standing. When I killed the buck your cutting up right now, there were three deer nearby. They all ran right towards me. If I wanted I could have taken them all down."

Archie finishes making the calls to Jimmy and Nick. He returns to the room and says, "That's quite a weapon."

With a big grin of his face, Danny proudly says, "We were shooting clay pigeons last night."

His Uncle Archie replies, "No way."

"I'm up to almost 50%."

"You can't hit a clay pigeon with an arrow. I don't believe you."

With complete confidence Danny challenges his uncle, "I know I've never beaten you in a bet, so let's put our money on the Thanksgiving table. Wild turkey tomorrow."

"With an arrow?"

"Yes, with an arrow."

"Standard bet?"

"Standard bet. Sun-up to sun-down time limit."

Archie smiles and says, "This is one bet I hope I lose. Wild turkey on Thanksgiving would be quite a treat."

Danny grabs a Red Bull enery drink out of the fridge and heads back downstairs to be with his cousins, Howie and Bobby. They are playing pool in the basement.

Big Game CEO

Joe finishes packaging the deer meat while Charlie and Archie clean up the remains of the carcass. Joe puts 15 pounds worth of steaks in the refrigerator, places the ribs and a few pounds of meat for venison chili on the counter for tonight's barbeque, and then takes the remaining cuts downstairs to the freezer. When he returns Archie and Charlie are having a beer. Joe says, "Only twenty-five minutes. We should get a job on the NASCAR circuit." Charlie and Archie just smile.

Charlie tips his beer and says, "This definitely beats church."

That Sunday over lunch Archie, Charlie, and Joe talk about hunting – they discuss if they have enough meat for the year, which they already know the answer. The three brothers just enjoy saying over and over again that rifle season is still two weeks away and anything they get this year they will have to give away. It is their polite way of bragging about their sons, and their sons' hunting prowess.

For the fathers that Sunday afternoon before Thanksgiving is spent lounging around, watching professional football on television, preparing for the evening barbeque, and admiring the construction of Joe's new lodge. For the cousins they work a catered event at the Lake Isle Country Club in Eastchester. The boys don't even know what the event is about other than it has something to do with hedge fund managers.

Lucille McKee, the caterer, likes Bobby and the boys. She pays them $200 each for making the extra long trip to that part of the City from Lords Valley, Pennsylvania. The boys don't mind the hour-long road trip. Since the money is under the table and tax free, it is an excellent paycheck for an afternoon's work.

Howie and Danny constantly joke that Bobby and the fifty-something Lucille, with her black and silver hair, are having an affair. Howie and Danny's favorite jab is, "Hey Bobby, isn't it time to service the salt and pepper." But Bobby and Lucille aren't having an affair. Lucille knows it is difficult to find hard working, clean-shaven, polished and polite white boys to cater events. Plus, they are all handsome, especially Howie. Lucille isn't stupid. Howie always works the bar, and for women's events she positions the bar in a prominent location so the ladies have a constant view of his eye-candy. Those three boys, especially Howie, give her catering business a leg up on the competition. Her

Chapter 1: The Fathers

reputation is growing. Even with the downturn in the economy she is able to charge more, and land more exclusive events. With the holiday season coming up she wants to stay on the boys' good side.

That Sunday before Thanksgiving is unusually warm. The sun is shining, there is a slight breeze from the south, and the high reaches 70 degrees. Howie, Danny, and Bobby return to the lodge around seven o'clock. Their fathers have just put the second set of ribs on the grill.

Everyone is on the deck, including their dads' friends Jimmy and Nick. As Danny walks up the stairs of the deck to the all male affair, Jimmy reaches into a cooler and tosses Danny a beer. Nick whispers to Jimmy, "I don't think he's 21 yet."

Jimmy replies, "Give me a break. Are you a woman? He's working. How much older do you have to be?"

Howie's father, Archie, overhears Nick's comment and chimes in, "Age laws are for losers. If the politicians had their way they'd make us all wear diapers."

Bobby sets a large container of coleslaw and another container of fruit on the table. The food was leftover from the Lake Isle Country Club event. No one touches the coleslaw or fruit. Tonight's dinner is simply deer ribs and beer. Charlie holds up his beer and says, "It doesn't get better than this."

After dinner Charlie starts a fire in the fire pit. Archie and Nick set up the poker table on the deck. Joe brings out the cards and poker chips. The men ask the boys if they want to join them. Charlie's son Danny jokes, "Would I have more fun losing my money here, or in Port Jervis at Johnnie's Topless Go-Go?" The men laugh. They then spend a few minutes discussing the local strip clubs and how things have and haven't changed since when they were nineteen.

Howie, Danny, and Bobby then head over to the north side of Joe's forty-two acres. The north side of the property is where they practice shooting clay pigeons with their new compound bows. There is a steep hill they can shoot into. This way they don't have to chase the arrows very far.

The fathers, Jimmy Gatz, and Nick Carraway are dealing their second hand of Texas hold'em when they hear Howie yell "Pull!"

Jimmy asks, "Where's the gun shot?"

Archie proudly says, "They're shooting clay pigeons with arrows."

Nick says, "I can't believe that. I've got to see this."

The men stand and walk around Joe's wrap-around deck to the north side of his house. Jimmy says, "This is the most beautiful deck I've ever seen."

Nick asks, "Who built it?"

Joe replies, "We built it Labor Day weekend. The three of us and the boys."

Archie proudly adds, "My son Howie designed it."

Jimmy says, "He designed a hell of a deck. Two years ago I could have used him. Now there's no business."

Archie says, "I know. Everybody knows there's no new construction."

From the north side of the house the men can see everything. The boys have parked everyone's truck facing the field, and turned on all the brights, fog lights, and spot lights. The field is lit up like a high school football field in Texas on a Friday night.

Bobby is to the right of Danny manning a clay pigeon thrower. Howie is to the left manning a second. Danny readies his IceMan compound bow and yells, "Pull!" Bobby launches a clay pigeon. Danny shoots an arrow. He hits the clay pigeon. A small piece of clay breaks off. The main body of the clay pigeon ricochets slightly to the left and the arrow ricochets downward. It is not like shooting a clay pigeon with a shotgun where the clay pigeon breaks into a hundred pieces but everyone there understands this is a thousand times more impressive.

Danny quickly and smoothly pulls a second arrow from the pack on his back, reloads, draws the compound bow back and yells, "Pull!" Howie launches a second clay pigeon. Same result, the arrow hits the clay pigeon. Danny pulls a third arrow from the pack on his back, reloads, and yells, "Pull!" Bobby launches another clay pigeon. Same result, the arrow hits the clay pigeon. Danny pulls a fourth arrow from the pack on his back, reloads, and yells, "Pull!" Howie launches another clay pigeon. This time he misses. Danny stomps his foot once and yells, "Damn It!"

Bobby says, "Your record is still four in a row."

Chapter 1: The Fathers

The five men standing on the deck look at each other in disbelief. Nick Carraway breaks the silence and says, "Jesus Christ, what was that?"

Jimmy adds, "I've never seen anything like it."

Hearing the voices, the boys realize the five older men are watching them. The boys move away from the beams of truck lights and adjust their eyes to the surrounding darkness. Howie, the leader of three, yells to the deck, "Do you want to try?"

Jimmy yells back, "That's some pretty impressive archery!"

Danny yells, "We're practicing for tomorrow's bet!"

Nick asks Archie, "What bet?"

Archie answers, "That they can kill a wild turkey tomorrow with an arrow."

Jimmy says, "This is classic."

The men and the boys talk for about ten minutes. They discuss the bet. Jimmy mentions he saw a group of wild turkeys in the morning over by Billings Pond. They spend most of the time discussing the best hunting locations. Danny mentions they plan to split up to cover more ground. Nick questions the strategy, suggesting it is better to form a line. Howie supports Danny's plan. Danny's father, Charlie, just says, "By tomorrow evening we'll know if the plan worked." The conversation ends. The boys go back to their target practice. The men resume their poker game.

After a half hour of target practice the three cousins head back to their apartment in Port Jervis. They want to get to bed early since the plan is to be in the woods before sunrise. The five older divorced men play poker until 11 PM, talking about what five divorced men in their early fifties typically talk about – business, government, sports, their sons, their ex-wives, and other divorced women. Here's a portion of the conversation from the poker game.

Archie says, "Someone's not in."

Charlie pushes his chips to the center of the table, "Sorry about that."

While Archie is dealing Nick asks, "So, is your son Howie still dating that billionaire's daughter?"

Archie answers, "He hasn't talked about her in a while. I don't think they were ever really dating. He was more like her boy toy."

Nick replies, "When I was his age I wish I was some hot heiress's boy toy."

Joe says, "Why his age? I wish I were the boy toy of some hot heiress right now. It would sure beat playing poker with you guys."

Archie asks, "What heiress is going to chase a fifty year old man?"

Joe answers, "You know what the people at the New York Lottery say, 'A dollar and a dream'."

Archie says, "You writers are always dreaming."

Charlie asks Jimmy Gatz, "Speaking of billionaires and dream homes, is Toll Brothers going to resume the Sparrow Bush development?"

Jimmy answers, "I just talked with their management team Friday. It will be at least another two years before they restart Sparrow Bush."

In a disheartened tone Nick says, "Tell them what else they told you."

Jimmy looks around the table, "They showed me their latest market analysis. Bottom line is the U.S. is turning into Europe. Most kids will live with their parents until they're forty before buying their first house."

Archie says, "Now that's a scary thought."

Charlie adds, "I keep wondering if Danny's going to move back in with his mother. Ever since his career in retail ended when Circuit City closed down I don't know how he's making it. Must be selling pot or something."

Joe says, "You heard the boys today. They're making good money waiting tables."

Charlie sarcastically replies, "Now that's another long-term career option."

"Danny will be fine." Joe's happy-go-lucky smile widens. He tosses two chips in the pot and says, "I bet two dollars."

Nick continues, "I don't know if there's a light at the end of the tunnel to this housing crisis. That's the problem with subcontracting work. It's all boom or bust. And when things go bust the big guys cut you off immediately."

Jimmy adds, "This downturn feels different."

Chapter 1: The Fathers

Archie says, "I read that 75% of the people laid-off during this recession have been men. That's because manufacturing and finance have been hit hard."

Charlie says, "No, it's because the country's built. Women don't need real men anymore. All the jobs are in health care and education. Just look at the table. I work as a maintenance man at the Orange Regional Medical Center and Joe teaches at Luzerne."

Nick tosses two chips into the pot and says, "In." Nick then shakes his head and continues, "Joe, you're lucky teaching at the community college. The work is steady."

Joe says, "But the pay sucks. I have to supplement my income working summers, stealing office supplies, and playing poker with you guys. And that barely pays my property taxes."

Nick asks, "So what was the assessment?"

The smile on Joe's usually upbeat face disappears. He sighs and answers, "$790,000."

Jimmy yells, "That's ridiculous! How much did you spend on building supplies?"

Joe answers, "I shopped around. Only $215,000. I even drove all the way over to Kellogg to cut down the oak tree that I used for the cabinetry and bookcases, and all the way to Canada to get the composite material for the deck."

Charlie says, "Don't get Joe started on the cabinetry and bookcases. He'll bore us for hours."

Nick says, "The woodwork is gorgeous."

Charlie cuts Nick off, "Don't get Joe started."

Jimmy says, "You should have got the appraisal before you built the deck."

Archie says, "It ain't right. A man does the right thing by building a house with his own two hands and not taking out a loan. Then the government tries to steal his hard work through taxes."

Nick says, "At least your not paying property tax in New York."

Jimmy tosses his cards in the pot and says, "Just like my business, I'm out."

Archie asks, "What do you mean, just like your business?"

Jimmy replies, "There's no work. I'm laying off everyone but four guys tomorrow. Nick's the only one that knows."

Knowing that his primary job function is to support his boss, Nick says, "The guys aren't stupid. They've been sitting around on their butts for the last two months. We've already had two rounds of layoffs. The handwriting is on the wall."

Jimmy replies, "It's painful. I spent thirty years building up my business. Right now I'm bleeding money. I could make more money as a Wal-Mart greeter."

Trying to lighten the conversation, Joe asks, "Since when did Wal-Mart greeter become everyone's fallback job?"

Charlie, trying to be funny like Joe, answers, "Since China's colon, I mean Wal-Mart, took over the damn country like a virus." However the joke comes off as mostly bitter.

Joe, not wanting Charlie to start into one of his angry tirades, jokes, "If Wal-Mart is China's colon, does that make a Wal-Mart greeter an anal polyp?" Everyone laughs.

Archie deals the next round of cards. Joe tosses two more chips in the pot and says, "Two more dollars to stay in." He then says to Jimmy, "Sorry to hear about your business."

Jimmy replies, "Don't worry about me, I'll be fine. Even with the beating my 401K has taken the last few months, I've still got enough stashed away. I'm just worried about all the guys I'm laying off."

In a clearly bitter tone Charlie says, "We don't build a damn thing here anymore. What kind of future are we leaving our sons?"

Jimmy says, "And our sons, sons? They'll all have to join the Taliban to rediscover their manhood."

Joe replies, "Now that's warped."

Charlie adds, "But there's a lot of truth to what Jimmy just said."

Archie subconsciously sits up straight to let everyone know he is the tallest man at the table. There is an unwritten competition between Jimmy and Archie. The competition is friendly but intense. Both played football in college and today both are businessmen. Jimmy is far and away the most successful of the group, but everyone at the table knows Archie's business is on the way up and Jimmy's is on the way down. Unaware of his highly competitive nature, Archie looks Jimmy straight in the eye and boasts, "I'm thinking of buying an old apartment building. If I do then I'll make sure you get all the renovation work."

Jimmy says, "Thanks."

Chapter 1: The Fathers

Nick asks, "So how's the apartment business?"

Archie answers, "The bright side of this mortgage meltdown is everyone is moving back into apartments. Two years ago my vacancy rate was 20%. I thought I was going to have to file for bankruptcy. Now my vacancy rate is below 5%."

Jimmy asks, "Where are you looking to buy?"

Archie answers, "College district in Scranton."

Nick replies, "Smart move. College students always rent. With the market depressed now's the time to buy."

Archie deals the next round of cards. Joe says, "Another two dollars." Archie and Nick each toss two dollars in the pot. Charlie nervously peels small pieces of the label off his beer bottle. He fidgets, as if worried about being laid-off again. Joe again says, "Another two dollars."

Charlie starts to fold but then tosses two dollars in the pot.

Nick asks Archie, "You worked on Wall Street for a while. What's your take on this financial mess we're in now?"

Archie, subconsciously wanting to establish that he is the intellectual alpha-male of the group, answers, "The financial wizards on Wall Street aren't the geniuses they claim to be. The based all their hedges on the Black-Shoals equation. But the noise in the stock market has a 1/f distribution. That's the same noise distribution as earthquakes. And every once in a while you get a big earthquake. They knew full well that a highly leveraged system had to collapse at some point."

Nick blurts out, "What the hell are you talking about?"

Jimmy answers, "In other words those managers only care about their next big bonus. Why the hell should I or anybody else work when they simply steal from the system left and right?"

Charlie says, "The rich are rich because they're spoiled brats. They cry and cry unless they have everything for themselves."

Joe says, "Hey Uncle Sam, give me, give me, give me."

Nick adds, "When economic times get tough it is socialism for the rich and capitalism for the poor."

Charlie adds, "The rich are nothing but socialist thieves."

Archie continues with his alpha-male editorial, "Look at Goldman Sachs. They drove Long-Term Capital, Bear Stearns, Lehman Brothers, and many other smaller companies out of business. When Goldman Sachs sees weakness they execute a short squeeze. For the executives

Big Game CEO

at Goldman Sachs moral behavior is destroying other companies to make a profit. But when they find themselves in a vulnerable position to a short squeeze with the imminent collapse of AIG, they run to the government to bailout AIG and save their own ass."

Charlie says, "Politicians are financial amateurs. They have no clue when they are getting grifted."

Nick adds, "Yeah, where's my bailout?"

Charlie says, "Those Wall Street types don't give a damn about this country."

Jimmy says, "You know the system is in trouble when the government starts playing favorites. Why should Wall Street get bailed out in favor of Main Street?"

Charlie says, "This is why our ancestors left Europe. To get away from Old World Trash like Goldman Sachs and their game playing."

Nick says, "Yeah, where's my Main Street bailout?"

Charlie asks the rhetorical question, "When's the last time you saw an executive drive an American made car?"

Joe jokes, "Come on. Everyone knows they only care about getting a bigger bonus so they can buy a bigger yacht named the S.S. Fellatio. And if we were in their position we would be doing the same thing." Everyone laughs.

Charlie mutters, "S.S. Fellatio, I like that."

Nick says, "It is true. I'd do the same thing. I'd want to take a ride on the S.S. Fellatio."

Jimmy says, "It's still not right. Why should any of us work when the guys on the inside simply steal from the system?"

Nick says, "To change the subject slightly, you know Sydney Carton. He lost all his money day trading."

Archie says, "That's the problem with Wall Street. Over the last thirty years it has changed from an investment market into a speculation market."

Nick says, "It's all the Internet's fault. The only thing meaningless information is good for is speculating and grifting."

Joe says, "You should say, 'It's all the Internuts fault'."

Jimmy adds, "My kids are a couple of Internuts. They spend all their time on the computer. My youngest is into online poker."

Chapter 1: The Fathers

Charlie sarcastically adds, "What do you expect? Even the government is pushing get rich quick schemes. They should change the New York Lottery slogan to *you've got to be in it to win it – sucker*."

An uncharacteristically depressed look comes over Joe's face. He says, "I feel sorry for Sydney's family. Day trading is like the slots; it's a lonely mental illness. No one is there to tell you that you've gone to far. So did he lose his business?"

Jimmy answers, "Both restaurants."

Charlie says, "That's a shame."

Archie, still in his alpha-male mode, drops in one of his editorials, "The whole damn market is an out of control fraternity house. The people running the show have no clue that it took generations to build the stock market to where it is now, and that the purpose of the stock market is about handing off control of society to the next generation."

Nick asks, "Again, what the hell are you talking about?"

Archie deals the next round of cards and says, "Each generation passes their knowledge and know how to the next generation before they retire. Problem is all our high level managers were busy pushing worthless paper as reality, and those managers ordered us grunts to pass all our knowledge and know how to China."

Charlie adds, "And are the Chinese going to pay for our Social Security with their taxes when were old? I don't think so."

Joe says, "You two should get a show on Fox News." He tosses some chips into the pot and says, "Two more dollars."

Charlie peels the remainder of the label from his beer bottle. After a sigh he tosses his cards on the pile, "I'm out."

Archie says, "I'm out too."

Nick says, "Joe, I don't like the look on your face, but here's two dollars just to keep you honest. What do you have?"

Joe turns over his cards and says, "Full house."

Nick tosses his cards to the center of the table and says, "This is clearly your night." Joe rakes in his winnings.

Everyone throws money into the pot. Jimmy starts to deal the next hand and says, "Back to basics. Five-card draw. Jacks or better, trips to win."

Charlie says, "I can't stand that Fed Chairman, Ben Bernanke. Economists."

Big Game CEO

Jimmy interjects, "Yeah, economists are nothing but grifters with a pedigree."

Charlie continues, "All a Harvard education teaches you is how to be a grifter. Investment bankers live in a fantasyland. How can you give Bernanke that much power when he never managed a real business?"

Joe adds, "I heard that when Bernanke was in his early twenties he worked at South of the Border."

Nick asks, "You mean that tacky tourist trap in South Carolina on I-95?"

"Yes."

Archie says, "Figures. Bernanke is a tourist trap. The last thing this country needs is more consumer credit. Consumer credit is Wall Street's version of welfare. The last thing our culture needs is more dependency."

Charlie says, "People should get paid for work and that's it."

Archie agrees, "Exactly. They've got to start paying people more money for doing honest work."

Jimmy adds, "Instead of paying rich boys and government officials to steal from the system."

Charlie continues, "And tell me a government employee that does an honest days work."

Nick adds, "If you want to spend your life doing meaningless work then take a job with the government."

Jimmy asks the table, "Can anyone open?" Nobody replies. Everyone tosses Jimmy their cards. Jimmy says, "Two more dollars to stay in." He then deals the next hand.

Nick says, "Changing the subject, did you hear that Ellsworth Toohey is having an affair with Council Woman Wilson."

Joe asks, "You mean Myrtle Wilson?"

Nick answers, "Yes."

Charlie asks, "I thought he was having an affair with Maria Ruskin over at the Development Board in White Plains."

Joe says, "I guess some guys just love the ins and outs of City Hall." Everyone smiles.

Jimmy adds, "If you're going to get screwed by government."

Nick adds, "It's good to see that someone is getting a return on their taxes." Everyone laughs.

Chapter 1: The Fathers

Joe says, "The next time I see Ellsworth remind me to call him Mr. Pool Boy."

Jimmy says, "Can you imagine that fat bastard with his handlebar mustache in a Speedo swimsuit?"

Joe raises his beer, "A toast, to us angry tax paying middle-aged males who have to support everyone."

The others reply, "A toast."

They clink their beer bottles over the table. Joe's bottle foams up and spills over, dripping beer on the chips. He pulls it back quickly. Jimmy says, "Hey, be careful. I don't like playing with wet chips."

Joe laughs and says, "Sorry about that."

Nick says, "At least you didn't get any beer on the cards."

Charlie asks Nick, "Speaking of Myrtle Wilson, what do you think about her cousin, Sairy Wilson?"

"From high school?"

Charlie answers, "That's the one."

Joe asks, "Is she divorced?"

Charlie replies, "Almost two years."

Nick replies, "I was checking out her Face Book page the other night. Sairy is still cute. I wouldn't marry her but I'd do her."

Joe adds, "I'd do her too."

Charlie turns to his younger brother and says, "If no one was looking you'd do a dead deer on the side of the road."

Knowing humor is the best way to deal with Charlie, Joe takes a big swig of beer to collect his thoughts, then replies, "Depends on whether it was a good looking deer and how many beers are in my system." Everyone laughs.

Jimmy says, "Speaking of women and getting screwed, there's a new hair salon in Port Jervis that charges $350 for a hair cut."

Archie asks, "How the hell do you know about this place?"

Joe adds, "Yeah, that's a pretty crappy haircut for $350."

Jimmy smiles and says, "It's because my ex-wife is using my alimony money to get her hair cut there."

Charlie asks, "How can they charge $350?"

Jimmy, with a gay affectation, says, "They serve wine when they style your hair."

Charlie says, "You've got to be kidding."

Big Game CEO

Archie asks, "Sure they're not serving cocaine?"

Joe says, "Hey Archie, you should become a metrosexual. With the right superficial renovations I bet you could add $200 a month to your tenants rent."

Archie just shakes his head. He then says, "It's true, homosexuals are my best tenants. They don't have kids to destroy the place, and since they don't have kids they have extra money to spend on the nicer apartments."

Nick says, "You know what I hate about my ex-wife. She has no clue she is a lousy driver. Every time she came home she'd tell these horrendous stories of how somebody almost hit her. Then she would start rambling on and on about how no one knows how to drive."

Charlie says, "My second wife did the same thing. Drove me up the wall."

Archie adds, "If the government ever did what was right they'd outlaw women from driving and talking on a cell phone at the same time."

Nick says, "I'd support that law."

Charlie says, "Imagine the uproar if they tried to pass a women's only law."

Archie adds, "But the uproar would be fun. It's always fun when women are forced to confront the truth. They make up the craziest stories."

Nick says, "Like how everyone else is a lousy driver."

In an effort to show the table that it is not only Archie who understands how the world works, Jimmy says, "I bet car insurance companies have data on accidents and cell phone use."

Nick says, "I'd like to see a male / female breakdown of that data."

Jimmy says, "Back to business. Can anyone open?"

Archie says, "Two dollars."

Joe smile widens as he says, "Here's two, and I'll raise you five dollars."

Archie, in his alpha-male tone, asserts, "You're an easy read younger brother. You're bluffing. You don't have three of a kind. I'll see your five dollars."

Nick tosses his cards on top of the pot, "I'm getting while the getting is cheap."

Chapter 1: The Fathers

Jimmy puts seven dollars in the pot, "I'll stick around."

Looking at his beer bottle with no label, Charlie says, "I'm with Nick. I'm out."

Archie draws three cards, Jimmy three cards, and Joe two cards. Nick says, "He only drew two cards. He must have three of a kind."

Archie asserts, "He's bluffing. You can tell by his shit eating grin."

Joe doesn't even look at the two cards he drew, "Five dollars."

Archie and Jimmy, each with a competitive look in their eye, push five dollars into the pot and say, "In."

Joe says, "Let's see you're openers."

Archie turns over a pair of kings.

Joe then turns over his cards. He has a 2, 3, 5, 7, and 9. Jimmy laughs and then says to Nick, "At least you got out early."

Jimmy deals a new hand to just Joe, Archie, and himself. Charlie stands and walks over to the cooler to get another beer. Joe says, "Get me one too."

"What kind?"

"Saranac pomegranate wheat."

Nick exclaims, "Pomegranate wheat? You know how gay that sounds."

Joe replies, "It's really good." He then yells across the deck to Charlie, "Bring Nick a pomegranate wheat also."

Charlie returns. Nick takes a sip. "This is good."

Jimmy says, "Maybe you're both becoming metrosexual in your old age."

Archie adds, "Or 100% gay."

Charlie says, "Speaking of gay, so when did all the council men become council women?"

Archie answers, "It's all part of their master plan to take over the country."

Jimmy says, "That's the problem with America these days. We are becoming a country run by a bunch of women."

Joe says, "I just heard a few days ago that at most colleges the female co-ops are now making more money than the male co-ops."

Archie says, "That's because we are becoming a country run by a bunch of women, and all women do is value unnecessary work. They love coming up with new programs that create new dependencies."

Nick asks the rhetorical question, "You know why women love creating a culture of dependency? It's in their genes. They're all mothers at heart. And they only find value in their lives if they think someone needs them."

Jimmy says, "It's all G.I.D., Government Induced Dependency."

Charlie says, "Next time I see my bitch ex-wife Jordan, I'll call her my giddy girl."

Nick asks, "Jordan still work for the Department of Social Services?"

Charlie looks down and answers, "Yes! And she still has Danny collecting welfare checks. Bitch is gaming the system and Danny's becoming a sponge."

Nick says, "It's just wrong for a 19 year-old white boy to collect welfare."

Archie says, "What do you expect? Just look at how complicated the tax laws are. Every time the government makes the system more complicated, they are telling their citizens to game the system. The government rigs the system for conniving spineless bastards to succeed. Most people don't even realize they can't tell the difference between moral and immoral behavior any more."

Charlie adds, "Pretty soon the whole country will be like the 'we cash checks here' part of White Plains."

Joe replies, "Now that's a scary thought."

Nick says, "Don't you mean the 'we cash checks here' part of Black Plains?"

Charlie answers, "Exactly."

Archie says, "Government is only good for lazy or old people who have time to waste standing in line, filling out forms, and listening to meaningless debates."

Jimmy says, "I was up in Brewster a few days ago. That place has gone down hill in a hurry."

Charlie asks, "Spics?"

Jimmy answers, "Spics."

Joe, not wanting Charlie to start into one of his blue-collar editorial tirades, says to Charlie, "Do you mind tossing a few logs in the fire pit?"

Charlie says, "No problem."

Chapter 1: The Fathers

Nick says, "This is the warmest November I can remember. Think there's any truth to this global warming?"

Joe is bored with the topic of global warming. Knowing that the conversation will end with statements such as 'Nothing leaves a larger carbon footprint than flying in a yuppie corporate jet', 'Greens never had to worry about paying for their grocery bills', 'Politicians would have you believe that the Earth is going to hurl itself into the sun and spontaneously combust', and 'For liberals global warming is the cult equivalent to the Ends of Days and the rapture' he cuts the discussion short with a joke, "Hope global warming is true. I'm tired of hunting deer. We need the dinosaurs to return. The added challenge will spice things up a bit."

Jimmy asks Joe and Archie, "Either of you have openers?"

Both reply, "No." Jimmy gathers the cards and deals again.

Nick says, "Times have changed. I read last week that more and more women are using sperm donors."

Joe says, "Look on the bright side. That means there are more and more women looking to have meaningless sex."

Nick says, "I also read that if you're not over six feet tall there's zero chance of a women selecting your sperm from a catalog."

Joe adds, "Sperm from a catalog? Since when did L. L. Bean get into the reproductive business?"

Jimmy says, "I guess size does matter."

Charlie adds, "I guess that means I'll never be a grandfather. Danny is only five ten." The table is quiet for a moment. Everyone looks at Archie. He is the only one at the table over six feet tall. At 6'3", Archie is an imposing figure. And at 55 years old he is still in remarkably good physical shape. The only one in the family that is more imposing that Archie is his 6'4" son, Howie. Although they would never admit it, both his brothers, Charlie and Joe, are jealous of Archie and his son Howie.

Jimmy breaks the silence and asks Joe and Archie, "Either of you have openers?"

Again both reply, "No." Jimmy gathers the cards and deals again.

Nick asks Archie, "So how's Howie doing?"

"Right now he's living with his cousins, Bobby and Danny, in my apartment complex in Port Jervis."

Nick replies, "I didn't know that."

Archie continues, "He's planning on going back to Cornell next year to finish his degree."

Joe looks at Archie and adds, "Getting hired by a big firm and then immediately laid-off has to be tough."

Archie says, "I can tell he's changed."

Nick asks, "What do you mean?"

Archie answers, "I can't put my finger on it."

Joe adds, "He used to be totally focused on architecture. Now he's into hunting and playing with Danny and Bobby in a band. I think the lay-off and the year out of school will turn out to be a good thing in the end."

Archie says, "Maybe. But he does owe almost three hundred thousand in loans."

Jimmy says, "Holy shit!"

Archie says, "If they'd quit giving out all these government backed loans the price of college would come roaring down."

Nick says, "Dependency."

Charlie adds, "Bankers and the government, they're nothing but a bunch of criminals pimping immoral behavior."

Archie says, "Criminals of dependency."

Nick adds, "At least when the criminals ran the lottery you got 85% of you're money back."

Archie says, "The root cause of the problem is that investment bankers see America as one big war zone, and each household as a battlefield. Their strategy is to get each family to owe them as much money as possible. Don't you feel like you're constantly under assault?"

Nick replies, "Not just investment bankers. The government, hospitals, insurance companies, credit card companies, and colleges – seems like they all want a piece of me."

Jimmy says, "Debts been a part of life for thousands of years. Archie, I wouldn't worry about Howie. That son of yours is one hell of an architect. This deck is amazing. He'll have those loans paid off in no time."

Archie proudly says, "You should see his portfolio. It's incredible."

Talking like a businessman, Jimmy says, "If you get a chance bring his portfolio by my office."

Chapter 1: The Fathers

Archie replies, "How about next week?" Jimmy nods in agreement.

Jimmy then asks Joe and Archie, "Can either of you open?"

Both say no. Jimmy then says, "I can. Five dollars to you." Joe and Archie each put five dollars in the pot. Next Joe draws three cards. Archie shows Jimmy an ace and draws four cards. Jimmy draws zero cards.

Jimmy tosses five dollars in the pot, "Five more dollars to you."

Joe says, "I'll raise another five dollars."

Archie says, "Unfortunately I've come this far." He tosses ten dollars in the pot.

Joe says, "Let's see the openers."

Jimmy turns over his cards, "King high straight."

Archie says, "Jesus, you dealt yourself a king high straight."

Nick says, "Sweet."

Jimmy starts to rake in the pot. Joe yells, "Wait!"

Jimmy says, "Now what?"

Joe says, "I've got a full house."

Jimmy says, "Another full house. You lucky son of a bitch."

Joe says, "You're the one who dealt me three sevens on the draw."

Charlie says, "I guess it's your night."

The deal passes to Charlie. He says, "Let's spread the wealth a little bit. High Chicago."

Archie asks, "Is the ace of spades high or low?"

Charlie sarcastically replies, "Of course it's high." Charlie deals two cards down and one up to each player. Charlie says, "King of spades is high. Archie starts the betting."

Archie says, "Why couldn't that king of spades been dealt face down. Oh well. Two dollars to get things started." Everyone tosses two dollars in the pot.

Jimmy says, "Speaking of Ellsworth Toohey, I ran into him a few weeks ago."

Charlie asks, "How's he doing?"

Jimmy answers, "Pretty darn good. He has several businesses now. His construction business just landed a fat government contract to resurface 15 and 206."

Nick says, "All part of the federal government's stimulus plan."

Archie asks, "What other businesses does Ellsworth own?"

Jimmy answers, "I know he also has a machine shop making specialized parts for some big defense contractor. He's also into big building construction. He owns a few other businesses but I don't know what they are."

Archie says, "Back in high school I always thought Ellsworth was gay."

Joe replies, "You think everyone is gay."

Charlie says, "He should be gay with a name like Ellsworth. I can't believe he has two mistresses."

Nick says, "That's not all. I heard he has a college-aged mistress and that she is drop dead gorgeous."

Charlie asks, "Where does this guy find all the free time?"

Jimmy says, "He doesn't need any free time. It's the money. Money is like a magnet when it comes to women. "

Joe says, "Yeah, men think with their penises and women think with their credit cards."

Archie asks, "And where did he find a college-aged mistress?"

Nick replies, "Where else, the Internet."

Charlie asks, "At eHarmony or Match.com?"

Joe says, "Probably from SeekingArrangement.com."

Jimmy asks, "What's that?"

Joe says, "One of my students brought up SeekingArrangement.com a few weeks ago in class. I've never seen such a heated debate among the students. It's a website for sugar daddies."

Jimmy asks, "What do you know about the site?"

Joe replies, "I did some research. SeekingArrangement.com advertises on websites for student loans. College women see the ads and investigate. It's an easy way to make money. Over 300,000 younger women and 30,000 older men use the site."

Charlie exclaims, "Jesus, 300,000!"

Joe says, "Some of my female students saw no problem sleeping with an older man if he paid for college tuition."

Nick says, "And I bet those were the good looking co-eds. And I bet the ugly ones were against the idea."

Joe replies, "Bingo."

Charlie asks, "What about the guys in your class?"

Chapter 1: The Fathers

Joe says, "It was funny. The girls were arguing back and forth. I thought a fight was going to break out. All the boy students just sat there and didn't say a thing."

Nick says, "They were probably hoping for a cat fight."

Archie says, "You know, I remember Bobby mentioning SeekingArrangement.com when we were up in Boston last month."

Joe asks, "Why'd he mention that?"

Archie answers, "I have no idea. Back to reality. If we are going to make enough money so we can each afford a hot college-aged mistress then we need to focus on the business at hand. So Jimmy, are you trying to get some of Ellsworth Toohey's road work from the government stimulus plan?"

Jimmy says, "Working on it. It's complicated. Roads aren't my specialty. I'll have to lease some new equipment. Credit is tight right now."

Charlie says, "I can't believe Ellsworth is making parts for a defense contractor. Back in high school he seemed like one of those pacifist, hate America types."

Jimmy says, "Well he's 100% red, white, and blue these days. Becoming rich will do that to you."

Nick adds, "And getting your horn waxed by a hot All-American college-aged girl will do that to you too."

Joe asks, "I wonder if he wears a red, white, and blue condom?"

Charlie deals another card face up to each player. Archie is dealt the ace of spades. Charlie says, "Queen of spades in the hole is looking good."

Archie looks at Charlie and says, "I'm your brother for crying out loud. At least deal me one spade in the hole." Archie then says, "Another two dollars." Everyone tosses two dollars in the pot.

Charlie deals another card face up to each player. Archie says, "I've been thinking. You know how the rest of the world thinks Americans are a bunch of imperialistic pigs."

Nick replies, "Yeah."

Archie, in his alpha-male tone, continues, "We should reap the rewards of being imperialistic pigs. Enough with this Afghanistan and Iraq crap. They're hellholes. We should take over all the nice places on the planet. You know, like Eastern Australia, the coasts of Argentina and Brazil, the South Sea Islands, all of the Caribbean, and the South of France."

Joe asks, "And if we take over the South of France what the hell are we going to do with all the French?"

Archie replies, "The French are different, aren't they?"

Nick adds, "The French are different like Texans. Rude and really annoying."

Jimmy says, "We could just get rid of the French. Send them all to Iraq."

Joe adds, "Or send them to Texas. They'd blend right in." Everyone laughs.

Charlie says, "Jimmy, you are now high with two sevens. Your bet."

Jimmy says, "Five dollars." Everyone throws five dollars in chips into the pot.

Charlie replies, "Everyone is still in." Charlie deals another card face up to each player.

Nick says, "Speaking of the French being different, I hear Archie has a new girl friend."

Joe asks, "Is this true?"

Archie says, "Nick, how the hell did you find out?"

Nick answers, "I have my sources."

Joe replies, "And you didn't even tell your brothers. I thought we were family?"

Archie says, "Give me a break. The only thing you and Charlie want to know is if she has any friends that will put out."

Charlie smiles and says, "Well does she?"

Archie answers, "Let's table that discussion."

Nick says, "And the best part of Archie's new girl friend is that she's French. Her name is Ladonna Cunegonde."

Jimmy says, "Now that's a sexy name."

Joe says, "I thought Ladonna is Italian."

Jimmy says, "You know what they say, the French are different." Everyone laughs.

Nick asks, "So is it true?"

Archie asks back, "Is what true?"

Nick responds, "That the French are different."

Chapter 1: The Fathers

Archie answer, "Oh yeah, they are very different."

Nick says, "You lucky bastard."

Joe says, "You know, Cunegonde means 'big bum' in Persian."

Archie, "How the hell do you know that?"

Joe answers, "Because I'm a writer. I study languages."

Nick starts singing the Sir Mix-a-Lot rap song, "I like big butts and I can not lie. You other brothers can't deny." Everyone laughs.

After a pause, Joe asks, "Where'd you meet her?"

Archie answers, "She works for a large property management company. We crossed paths a few times. I finally decided to ask her out."

Nick says, "You really are a lucky bastard."

Archie says, "Not tonight. I haven't won a single hand."

Charlie says, "Jimmy is still high with a pair of sevens."

Jimmy says, "Five dollars if you want to see your last card." Everyone tosses five dollars in the pot. Charlie deals the seventh and final card face down.

After the deal Jimmy says, "Another five dollars."

Charlie says, "I'll raise you five dollars."

Archie says, "I'm out."

Nick says, "I'm out too."

Joe tosses ten dollars into the pot and asks, "What do you have?"

Jimmy says, "Three sevens and the two of spades in the hole."

Charlie says, "Three eights."

Joe asks, "Any spades in the hole."

Charlie answers, "None."

Joe says, "Looks like I split the pot with Charlie. I have the four of spades in the hole."

Archie says, "You won with the four of spades in the hole. Jesus, this is your night. I tossed away a hand with the five of spades in the hole. I've got to get another beer."

Nick says, "So tell us more about this Ladonna."

Standing by the cooler, Archie replies, "We are talking about going to South America on vacation for three weeks after the holidays."

Nick says, "Now that would be sweet."

Jimmy asks, "How's the sex?"

Archie, in his typical alpha-male tone, replies, "Best damn sex I've ever had."

Joe asks, "Thinking about getting married again."

Archie says, "Hell no. Ladonna is extreme high maintenance."

Jimmy says, "Show me a woman that isn't high maintenance."

Nick replies, "Maintenance is why I'm three times divorced."

Charlie says, "The worst part is all the emotional support you have to constantly feed them. Honey you look great. Your new hairstyle is spectacular. I love your clothes. You're doing a great job with the kids. Your redecorating has added value to the house. At some point you'd think they'd realize that I don't give a damn what color the curtains are! Just buy the beige ones so I can get home and watch the game!"

Nick says, "Amen to that."

Joe adds, "No, the worst part is when they ask you, 'If you still find me attractive then why do you always close your eyes when we make love?' There's no escape from that question." Everyone laughs.

Jimmy adds, "Maybe I should look into this SeekingArrangement.com site. Subsidizing a coed's college education is more satisfying that subsidizing my ex-wife's $350 hair cuts."

Joe says, "We should start the Dirty Old Guy Student Loan Foundation. I'll be in charge of admissions. My main job will be to personally interview all the applicants." Everyone laughs.

Archie sits back down, lifts his beer, and says, "A toast to low maintenance friends."

Jimmy says, "I'll drink to that." Everyone toasts.

Nick says, "It's getting late. I got about another half hour in me. Let's get to the $20 limit black jack. Joe's the big winner so far so he's the house."

Joe says, "Toss me the cards so I can deal."

They play black jack for another forty-five minutes. Joe is the big winner overall, making $550 on the night.

At this point in the story a little background about the three fathers is in order. Archibald Roark, Charles Roark, and Joseph Roark are brothers. They grew up not far from the New Jersey border in Warwick, NY. Their family is traditional. Their father works at IBM's Thomas J. Watson Research Center in Yorktown Heights as a technician. He

Chapter 1: The Fathers

works for IBM his entire career. Like most women in the 1960s their mother stays at home and never takes a job outside the house.

Archie, the oldest, is his father's favorite. He is an above average student. More importantly, at least in his father's eyes, he is a very good football player. Archie is good enough to get a football scholarship to Boston College. He plays outside linebacker and starts his junior and senior years. Archie majors in business and minors in math. After graduation he takes a job on Wall Street as a stockbroker in the late 1970s during a bear market. When the stock market starts to take-off in the mid 1980s he starts making very good money. At the age of thirty-one he marries a social climber by the name of Daisy Buchanan. Soon after getting married they have two children, first Howard Holden, and then a girl, Phoebe, the following year.

Archie and Daisy go through an ugly divorce when Howie is seven and Phoebe is six. At this time Daisy is romantically involved with a wealthy investment banker by the name of Meyer Wolfsheim. Meyer comes from old money. He lives in the penthouse apartment three floors above Daisy and Archie. Their apartment complex is the upscale Manhattan House at 200 East 66th Street on the Upper Eastside. When Daisy asks for a divorce Archie finds out about Meyer. He goes crazy. Immediately marching up to Meyer's penthouse apartment he kicks in the door and attacks him. Meyer, being a slender man, doesn't stand a chance. After breaking Meyer's nose, Archie holds Meyer by his ankles, dangles him over the balcony, and threatens to drop him. Meyer begs for mercy. He promises Archie he'll do anything. He'll give Archie all his money. Meyer starts to cry.

Daisy rushes into the apartment. She pleads with Archie not to drop Meyer onto the street below. Archie pulls him back over the rail. To showoff his physical superiority, he tosses Meyer like a rag doll into the balcony's sliding glass door. Fortunately for Meyer the glass door doesn't break. But Meyer's ego is shattered. He never gets over crying like a baby and being tossed around like a rag doll in front of Daisy. Archie storms out of the apartment.

Immediately after leaving Meyer's apartment Archie makes several phone calls. He manages to move all his money into off shore accounts. This amounts to a little over two million dollars. Archie is arrested the next day trying to board a plane for the Bahamas.

Big Game CEO

Angry, Meyer hires the best divorce lawyer in town for Daisy. Meyer then hires the best lawyers to sue Archie for pain and suffering. Meyer's lawyers have numerous eyewitnesses that testify seeing Archie hold Meyer by his ankles and dangle him from the penthouse balcony. Archie's lawyers don't stand a chance. Archie serves all of a six-month prison term. He is ordered to pay Meyer one and a half million for pain and suffering. In divorce court Archie is ordered to pay Daisy another two million, one million for her, and another million for the children. Archie is also served with a restraining order to never come within a hundred feet of Daisy, Meyer, and the children.

During his prison sentence Archie does two things. First, he files for bankruptcy. Second, he becomes an anarchist. Not just a run of the mill, angry white male, gun toting, Michigan Militia-style Libertarian. Not just a run of the mill 1930s Depression Era anarchist. Not even a flamboyant anarchist. He becomes a full-fledged flaming anarchist. He believes, rightly or wrongly, that the entire purpose of the government, taxes, and the judicial system is to let the weak survive and prosper in the world through game playing, networking, and conniving. And letting the weak prosper is Archie's definition of evil.

After getting out of prison Archie does his best to disappear from the system. He spends over a year in the Bahamas, bartending and living in a small bungalow. After a year Archie is starting to get bored with his beach bum life when he discovers Meyer has tracked down one of his off shore accounts. Archie decides to fight the system. He heads back to New York.

Back in New York, Archie moves in with his recently divorced brother Charlie. They were good friends growing up but drifted apart after Archie left home. They kept in touch at most three times a year. It is during this period that Archie and Charlie become good friends again. To support himself Archie works construction for Jimmy Gatz, and friend of Charlie's. Jimmy pays Archie off the books.

With Meyer pulling all the strings for Daisy, the fight between Daisy and Archie in divorce and bankruptcy court lasts for seven years. Meyer tracks down over a million dollars Archie has hidden in off shore accounts. In the end Archie still has $800,000 hidden in the LGT Bank in Liechtenstein. What ends the feud between Archie and Meyer is the stock market crash in 2001. Meyer has much of his money invested

Chapter 1: The Fathers

in technology companies. When the market crashes Meyer loses over 60% of his worth. With diminished savings he decides to call off the lawyers and financial detectives.

While living with his brother Charlie, Archie slowly starts to put his life back together. He moves the $800,000 back into America. He uses it as a down payment for a 75-unit apartment building in Scranton, Pennsylvania. After five years Archie saves up enough money to buy a second apartment complex thirty miles away in Port Jervis, New York.

One day between the time of purchasing his first apartment building in Scranton and his second apartment building in Port Jervis, Archie is reading the sports page of a local paper. To his surprise he sees his son's name. It turns out that Howie, as only a junior, is a star lacrosse player at Manhasset High School on Long Island. Archie starts attending all of Howie's lacrosse games. During one of the final games of the season Howie notices Archie in the stands. He recognizes Archie from the lone picture of his father Howie keeps hidden in his nightstand. After the game Howie tracks down his father. The pair goes to dinner. They try to catch up on lost years. During dessert it is the first time in Archie's life that he cries.

For Howie it is the first time he hears about the divorce from his father's point of view. Meyer and Daisy have indoctrinated Howie that Archie is an evil man; and because of this indoctrination Howie often wonders if he is half evil. But Howie now realizes that Archie must care about him. Why else would Archie attend his lacrosse games? His mother and his stepfather never once watched him play.

During the summer between Howie's junior and senior year in high school, he and Archie secretly play golf twice a week. They become good friends. For Howie, Archie's alpha-male view of the world is a welcome change from Meyer's liberal Manhattan perspective. Archie tries talking Howie into going out for the football team. Howie counters, saying, "Football is so 20th Century."

Archie pushes the issue, telling Howie, "With your height and speed, you could easily get a college scholarship playing wide receiver or free safety."

But Howie could care less about football. During one of their rounds of golf, Archie, as Howie's father, feels obliged to give his son the 'don't use drugs' talk. Half way through the speech, Howie says,

"Dad, what is more damaging to my body, smoking pot or playing football?" It is at that moment that Archie realizes his son is smarter than him. Archie never brings up the football issue again.

They talk about all kinds of subjects as they walk the golf course again and again that summer. Archie tells Howie all about his life. Without realizing it, Archie teaches Howie all about the stock market: how to turn a fast buck by selling short; how to use dark pools to hide your transactions; and how to hide money overseas. He also indoctrinates his son with his anarchist philosophies.

Howie tells his father all about his passion for architecture. He is thinking about going to college at Columbia, Princeton, or Cornell. All have good architecture programs, but he is leaning towards Cornell because they have a better lacrosse team. To make up for Christmases missed, Archie buys Howie the latest state-of-the-art workstation computer, with a high-end graphics card, and the most recent version of AutoCAD. Howie thinks it's the greatest gift ever. During his senior year in high school, Howie gives up video games and spends his free time teaching himself to design buildings.

That summer Archie also learns through Howie that Daisy and Meyer have had two children, a daughter and a son. During one round of golf Archie asks Howie, "Do you and Meyer get along?"

Howie answers, "We never talk much. It's clear that Jacob is his favorite. I swear Meyer's scared of me ever since I became taller than him."

Archie says, "I can believe that."

Charlie Roark is two years younger than Archie, and has always lived in Archie's shadow. Archie takes after his mother's side of the family, with his high cheekbones, broad shoulders, and above average height. Charlie takes after his father's side of the family, with his round face, narrow shoulders, and merely average height. Archie and Charlie are good friends growing up, but drift apart in high school. Charlie isn't book smart like Archie, and has a difficult time in school. He knew by 10th grade that college is not an option. Secretly, Charlie starts to resent his older brother just after Archie leaves home for Boston College.

Graduating high school in the mid-1970s, Charlie takes a job at an automobile parts plant in northern New Jersey. The plant is brand

Chapter 1: The Fathers

new and makes small electrical motors for power windows. At the time power windows are a new feature only found in luxury cars.

Like his father, Charlie is a natural technician. In two years he moves from the assembly line into a job as a technician for the product development group. One night while watching the evening news he sees a story about a four-year-old boy who dies on the highway after falling out a car window. The next day Charlie takes his idea for a patent to his boss. Charlie's patent idea is a safety switch that turns off passenger control of the power windows. With a flip of a switch only the driver can control the windows. Charlie's boss steals the idea and patents it for himself. This incident is the beginning of Charlie's intense distrust of management types.

Charlie marries his high school sweetheart, Lucie Manette, at the age of twenty. A year later they have a daughter, Annette. Their marriage is going so-so for three years. They're happy but not close. Charlie isn't a warm, affectionate man. Lucie often feels like she is living alone.

In 1979, the first in a series of recessions hit America. Charlie is laid-off. To help pay the bills Lucie takes a job at Macy's. Charlie can only find odd jobs. Lucy becomes good friends with a manager at Macy's. She never cheats on Charlie but the opportunity for greener pastures is there.

Finally, Charlie and Lucy lose their house to foreclosure. Lucie asks for a divorce. For the next six months Charlie jumps from odd job to odd job, living with friends. Then he is rehired at the parts plant. Then laid-off again in 1982. This time he spends a year and a half working odd jobs and living in a run down apartment before he is hired back at the plant.

By 1988 things are going pretty well for Charlie. Working steadily for five years, combined with the fact that his child support payments are becoming a smaller and smaller part of his paycheck, he manages to rebuild his savings. Lucie remarries and Charlie no longer has to make alimony payments. That summer he buys a house and twenty acres just outside of Port Jervis, across the New York border in Pennsylvania. It is during this period in his life he becomes a fan of NASCAR and joins the Republican Party. Many Liberals would consider Charlie to be an unthinking 'NASCAR and apple pie' conservative. Charlie considers himself to be someone with clear priorities in life.

That summer he also meets Jordon Baker, a one-time divorcee who works for the Department of Social Services. They marry six months later. They are an interesting odd couple, Charlie being a die-hard Republican and Jordan a staunch Democrat. In August of 1989 Jordon gives birth to their son, Daniel Crockett.

In 1992 another recession hits. Things are different this recession for Charlie. Corporate decides to shut down the plant and move operations to the Philippines. The workers protest out of frustration. Charlie and the other technicians are discouraged because their livelihood is moving overseas. Subconsciously they know it is the end of their way of life. They are furious because upper management reduces the workers' pension benefits by 50%. Legally, management can get away with it. With only 15 years at the company, Charlie's severance package goes from small to really small. With all the tough talk and bad blood, the only violence that erupts is one technician throwing a large rock through a manager's car window. Seeing upper management walk away with his pension money is something that haunts Charlie for the rest of his life. He feels like he lost part of his manhood those few weeks because he didn't fight.

Charlie can't find a job in 1992 or in 1993. They are now living on Jordan's salary. He starts to drink. In 1994 they get a divorce. Charlie doesn't have to pay alimony or child support. However, Jordan gets the house, the car, and the twenty acres.

After the divorce Charlie starts working construction for Jimmy Gatz. The pay is OK but there are no benefits. He gets a two-bedroom apartment in Middletown. The following year Archie, going through a difficult divorce of his own, and trying to hide from the government, moves in with Charlie. Charlie gets Archie a job with Jimmy, and Jimmy agrees to pay Archie off the books. Archie gets Charlie's drinking problem under control, allowing Charlie only one beer after dinner. One day when he finds Charlie sneaking an additional beer, Archie drags Charlie outside and says, "You're not drinking yourself to death on my watch. If anything is going to kill you it is going to be me." Archie then beats him up. Charlie knows it is for his own good. After that Charlie doesn't touch a beer for over a year.

In 1997 Charlie and Archie get a larger apartment in Middletown. In 1998 Charlie takes a job as a maintenance man for the Orange

Chapter 1: The Fathers

Regional Medical Center. The job pays the same as working construction with Jimmy plus there are health and retirement benefits.

In 1999 Charlie gets caught up in the Y2K hysteria. He joins a local militia, buys all kinds of guns and supplies, and prepares for the end of society with coming of the year 2000. Archie enjoys going to the shooting range with Charlie and his friends in the militia, but Archie thinks the Y2K hysteria is a joke. He keeps telling Charlie, "You and your militia friends are wasting your time with this end of the world crap."

On New Year's Day, 2000, nothing happens. Charlie feels like a fool. Archie doesn't say a word. To relieve the tension Archie pays for a two-week ski vacation in Colorado. Archie says it's a gift for helping him hide from the government. It is the second time Charlie has traveled outside the New York City area, the first being the one time he visited his brother Joe in Los Angeles. After the ski trip neither mentions the militia or Y2K again. However, Charlie and Archie keep the guns. The lasting impact of the militia experience is that it turns both Charlie and Archie into avid hunters. Subconsciously they enjoy hunting because it reminds them of their childhood when their grandfather took them hunting every fall on his farm in Upstate New York.

By 2002 Archie is not afraid of Meyer coming after him anymore. The brothers get separate apartments.

Unlike Archie, Charlie has a more traditional child sharing arrangement with Jordan. Danny stays with Charlie every other weekend and two weeks in the summer. Also, from a young age, Danny is interested in the cub scouts and boy scouts. Charlie becomes the den leader so he can see his son on Thursday nights during the school year.

Charlie realizes that like himself Danny isn't a good student or great athlete. Jordan realizes this too, and encourages Danny with his music. Charlie sees music as being for sissies, and encourages Danny with his love for scouting. He also sees scouting as a way to keep Danny off drugs. He even helps Danny train to become an Eagle Scout.

Joe Roark is born two years after Charlie. Being the youngest, he adopts the natural position of family comedian. From the age of four Joe could make anyone laugh. And the person he loves making laugh the most is his mother. Everyone in the family understands Joe is his mother's favorite.

Joe takes after his father with merely average height. He is only 5'10", just like Charlie. But like Archie he has his mother's high cheekbones and broad shoulders. Being only two years apart Charlie and Joe become good friends, sharing comic books in elementary school, bikes in middle school, and cars in high school. Archie, being four years older, is always more of an idol than a close friend to Joe.

Joe's personality is more complex than his brothers. Archie is an always-on alpha-male. Charlie is unsure of himself, and always looking for reassurance with his decisions. Joe, on the other hand, suffers from manic-depression. When people are around he lights up the room with his smile and sense of humor; but when everyone leaves the lights go out. At night the only thing darker than the room is Joe's bleak outlook on life.

Being a comedian, Joe's natural talent is story telling. But it takes Joe a while to realize he wants to be a writer. After high school he attends community college for two years before transferring to SUNY Binghamton. There he gets a degree in English in 1979. Just before receiving his degree Joe and his girlfriend of two years go through a bitter break-up. Heartbroken, Joe ponders suicide for a few hours one evening.

Looking for a change Joe moves to Los Angeles with little more than the clothes on his back. For the first few months he shares a two-bedroom apartment with four guys, and supports himself delivering pizza in the evening. He spends his mornings writing and spends his afternoons pushing scripts at the studios to anyone that would talk to him. After six months he gets a break. The producers of *WKRP in Cincinnati* buy one of his episodes. Joe writes six episodes for *WKRP in Cincinnati* before the series ends in 1982.

In 1983 Joe finds steady employment with an advertising company. He goes to meetings and comes up with catchy slogans and funny ideas. However, he doesn't find the work meaningful. In his free time he writes movie scripts. On the weekends he promotes his scripts to his contacts at the movie studios.

One script that Joe is pushing in late 1983 is a coming of age story targeted for a teenage audience. The story revolves around five high

Chapter 1: The Fathers

school students. The teenagers are not complete strangers, but not close friends either. They come from different social groups and cliques. The five are reporting for Saturday detention. The students pass the hours in a variety of ways. They dance, harass each other, tell stories, fight, smoke pot, and talk on a wide variety of subjects. No studio is interested.

Then the movie *The Breakfast Club* is released in 1985. Joe immediately realizes it is a complete rip-off of his 1983 script. Joe is smart enough to copyright all his work. He talks to a lawyer. The lawyer tells Joe this is going to be a tough case since there is no solid evidence that Joe talked with writer and director John Hughes. But the lawyer decides to take the case anyway. The studio offers Joe and his lawyer $40,000 to just go away. After some soul searching Joe takes the offer. He gets $20,000 and the lawyer gets $20,000. At that moment Joe realizes it is highly unlikely he will ever make it big in Hollywood. He again contemplates suicide.

Still working for the advertising company in 1986, Joe makes the acquaintance of an actress from Philadelphia by the name of Marian Starrett. She is a so-so actress looking for that big Hollywood break. She scrapes out a living doing commercials and getting small parts in second-rate horror films. Six months after meeting they move in together.

By 1988 both are growing tired of the Hollywood scene. At 28 years old Marian realizes her window of opportunity for catching that big break is rapidly closing. Joe sees the advertising company as a go nowhere job. The pay is not great because in Hollywood clever writers are a dime a dozen, and there is zero opportunity for him to move over into management since the company is run by a group of University of Southern California graduates. Joe knows he can't break into that circle.

So in 1989, looking for a change, Joe and Marian get married and move back across the country to Red Hill, PA, a small community just north of Philadelphia. Marian starts nursing school. Joe takes a job with the Philadelphia Inquirer. Joe quickly becomes a jack-of-all-trades reporter. He reports homicides, court cases, film festivals, restaurant reviews, special interests stories, and every March he even

Big Game CEO

does basketball games during the first week of the NCAA tournament. Basically Joe goes where they tell him to go.

In October of 1989 Marian gives birth to their son, Robert Edward. His nickname soon becomes Bobby. Bobby is two months younger than his cousin Danny. Growing up Bobby and Danny see each other often and become close friends.

Everything is going smoothly in Joe and Marian's life during the 1990s. Marian finishes her nursing degree and starts work at Montgomery Hospital and Medical Center. Joe is slowly advancing at the paper, hoping to soon become editor. He also spends his free time writing novels. Most of these novels are based on homicide cases that he covers as a reporter. Joe and Marian both know that his novels are never going to make it big, but as Marian often says, "At least they keep Joe out of trouble."

'Keeping Joe out of trouble' turns out not to be the case in 2002. Partially because Joe is bored with married life, and partially because Joe is afraid of growing old, that spring he has an affair with a young staff reporter. Marian finds out. With one of the lamest excuses of all time Joe tries to justify the affair to Marian by arguing that his latest book is about infidelity and murder and that he was simply doing research. Marian looks at Joe in disbelief and says, "That's it." She grabs Bobby and leaves for her parent's house. Besides losing Marian, Joe also loses his job. Again Joe contemplates suicide.

Six months after the divorce Archie's, Charlie's, and Joe's mother dies of a heart attack. However, everyone knows she really died of a broken heart. She couldn't believe that the marriages of all three of her sons, especially her favorite, Joe, ended in divorce. She couldn't figure out what she did wrong. Every Sunday she took the boys to church.

Soon after the divorce, Joe takes a job teaching English at Luzerne Community College in Scranton, Pennsylvania. The pay is not great but the work is meaningful. The only time Joe smiles during his first year in Scranton is when he is talking with his students about writing.

In the spring of 2002 Archie introduces Joe to Jimmy Gatz. In the summers of 2002 and 2003 Joe supplements his salary working construction for Jimmy on a Tolls Brothers development in New Jersey.

Chapter 1: The Fathers

In January of 2004, Archie's, Charlie's, and Joe's father passes away. Everyone knows he missed his wife and died of loneliness. At the funeral Joe notes that over 200 people attended their mother's funeral but only 70 attended their father's. Talking with friends of his father, the brothers discover the old neighborhood is rapidly changing, and many of the old neighbors have moved further Upstate or to Florida.

After the funeral the brothers decide to visit their old neighborhood. The neighborhood has indeed changed. The empty nesters that remain are getting older and are now having difficulty taking care of their yards. There is a lot of turnover in the neighborhood; some young families with children have moved into a few houses. These new families are predominately Puerto Rican.

Archie, Charlie, and Joe stop into a bar to talk about the old neighborhood and the passing of their father. What they are subconsciously drinking to is the fact that with their father gone they are next in line to meet the grim reaper. They reflect on their lives. Then Charlie makes the uncharacteristically astute observation, "You can tell whether a community is thriving or dying by how many people attend the funerals."

Archie, Charlie, and Joe were unaware that their father had a fairly large investment portfolio. After the brothers sell their parents' old house, settle the estate, and pay taxes, each receives a little over $270,000 in inheritance. Joe uses the money to buy 42 acres just north of Lords Valley, Pennsylvania near Lake Giles. On the property is a dilapidated old farmhouse built in 1876 that is beyond repair.

Joe selects this isolated location just north of Lords Valley for two reasons. First, it is half way between Scranton and Port Jervis. Second, he wants to build a fortress of solitude where he can live out the remainder of his days writing novels.

But before writing any novels Joe must serve his penance for cheating on Marian and breaking his mother's heart with the divorce. This penance is a way for him to keep his mind away from suicide. The spring of 2004 Joe bulldozes the dilapidated old farmhouse to the ground.

That summer he starts building a new house on the western edge of his property overlooking Lake Giles. He gets the plans for a rustic yet modern cedar home from Jimmy Gatz. The plans are from Town and Country's Colonial Lodge series. The 2350 square foot lodge will contain 3 bedrooms, 2.5 baths, a library, a great room with large windows overlooking Lake Giles, and a three-car garage. The design is for construction on the side of a hill and thus includes a walk out basement. Joe plans to make the basement into a bar and game room.

Jimmy Gatz and his crew lay the foundation for the lodge in June. Starting in July, Joe works on the lodge every day. The first thing Joe builds is the garage in order to move the tools from his father's old tool shop indoors. On the weekends his brothers visit and help with the project. The only thing Archie and Charlie ask is that Joe buys the beer. Even though the work is hard they have a good time because the work is meaningful.

That summer the three brothers reconnect. Joe no longer views Archie as an idol. Without realizing it all three become best friends. Deep down they know that in an increasingly lonely world their friendship is the only meaning they have left in their lives.

In August, Joe's son Bobby and Charlie's son Danny stay with Joe the entire month. Both are now fourteen and old enough to be useful. They help Joe put in the plumbing and roof the house. By Labor Day the rough plumbing, the shell of the house, and the instillation of the windows are complete.

Since there is no electricity or running water Joe stays in his one-bedroom apartment in Scranton during the school year. Burnt out from working 14-hour days, Joe does very little work on the lodge until the following summer. In 2005, Joe, Archie, Charlie, Bobby, and Danny run electricity and water to the lodge, wire the lodge, add a septic tank, add insulation, and finish most of the kitchen. Everything in the kitchen is either oak or stainless steel.

The fall of 2005 Joe moves in to the unfinished lodge. That Thanksgiving Joe, Charlie, Archie, Bobby, Danny, and Archie's son Howie start the tradition of spending holiday weekends there. Besides eating, they spend most of their free time hunting on Joe's property.

That winter Joe custom builds oak cabinetry for the kitchen and oak bookcases for his library. The following summer Joe, Archie, Charlie, Bobby, and Danny finish the interior of the upstairs, including a heated tile floor in the kitchen and great room. In the summer of 2007 they finish the game room and add a paved driveway.

Chapter 1: The Fathers

The summer of 2008 they take it easy. Charlie finally decides to spend part of his inheritance money. He buys a Suntracker Party Barge Pontoon Boat with NV performance pontoons and 90 HP OptiMax engine. It is an unusual pontoon boat capable of doing 40 mph. The pontoon boat is good for water-skiing, fishing, or just hanging out on the lake while barbequing. Charlie also buys a brand new and fully loaded Dodge Ram 3500 Quad Cab Truck for hauling his Party Barge Pontoon Boat.

The sons, Bobby and Danny, borrow the boat often to go water-skiing with their numerous girl friends. The fathers, Archie, Charlie, and Joe, spend their free time fishing, barbequing, and hanging out on the local lakes. When Joe is free in the evenings, he starts work on all his unfinished novels. Occasionally on the weekends the fathers hook-up with some local divorcees using one of the many popular online dating services for older singles.

In late July of 2008 Howie is laid-off from his new job at an architectural firm. Temporarily living with is father, Howie starts hanging out with Bobby and Danny. Bobby and Danny like Howie's company. He is Ivy League educated, good looking, and 6'4". With Howie, Bobby and Danny are able to attract a better-looking group of girls. Soon Howie, Bobby, and Danny decide to move in together. Archie gives them a good deal on a three-bedroom apartment in his complex in Port Jervis.

At their summer barbeques a common topic of conversation is the last piece in Joe's lodge – the unfinished deck. Without telling a soul Howie designs a beautiful three-tiered wrap-around deck that enhances the scenic view of Lake Giles and seamlessly flows from the lodge to the hillside below. He shows everyone the plans at a barbeque in August. Starting the Thursday before Labor Day the six of them make Howie's design a reality. Working 12-hour days they finish early Monday morning. With a keg of beer and a barbeque they christen the completion of Joe's lodge.

Without realizing it Joe's dream lodge, his fortress of solitude, has turned into a real fortress of solitude for the three brothers and their three sons. It is a place for them to hunt, fish, barbeque, ride motorcycles, work on cars, play pool, play poker, play video games, and escape the constant annoyances of the modern world.

More importantly it is a place for the six of them to be men. A place where they are the kings of their own world. With the suburbs of Scranton spreading eastward and with the suburbs of New York City moving westward beyond Port Jervis, the brothers know their fortress of solitude will eventually be a thing of the past. They estimate fifteen to thirty years before suburban sprawl surrounds the property.

But for now it is a place for the brothers to forget about their failures in life. For all three to forget about their failed marriages. For Archie to forget about his dream of being a power player on Wall Street; for Charlie to forget about the moving of the automobile parts plant to the Far-East and his wish of being a company man for his entire career like his father; and for Joe to forget about his failed attempt to make it as a writer in Hollywood.

But enough about the fathers, for this is not a story of what could have, would have, and might have been. Instead this is a story about the sons, and what can be, will be, and shall be.

Chapter 2: The Sons

At 4:40 AM on Monday morning Danny's alarm goes off. He slams it off, rolls out of bed, immediately puts on his camouflage-hunting outfit, and slips into his Chippewa hunting boots. He walks down the hall, bangs on his cousins' bedroom doors, and yells, "Let's go."

Howie is already dressed and awake. He is working at his computer, studying the CAD drawings for an art museum that was recently designed for a site in Rio de Janeiro by Henry Cameron but never built. He takes a Dexedrine from the pillbox on his computer desk. Ever since his junior year at Cornell, Howie's been taking these go-pills to help stay awake and focus.

Howie gets up, follows Danny down the hall to the kitchen, and yells, "Toss me a Red Bull."

Danny opens the fridge, throws it over his shoulder, and asks, "Do you ever sleep?"

With a quick sweeping motion Howie grabs his lacrosse stick next to the three empty pizza boxes on the kitchen counter with his left arm and catches the Red Bull in the stick head. He answers, "About three hours a night." When Danny isn't looking Howie pops the Dexedrine he's holding in his right hand into his mouth. Next he washes it down with two big gulps of the energy drink.

A few minutes later Bobby staggers out of his bedroom in just his underwear and carrying his hunting clothes. Danny says, "You can dress in the truck."

Big Game CEO

Bobby throws Danny the keys to his truck and groggily mumbles, "You drive and grab me a Vitamin Water."

Howie grabs the three camouflage equipment bags next to the door and heads out with Danny. Each large bag is packed with their IceMan compound bows, twelve RedHead Carbon Fury arrows, field binoculars, cell phones, and other supplies. Danny starts Bobby's black 2005 Ford King Ranch F-150 Super Crew Pickup Truck.

Bobby, now wearing just his camouflage hunting pants, slams their apartment door, runs across the frost covered grass with his bare feet, tosses the rest of his clothes in the back of the crew cab, dives in the back seat, and covers himself with a blanket. He yells, "Turn on the heat and toss me the Vitamin Water." Bobby quickly puts on his clothes and sleeps for most of the twenty-five minute drive to Lords Valley.

Along the way Danny and Howie discuss their hunting plans. Danny and Bobby will take two of the three Kawasaki KLX dirt bikes in the back of the truck to cover more ground. Danny will start on the south end of Beaver Lake, head north on foot, and then cut over towards White Deer Lake. Bobby will start at the east end of Billings Pond where Jimmy Gatz saw the group of wild turkeys the day before and then head south on foot towards Piersons Pond. Howie will circle Lake Giles on foot and head west towards Fairview Lake. If any of them spies a group of wild turkeys from a distance they are to call the others on their cell phones so the three of them can surround the turkeys. Danny says, "Make sure all your cell phones are set to vibrate."

They are to meet back at Joe's lodge at 10:00 AM. They promised Lucille McKee they would work a luncheon event at the Otterkill Golf and Country Club in Campbell Hall, NY. With the holiday season approaching Bobby wants to stay on Lucille's good side. If they are unsuccessful in the morning then they figure that they can be back in the field by 3:00 PM for a second go of it.

At 5:20 AM they pull into the winding driveway that leads to the lodge. No lights are on. Joe is clearly asleep.

From the east the first rays of sunlight cut through the darkness. The boys unload two of the three dirt bikes from the back of Bobby's truck. Each with an equipment bag slung over their left shoulder, Bobby and Danny are off.

Chapter 2: The Sons

    Howie walks across the frost-covered field and down to the edge of Lake Giles. Standing perfectly still he surveys the situation. There is no wind. There are no clouds in the sky. Everything is perfectly still except for the mist rising up from the lake and the fog of his breath. The sun breaks the horizon. The water is completely calm, reflecting the sunrise like a perfect mirror. Like the architect that he is, Howie looks across the lake at a 40-foot high pine tree, and calculates in his head the length and position of the shadow this tree will cast from sun up to sun down that day. He notes to himself that Lords Valley is at 41.4 degrees latitude. Next he calculates in his head how the position of the shadow's daily path will change from fall, through winter, spring, and summer. Thirty feet away from Howie a large mouth bass jumps out of the water. The big splash startles him, breaking his intense concentration. He studies how the ripples propagate across the lake and reflect off the shore, forming an interesting interference pattern that makes the reflection of the sunrise seem to dance across the lake. He takes a deep breath and heads north and west around the lake.

    Making a straight path towards Beaver Lake, Danny reaches the southern rim in three minutes. He parks his Kawasaki KLX dirt bike next to a maple tree. He quickly puts the small pack with 12 arrows on his back, attaches his binoculars, knife, and cell phone to his belt. He firmly grabs his compound bow with his left hand and proceeds by foot. Soon standing at the south edge of Beaver Lake he stops to survey the situation with his binoculars. A group of deer is drinking water on the far north side of the lake. He mumbles to himself, "Not today." Next Danny asks himself, "What do wild turkeys like to eat?" From his Eagle Scout training he remembers that adult turkeys consume mostly acorns, nuts, leaves, buds, seeds, and fruit. Young birds tend to eat mostly insects, snails, and spiders. He doesn't spy any acorn trees. Since it is late fall almost all the trees are bare. Along the west side of the lake Danny notes a small groove of white maples that still have about half of their leaves. He marches off in the direction of the white maples.

    Bobby's hunting style is unique. When he is outdoors he becomes like an alpha-dog whose instincts forces him to leave his mark everywhere he visits. About half way to Billings Pond, Bobby comes upon a frost-covered field. He stops the dirt bike in the center of the field. He mumbles to himself, "Time to wake up the turkeys." Firmly grabbing the hand brake to the front wheel, he guns the engine and does doughnuts for a few minutes. Grass and dirt fly from the spinning rear wheel. After spelling his name "Bobby" in the field, he heads over to a small dirt bike course along the west edge of Billings Pond.

Reaching the dirt bike course he stops and stares into the breaking dawn. Bobby grabs his white Julbo Explorer Glacier Sunglasses from his camouflage equipment bag and then tosses the bag to the ground. On top of the equipment bag he tosses his bright orange hunting baseball cap with the name *Zen Reaper* written in black ink across the front. He races around the loop of the dirt bike course seven times. Each time when he reaches the main jump on course Bobby attacks the jump a little more aggressively, flies into the air a little higher, and yells a little louder. For the seventh jump Howie and Danny can faintly hear Bobby's primal scream in the distance. At the same time both mutter, "Only Bobby."

Bobby puts his hunting cap on backwards, grabs the equipment bag and races over to the north side of Billings Pond. He parks the dirt bike next to a tree. He grabs a bottle of Vitamin Water and a can of Skoal from his equipment bag. After finishing the Vitamin Water he puts a pinch of chewing tobacco between his gum and left cheek, and mutters, "Breakfast of Champions." Then he mutters, "I see target practice." There is a rabbit about 50 feet away. Quietly he grabs his compound bow and lays three arrows on top of the equipment bag. Kneeling on his right knee he loads the compound bow. Sensing something is about to happen the rabbit races away. Bobby shoots. The arrow sticks in the ground just in front of the rabbit. The rabbit changes course. Bobby reloads and shoots again. He just misses, grazing the hair on the rabbit's back. The rabbit reaches some bushes and hides.

Bobby retrieves the two arrows. Walking back towards the equipment bag he starts dancing an Irish Jig, and loudly sings, "If I were a turkey where would I be? If I were a turkey where would I be? I'd be chasing a female turkey, that's where I'd be. I'd be chasing a female turkey, that's where I'd be. And if I were a female turkey, where would I be? And if I were a female turkey, where would I be? I'd be dancing with a pole, that's where I'd be. I'd be dancing with a pole, that's where I'd be." He stops singing and says to himself, "The turkeys will be in that groove of trees."

Chapter 2: The Sons

Bobby puts his knife in his thigh pocket, his cell phone in his vest pocket, and the small pack with 12 arrows on his back. He grabs the binoculars, looks at them for a moment, tosses them back in the equipment bag, and says, "I don't need these." He stands up straight, quickly surveys Billings Pond, and says, "It's showtime turkeys." From that moment on he doesn't say a word. He silently heads south along the ridge just east of the pond, moving from tree grove to tree grove.

Howie circles Lakes Giles one time before heading west. He makes the four-mile journey to Fairview Lake in nearly a straight line, periodically stopping every quarter mile for a few minutes to quietly survey the terrain in detail. He sees deer and rabbits but no turkeys. Reaching Mainses Pond, he methodically makes his way around the southern end. Two flocks of geese fly overhead. Howie studies their V-formation, and how the V-shape changes as the lead goose tires and a new alpha-goose assumes the lead. A third flock of over a hundred geese lands on the pond, filling the air with their calls. After stepping in a pile of geese poop, he observes inch long pellets of geese poop everywhere along the edge of the pond. Howie quietly mutters, "Note to self – never design a development with geese friendly ponds." He continues his path west reaching Fairview Lake at 8:10 AM.

Danny reaches the small groove of white maples, finds a vantage point with a good view, and quietly waits. Constantly surveying the area with his binoculars he sees rabbits, ducks, numerous deer, and even a 10-point buck on the other side of Beaver Lake. After 30-minutes of no turkeys he heads to the north end of Beaver Lake and again surveys the area from a good vantage point for 30-minutes. He then heads towards White Deer Lake. White Deer Lake is only 1.5-miles way, but Danny turns the journey into a three-mile trek, taking a long detour along a winding stream. At a ridge that overlooks a bend in the stream Danny stops for another 30-minutes, patiently waiting for the wild turkeys to arrive. After no luck he continues northwest. He reaches White Deer Lake at 9:05 AM.

Bobby never stops for more than one minute to survey the situation. He is constantly on the move. He walks around Billings Pond twice – once far away from the shoreline, staying in the trees, and a second time in the field next to the shoreline. Walking towards Piersons Pond he decides to take some target practice. He grabs an arrow from the pack on his back, loads the compound bow, and shoots a tree 150 feet in front of him. He rapidly repeats this for the remaining eleven arrows. All twelve arrows form a nearly perfect vertical line in the tree trunk. Admiring his marksmanship as he pulls the arrows from the trunk, Bobby whispers to himself, "Number seven was off a few inches."

After walking around Piersons Pond one and half times he heads south towards Interstate 84. Walking along a ridge overlooking the highway he ponders if he could kill someone driving by at 70 mph if the window is rolled down.

Knowing that the interstate forms a fence line that tends to coral the turkeys, he heads east along the interstate towards Dingman Turnpike Road. Thirsty, and knowing no boundaries, Bobby walks up to a house and takes a drink of water from a garden hose in the backyard. Next he heads northwest back towards Billings Pond.

Returning to the south end of Billings Pond, there are now fifty geese swimming on the water. He tosses a rock over the geese. It splashes into the water. The geese take flight and head south. Bobby grabs an arrow and loads his IceMan compound bow. A few fly just ten feet over his head. He shoots. One falls to the ground. He walks over to his victim. Barely alive, the goose tries to get away. Bobby grabs his knife and with one whack cuts off its head.

Holding his kill by its feet he heads back to the motorcycle and picks up a straight solid stick that is four feet in length. Back at the motorcycle he firmly positions the stick five feet above the ground between two branches of a small maple tree. With some rope he ties the goose's feet to the straight stick and begins field dressing his kill. Bracing the stick with his left hand, he quickly pulls out fist full after fist full of feathers with his right hand until the goose is almost bare. Next he makes a ½" deep cut from the base of the neck to the feet, making sure not to puncture the gall bladder. Uncle Charlie taught him that releasing the bile from the gall bladder always taints the meat. With his knife he removes the interior organs and tosses them against a tree trunk. He smirks as they slowly slide down the tree trunk to the ground. He walks over to his equipment bag and grabs a roll of paper towels and a pair of latex gloves. Wearing the gloves he wipes the blood from the inside of the body cavity and tosses the bloody paper

Chapter 2: The Sons

towels to ground. A gentle breeze slowly blows the paper towels to the east. Using a small stick, he holds open the goose's body cavity. This discourages bacteria by increasing air circulation inside the cavity and drying the remaining blood. He takes off the latex gloves and tosses them to the ground.

Wearing his white Julbo Explorer Glacier Sunglasses, with his equipment bag slung over his right shoulder, holding his kill by it's feet in his left hand, and the motorcycle throttle in his right, he heads back to his father's lodge. It is now 9:32 AM.

Howie returns to his uncle's lodge at 9:49 AM. He sees the freshly killed goose hanging from a tree with a rope tied to its feet. Bobby comes walking out of the garage holding a propane torch. Howie says, "We are suppose to get a wild turkey, not a goose."

Bobby replies, "Anything with wings is good enough for this silly $20 bet. Besides, I would rather have Canadian goose for Thanksgiving dinner."

Howie says, "Geese are all over the place right now. I could have easily killed ten by just randomly shooting into the air."

Bobby dismisses Howie's comment by saying, "Whatever." He then lights the propone torch and continues to dress the goose. Lightly running the flame over the goose's body Bobby removes any leftover down and tiny feathers. With the flame he burns the rope near the tree branch. The rope breaks. As it falls towards the ground Bobby grabs the rope near the goose's feet and walks up towards the garage. Just outside the garage is a large pot of water on top of a propane burner. The water is just starting to boil. Bobby dips the goose into the water three times to loosen any remaining quills, but not long enough to cook it. He runs his hand quickly over the skin to loosen the remaining few quills. He dips it a fourth time and quickly pulls it out of the water to rinse off the final quills.

Bobby's dad, Joe, opens the entrance way from the garage to the kitchen. He stands there sipping a cup of coffee, admiring his son's kill. Bobby walks over to his dad and says, "Can you toss this in the freezer. We have to run to work. "

Joe replies, "Sure."

Bobby then turns to Howie and says, "Call Danny. It's after ten. We don't want to be late and piss off Lucille. Holiday season is upon us."

Howie calls Danny. Danny answers by saying, "Leave without me. I just spotted two turkeys on the east side of Beaver Lake. I'm going to loop around."

Howie replies, "This is ridiculous. You need the money more than any of us. We can come back out after the luncheon."

Danny answers, "I'm staying out. I have to show-up Uncle Archie at least once before I die."

Bobby asks Howie, "What's going on?"

Howie replies, "He just spotted some turkeys on the east side of Beaver Lake. He's not coming."

Bobby grabs the cell phone out of Howie's hand and turns it off. Bobby then says, "Danny's stubborn-stupid. Get in the truck."

Driving his Ford F-150 Super Crew Pickup over fields, across a small creek, between rocks, and over numerous small trees, Bobby beats Danny to the east side of Beaver Lake. The wild turkeys hear the truck coming and like prehistoric birds, they fly across a narrow section of Beaver Lake to the other side. Howie exclaims, "I didn't know wild turkeys could fly that far!"

Bobby replies, "Freaky."

Danny comes running up to the truck and screams, "Why the hell did you do that?"

Bobby answers, "Because I love you man. Get in the back, we're running late for work."

With a disgusted look on his face Danny replies, "Fine."

As Bobby drives east over the fields toward Valley Road no one says a thing. Speeding south on Valley Road towards I-84 Howie breaks the silence, "I see four turkeys."

Danny asks, "Where?"

"To the east, over by that small pond."

As an offering to his cousin, Bobby says to Danny, "I'll cover this area after the catering event."

On I-84 Bobby speeds back towards their apartment. He tells Danny about killing the goose on the fly. Both Danny and Howie give Bobby a hard time, repeatedly telling him there are geese all over the

Chapter 2: The Sons

place right now – even our dads could kill one. The three then plan their hunting strategy for the afternoon. Bobby will cover the area near Valley Road by the small pond. Howie and Danny will team up and cover both sides of Beaver Lake.

Bobby slams on the brakes and skids into his parking spot back at the apartment. The trio manages to shower and change in twelve minutes. When Danny and Bobby aren't looking Howie takes another Dexedrine to stay alert. On the way to work Bobby lectures Danny and Howie about putting on a good show at the luncheon. He says repeatedly, "We need to get on Lucille's good side. I'll come up with a plan to get us out of there early."

Even after running two red lights the trio is twenty minutes late to the Otterkill Golf and Country Club. Lucille's mad. Bobby smiles and turns on his boyish charm, telling Lucille, "There was an accident on Route 207. We got stuck in traffic."

Lucille smiles and replies, "I understand."

Working double time, the boys help the other seven workers prepare the appetizer plates and set the tables. Howie takes his position behind the bar, Danny takes his position as one of the waiters, and Bobby assumes his natural position as host and headwaiter. Today's luncheon is for the Hudson Valley area leaders of the Red Hat Society. The Red Hat Society is a social club for senior women. Lucille is expecting a party of slightly more than 200 guests.

Bobby and the boys are in rare form with the senior ladies. From being outside all morning their faces are freshly suntanned, radiating youth and life. With a big smile, Bobby welcomes the women as they enter. He politely directs them to their tables, making small talk. His two favorite lines are '*I should hang out at the Red Light district more often*', and '*You look stunning. You must have cut a deal with the devil. Is that why you are all wearing red?*' The senior ladies love his compliments and all the attention. The hall fills with laughter. Everyone is in a good mood and Lucille clearly understands Bobby is the reason. Lucille whispers to herself, "Everybody loves Bobby."

Like usual for these all female events, Lucille positions the bar where everyone can see Howie's 6'4" tall eye-candy. Even the senior ladies that don't drink make at least one trip to the bar. And for the ladies that do drink they make two or three trips. Howie quickly serves the drinks while making his own brand of small talk. His two favorite lines are *'We're running a special on the Lady in Red, a perfect mix of cranberry juice, grenadine, coconut rum, and vodka. Perfect for a group of fun ladies like yourselves'*, and *'That's a sophisticated choice'*. Five of the ladies proposition Howie to go on a date with their granddaughters. Howie takes in over two hundred dollars in tips.

Danny works double time, serving appetizers, serving lunch, refilling water glasses, and clearing plates. He covers twice as many tables as anyone else on the wait staff. He doesn't make small talk. He just smiles and says, *'No mam'*, *'Yes mam'*, *'May I take that'*, and *'Please give me one moment'*.

After the event Howie and Bobby work double time boxing the liquor bottles and packing the bar into Lucille's catering truck. It's 2:15 PM and Danny looks anxiously at Bobby. Remembering what his Uncle Charlie once said, *'Hunters are the most discriminated group of people in this country'*, Bobby decides to make up a lie.

He waits until Lucille is all alone then walks up to her and says, "Today's my mother's birthday. The three of us are going to drive down to Philadelphia and surprise her for dinner. Can we leave now so we can beat traffic?"

Lucille smiles and replies, "No problem." She then slips a wad of bills into his pocket.

Bobby says, "Thanks." He quickly walks over to Danny, slaps him on the back, looks over at Howie, and says, "Let's go." The rest of the wait staff jealously watches as the trio heads for Bobby's truck.

As Bobby speeds back to Lords Valley, Howie and Danny change out of their wait clothes and into their hunting gear. No one says a word as Bobby weaves through traffic. Just before I-84 Bobby pulls over and jumps in back. Danny hops in the driver's seat and drives the rest of the way while Bobby changes.

Danny asks, "So how much did Lucille give you?"

Bobby replies, "$420." Bobby asks Howie, "How were the tips?"

Howie answers, "$220."

After doing a quick calculation in his head Bobby says, "$213 isn't bad for four hours of work. This sure beats the hell out of working at Circuit City."

Chapter 2: The Sons

Howie says, "$213 and thirty three cents. $213 and thirty four cents for me since I'm the oldest."

Bobby says, "You can keep your damn penny grandpa."

At this point in the story a little background about the three cousins is in order. Howard Holden Roark is currently 22 years old, Daniel Crocket Roark is 19 years old, and Robert Edward Roark is two months younger than his cousin Danny.

From an outsider's perspective, it appears Howie is living the most charmed life of the three. After his mother, Daisy, divorces his father, Archie, and marries Meyer Wolfsheim, he and his sister Phoebe live the life of luxury. Howard attends The Browning School from 3rd grade to 12th grade. The Browning School is an exclusive all boys preparatory school in downtown Manhattan. His sister Phoebe attends an exclusive all girls preparatory school. Vacationing in Europe every summer, in the Caribbean every Christmas holiday, and in Africa, Asia, or South America every spring, Howie is a world traveler, and speaks numerous languages fluently.

Various nannies effectively raise Howie and Phoebe. The two only see their mother, Daisy, on the weekends and holidays. Guilt causes Daisy to turn her limited time with Howie and Phoebe into forced quality time. Cultural events fill their weekends. Howie can't stand the Broadway shows, art galleries, and philharmonic concerts. Meyer hardly ever joins Daisy at any of these events. Half the time Daisy doesn't even go, leaving the nannies to chaperon the children.

As they grow older Phoebe becomes Howie's psychological counselor and vice-versa. Together they gain awareness that it is their mother who is responsible for their anxious-ambivalent sense of insecurity.

Searching for a man in his life, in 4th grade Howie becomes friends with Casey Hall, a young financial analyst who lives in Howie's apartment building. Casey also has a part-time job playing attack for the New York Titans, one of the twelve teams in the National Lacrosse League. As far as sports go, professional lacrosse does not pay much money. Most games are on the weekend since most players need to support themselves with a second job. Those that play do it because they love the game.

Casey only sees Howie a few times a week, usually coming in and out of the apartment building. Casey never realizes he is the main role model in Howie's young life. Casey's love of lacrosse rubs off on Howie. As a gift Casey gives Howie one of his old lacrosse sticks. Howie thinks it's the greatest gift ever. For the next month Howie plays wall-ball on the roof of his apartment, Manhattan House, for a minimum of one hour a day.

Howie begs his mother to sign him up for a spring lacrosse league. She refuses, seeing lacrosse as a waste of time. Then one Sunday morning during breakfast Meyer tells Daisy, "Oh, let him play." It is the first and only time in Howie's life that he hugs Meyer. Daisy tells Howie to find a league. He chooses Doc's New York City Youth Lacrosse. Practices are on 57th street, not far from Manhattan House.

For the few minutes they occasionally see each other, Casey gives Howie tips – how to hold his stick, how to gain leverage in a fight for a ground ball, how to pass over your back shoulder, and how to shoot hard, quickly, and accurately. Casey urges Howie to carry his stick everywhere for if you are going to be good then the stick must become an extension of your arms. Howie absorbs all of Casey's advice. He carries his stick everywhere. It becomes an extension of his body. By 6th grade Howie is far and away the best player on the field for his age group.

Casey Hall moves to Kansas City the spring when Howie is in 6th grade. Howie had always been more of a loner, but that summer he starts hanging out with a group of boys in the apartment building across the street. One July day they talk Howie into setting off the fire alarm in his own apartment building.

Mike Donnigan, the head maintenance man for Manhattan House is highly annoyed with the false alarm. Upon evacuating the building one of the senior tenants leaves their stove on. That starts an actual fire. The stove fire doesn't cause much damage because the firemen catch it early. However, it takes Mike most of the day to replace the stove and repaint the ceiling.

Studying the security tapes of the apartment building just before the false alarm Mike Donnigan determines Howie pulled the false alarm. Mike can't stand spoiled rich kids so he decides he is going to make Howie pay.

Chapter 2: The Sons

Three days after the fire alarm incident Mike confronts Howie just outside the north entrance. Mike tells Howie he has evidence that he pulled the fire alarm. Howie says, "That's a lie. Prove it."

Mike glances at the lacrosse stick Howie is holding in his left hand and says, "We can take this up with your lacrosse coach."

Howie, stunned that Mike didn't say he was going to take this up with his parents, blurts out, "You mean Coach Danny?"

Mike just smiles and comfortably tells the lie, "Coach Danny and I are good friends. It would be a shamed if you got kicked off the team."

Mike and Howie talk for the next ten minutes. Mike gets Howie to apologize for pulling the fire alarm. It is the first time in Howie's life he has ever apologized for anything. Howie agrees to work for Mike every morning for the next two weeks rewiring the building. Mike wants him to work for three weeks but Howie tells Mike that his family is vacationing in the south of France all of August. Mike asks, "What do you do with your parents all of August in France."

Howie replies, "Not much. At least two of our nannies come with us every time we go on vacation." Mike just shakes his head.

Starting the next morning Howie helps Mike and his assistant wire the building for high-speed Internet. The three run wires through pipe chases and crawl spaces of Manhattan House. Mike tells Howie that Gordon Bunshaft, the architect that designed Manhattan House, was a very good but not great architect. There is easy access to all of the apartments except those in the northwest corner of the building. It takes Mike and Howie more time to run wire to the apartments along the northwest corner than all the other apartments combined.

During their morning breaks Howie, Mike, and Mike's assistant hangout in the maintenance room in the basement. Mike always drinks a coffee, Howie a Pepsi, and the assistant enjoys a cigarette. Mike's favorite topics of conversation are building design and New York City's infrastructure. They talk about building airflow, heating, water pressure, New York City's underground electrical grid, and other maintenance related topics. Mike grows fond of Howie because Howie is interested in his every word. Mike can tell that Howie is very smart from his numerous intelligent questions. During the second week Mike shows Howie his collection of blue prints for Manhattan House. Howie thinks the blue prints are the coolest things ever. It is the beginning of a highly unusual friendship.

Before leaving for France, Howie talks his mother into buying him a Nikon D1, one of the best professional digital cameras available at the time. Besides taking pictures of the topless girls on the Mediterranean beaches, Howie spends much of his vacation taking pictures of old and new buildings along the south of France and in Paris. In Paris he decides he is going to be the greatest architect that ever lived. On the plane ride back to the States he tells his mother about his decision. Daisy smiles and says, "That's cute. But don't you know that you are being groomed to run America – not build it. Building is for people of ethnicity." For the remainder of the flight home Howie and his sister Phoebe discuss the motivation behind their parent's decisions. Phoebe, being a natural psychologist, has most of the insights. Their nannies listen in on the conversations and wonder how an eleven-year-old girl can be so perceptive.

Middle school and high school fly by. A natural student, Howie excels in all his classes at The Browning School. He learns Spanish, Chinese, and French. Since The Browning School doesn't have a lacrosse team he arranges through the school counselor to play for the Manhasset High School team on Long Island. Howie hand selects Manhasset because it is one of the premier high schools teams in the area. The Manhasset coach is against the idea until after the first practice. The coach quickly realizes that even in 9th grade that Howie is one of the best players on the field, and his assessment includes all the seniors.

During his down time in the evenings Howie often hangs out with Mike Donnigan. This amounts to one to two hours a week. Unlike his mother Mike nurtures Howie's love for architecture. Through his connections with other maintenance men Mike shows Howie the blue prints to other nearby buildings. He also introduces Howie to the underworld infrastructure of New York City – the endless tunnels of pipes, power lines, and communication wires. Most individuals would find the tunnels damp and dreary. For Mike and Howie the tunnels are a beautiful place – the primary arteries that provide life to the city above.

During the fall semester of his junior year in high school a male English teacher asks Howie to stay after class to make up an assignment.

Chapter 2: The Sons

Sitting at his desk and writing away he suddenly feels a man's breath on his neck and a hand rubbing against his thigh. Stunned, he just sits there for fifteen seconds. But for Howard Holden Roark those fifteen seconds feel like an eternity. As soon as the male English teacher puts his other hand on Howie's chest, Howie stands up and leaves. He never tells a soul about the incident, not even his sister. That night those fifteen seconds keep playing over and over again in his head. He wonders if he is gay. The next day after school he loses his virginity to a 12th grade girl that lives in the apartment building across the street. She's had her eye on Howie for a long time, and Howie decides today is the day. After they have sex she keeps trying to hook up with Howie for the next six months. Howie politely ignores her advances.

As you already know, late in Howie's junior year he reconnects with his biological father, Archie. Twice a week that summer they secretly play golf together. They become good friends. Archie encourages Howie's love of architecture. He also becomes Howie's first bridge to the America outside Manhattan. Unlike most people Howie knows, Archie does not view Manhattan as the center of the universe. He views his father's attitude about Manhattan as refreshing, and his anarchist ideology eye-opening. The largest impact Archie has on Howie is his attitude about his stepfather and his liberal Manhattan perspective. Howie's feelings about Meyer change from ambivalent dislike to hate.

During his senior year Howie applies to Columbia, Princeton, Cornell, and Boston College. Howie tells everyone he is leaning towards Cornell because they have a better lacrosse team but he secretly wants to go to Princeton. Little does Howie know but Princeton only plans to accept fifteen students from The Browning School this year. He doesn't make the cut. Disappointed, he accepts admission into Cornell.

With their loses in the stock market during the dot-com bust, Daisy and Meyer have gone from very wealthy to merely wealthy. The couple secretly decides that they want to focus their resources on Jacob and Jade, Howie's younger half-brother and half-sister. Also, Daisy isn't happy that Howie wants to major in architecture. So they inform Howie that since Cornell doesn't give athletic scholarships he will have to take out student loans. As long as he can go to college and focus on architecture and lacrosse he doesn't care about the debt. Howie views money as a means to an end. If he has to file for bankruptcy after graduating, so be it.

Living in a dorm room on west campus with two other guys, one from Boston, the other from Colorado, Howie slowly comes out of his loner shell. Howie is a morning person. He always finds early morning the best time to work at the computer and to surf the Internet. For his first semester his daily schedule is: 4 AM - 6 AM go to Rand Hall during the quiet time and design buildings just for the fun of it; 6 AM - 8 AM off season lacrosse training; 8 AM - 3 PM breakfast, lunch and classes; 3 PM - 9 PM study and dinner; 9-11 PM hang out with the people in his dorm; and 11 PM – 4 AM sleep. On Friday night he usually hooks up with one of the young coeds. Even though there are more men students than women students at Cornell, with his muscular build and curly blonde hair, Howie never has any problem attracting members of the opposite sex.

With his preparatory training from The Browning School, Howie's first year of course work is a breeze. The same isn't true on the lacrosse field. It is a shock to his ego to discover he isn't the star. In fact he doesn't even start. He still gets a lot of playing time, but he is unhappy because the coach moves him from attack to defense. At first he thinks that he will just ride out his freshman and sophomore years and play attack his junior and senior years. But half way through his freshman season he realizes that isn't going to be an option. Luke and Chris Fletcher are twin brothers from Maryland. Like Howie they are freshman. But unlike Howie the coach keeps them at attack. Half way through the season the twins are promoted to the starting line-up. Lightening fast, and playing as if they possess a single mind, the twins quickly become stars.

By May of his freshman year Howie is tired of the five plus hours a day spent practicing lacrosse during the spring season. At the end of the season he quits. He was rushing the Alpha Tau Omega fraternity, but since most members of Alpha Tau Omega are on the lacrosse team he decides not to join.

Since Howie isn't interested in the fraternity scene there is no solid reason for him to stay in Ithaca. To take his mind off lacrosse he studies abroad in Rome the fall semester of his sophomore year. In the spring he studies at Cornell's satellite campus in Washington DC. In addition

Chapter 2: The Sons

to his $55,000 in student loans from his freshman year, his vagabond sophomore year is another $95,000.

Returning to Ithaca his junior year Howie gets lucky. At the last minute a wealthy senior student decides to take the year off and travel around the world. Howie takes over her lease. The premier apartment at the corner of College Avenue and Dryden Road is on the top floor. High above Lake Cayuga's waters his corner bedroom overlooks the ivy-covered buildings on campus and the town in the valley below where the workers that support the university live.

Using the fire escape it is an easy climb from his bedroom window to the roof of the building. It is Howie's favorite place to read and study. He sets up his own little patio on the roof. He even buys a barbeque grill. From the roof he can see for miles in all directions, including Ithaca College on the south side of town. On Friday and Saturday nights the roof of his apartment is also his favorite place to make love to the many available young coeds. Howie never keeps an exact tally but he estimates that half the girls he hooks up with attend Cornell and the other half Ithaca College.

Most of Howie's numerous girl friends treat him like a pet dog – that is they expect loyalty. And the families of most of these girls encourage the pursuit of boys like Howie because marrying a handsome Ivy League educated boy is seen as a positive thing. Having no plans on developing a serious relationship Howie rarely returns calls because he finds most of their conversations boring. When he runs into one of his numerous conquests on campus or at the local bars, he is polite, smiles, and makes small talk. But he never opens up to any of these girls because he has no intention of becoming good friends. There is one exception to this rule. Her name is Dominique Francon.

Dominique is different. She is very different. Most women with widely separated eyes, a long thin nose, and narrow lips are typically considered unattractive. For Dominique these features make her exotic. She possesses the look of a heroine-chic supermodel. What makes her even more exotic is that her dying father is an eighty-one year-old billionaire, having made his fortune in the hotel and gaming industry. Her mother is thirty-five years younger than her father, a college educated trophy wife whose hobbies include writing romance novels, affairs with younger men, and grooming her daughter to marry into money.

Dominique and her mother are best friends. Together they carefully plan out Dominique's future. The next step in their plan is for Dominique to get a double major in philosophy and art history, and to make as many sisterhood contacts as possible within the sorority system at Cornell. Dominique and her mother discuss everything, including Howie. She tells Dominique to enjoy the sex but not to become emotionally involved with Howie or any of the other boys on campus. Her mother doesn't want any romantic ties holding her back once she graduates.

That is why Dominique treats Howie more like a pet cat than a pet dog. She never puts any effort into their relationship, but is happy when she runs into Howie and he shows her affection. They have a lot in common – both having wealthy parents, and both growing-up in Manhattan. Perhaps that is why Howie and Dominique often talk through the night on their occasional hook-ups. Or perhaps it is because they respect each other since both know exactly what they want out of life – Howie wants to become a famous architect and Dominique wants to become the next generation of power player in the global world of the 21st century.

Unlike most of Howie's girl friends, Dominique loves to discuss architecture. The walls of Howie's bedroom are covered with poster-sized photos of unusual European buildings he took while studying in Italy. Often they would spend an hour talking about a single photo, discussing the buildings practical purpose, its traffic flows, its structural stability, its beauty, and above all else its spiritual purpose.

When discussing philosophy they both agree that meaningful work is a person's noble purpose in life. Self-achievement is the highest form of morality. Dominique and Howie agree that the mass culture of Joe Public is a joke. People Magazine, cable news, reality television shows, MySpace, and FaceBook are nothing more than desperate people striving for attention in the theme park of Andy Wharhol's fifteen minutes of fame, and that the Internet is the ultimate tool for these mindlessly self-aborbed individuals. Fleeting fame is inauthentic. Authenticity is building something that can stand the test of time. And authenticity equals happiness.

Chapter 2: The Sons

On one of their first hook-ups Howie tells Dominique that he is having problems focusing late at night. He is not happy that he is sleeping more and more hours. He feels unproductive. Dominique introduces Howie to Dexedrine. Howie quickly becomes addicted to this mild form of amphetamine. It reduces his appetite, increases his energy level, increases his self-confidence, makes him feel happier, and above all else increases his libido and orgasmic intensity. He considers it the perfect dietary supplement.

In February of their senior year Howie runs into Dominque in College Town late one Saturday afternoon. They agree to an improtu dinner in Howie's apartment. After dinner they talk through the night and have sex five times. For the fifth act Howie shovels the snow off the roof of his apartment, lays out a blanket, and fires up a portable propane spaceheater. They make love with Dominique on top. They take their time, looking through one of Dominique's art history books on renassiance artists during their sex act. They discuss what is good art and what is bad. A gentle snow begins to fall. Afterwards they both agree it is the best sex they've ever had.

Late April of Howie's senior year there is a ground-breaking on campus for the new Architecture, Arts, and Planning building. That evening Howie is one of the few students invited to a private dinner held by the Dean of the Architecture School. The dinner is to celebrate one of the programs most famous students, Henry Cameron. Henry is sixty-two years old, works for the international firm Symanski and Nowicki, and has won almost every architectural award imaginable. Howie thinks it is cool that Henry, instead of donating money to the University, donated his design for the new AAP building.

After dinner the Dean introduces Henry to Howie. The Dean tells Henry that Howie is a master at computer aided design. He knows all the keyboard shortcuts. Freshman and sophmore students will often gather around his computer terminal to watch him create a new design. What takes most students one to two days to create Howie can accomplish in ten to twenty minutes. In his subtle way of bragging, Howie mentions that practice makes perfect. He estimates putting in over 7,000 hours designing buildings in front of the computer the last five years.

The Dean tells Henry that Howie is also the student that won the student design competition for the AAP building. As a guest judge, Henry acknowledges he voted for Howie's design. Henry loves the fact that Howie set-up a movie behind the model of his building showing a young man walking along a path. Walls and windows fly in from off the screen constructing the building as the man walks along. Henry says, "Steven Spielberg couldn't have don't a better job." Howie tells Henry that animating walk throughs into a Hollywood-like production is easy these days with the latest version of AutoCAD 3DS Max.

Henry and Howie talk and talk. As the evening winds down Henry and Howie decide to walk from the Dean's house in Cayuga Heights across campus to Henry's old watering hole, The Chapter House. Henry tells Howie the old legend that if a virgin walks across the Arts Quad at midnight on Halloween that the statues of Ezra Cornell and Andrew White come to life. The men shake hands and congratulate one another on the chastity of the university coeds. Howie comments, "I bet it's been a long time since they've shaken hands."

The two continue to discuss architecture. They agree the Arts Quad, looking out over Lake Cayuga, is what gives Cornell its character; the renovation of Sage Hall is an architectural success but too expensive and a waste of resources; the Engineering Quad is an architectural disaster; and the addition to the Law School is too 19th century.

Just before they enter the Chapter House, a brand new black BMW drives by. Inside are three members of the Sigma Alpha Epsilon fraternity. They toss two fist fulls of quarters onto Stewart Avenue. They laugh as some of the townies scatter to pick-up the money. Henry asks, "What was that?"

Howie replies, "What the frat boys call a drive by shooting. Someone I know once told me it is a training exercise."

Henry asks, "Training for what?"

Howie answers, "Training so they don't feel emotional pain when they hire, fire, and lay-off workers in the real world."

Inside at the Chapter House they share a pitcher of beer. They discuss Henry's four buildings in Manhattan. Henry is blown away when Howie tells him that the maintanence men don't like his apartment on 82nd Street because it is difficult to work on the plumbing on the west side of the building.

Chapter 2: The Sons

Henry asks, "How do you know that?"

Howie replies, "Growing up I became good friends with my building's head mainteneance man. Word gets around among the mainteneance men."

Henry then asks, "What about my other buildings?"

Howie replies, "No complaints that I know of."

They talk on and on. They discuss things like how developers constant focus on the bottom line is destroying the field. Developers want big, flashy, and inexpensive. Developers sell the units and make their fast money. The tenants are left absorbing unnecessary maintenaence and energy costs. More importantly the tenants are forced to live in a maze of boxes piled on one another, spiritually turning them into rats.

Henry and Howie quickly become soul mates. After his third beer Henry offers Howie a job. Howie replies, "Like most architecture students it's going to take me five years to graduate."

Henry laughs and says, "This place has nothing left for you. Your wasting your time here."

Tired of creating imaginary buildings, on the Wednesday after Memorial Day Howie starts work at Symanski and Nowicki. Howie doesn't even bother going through the new employee orientation at the main office in Manhattan. He flies immediately to China. Henry Cameron's latest project is a huge hotel complex along the waterfront in Shanghai. As he flies into the city the first thing that catches Howie's eye is all the construction cranes that dot the skyline. Howie mutters to himself, "If you are an architect in the 21st Century then China is the place to be."

When Howie joins Henry at the construction site Henry doesn't even say hello. He turns to Howie and barks, "We have problems. We just discovered city planners want to move the new subway line from the south side of the site to the north side of the site. We will have to split the main foundation. This requires a complete redesign. Here are my sketches. Get to work. If you have any questions ask Albert."

Working with two other architects they redesign the hotel in three days. Then the meetings begin. Howie quickly realizes that at this point in Henry's career he is more of a diplomat than architect. The client doesn't like the shopping area and restaurant on the first two floors. Henry negotiates another redesign. Six days later the client asks for more penthouse hotel rooms with views of the water. Henry negotiates another redesign. This goes on and on for six weeks until the client is happy. The plans are for Albert and Howie to stay behind and oversee construction of the complex through the end of the year while Henry flies to Rio de Janeiro to talk with a new client about an art museum.

However, before Henry boards the plane he discovers that because of the global economic downturn construction of the Shanghai hotel complex is being put on hold for at least two years. Henry and all of his staff are to fly immediately to New York City.

The last Friday in July there is a manatory meeting of all the employees. Since it is everyone, the company is forced to rent a music theater two blocks from their main office. Rumors are flying about layoffs. The CEO walks on stage. By the look on his face it is clear the rumors are true. The CEO says, "With all the uncertainty surrounding the economic downturn, two-thirds of our projects have been delayed or cancelled. As everyone knows there is a sharp downturn in the North American housing market. We project this will last for at least three to four years. Our recent market surveys project a similar market downturn in the commercial realestate market." A tear trickles down the CEO's eye. He continues, "We are either going to go out of business in one year or I have to lay-off half the work force now. This is the most painful thing I've ever had to do because I know you are all good people. Your instructions are to go home. Your manager will call you tonight. In the unfortunate event that you are laid-off, you are to meet here Monday morning at 9 AM. Everyone gets 2 weeks salary for every year at the company. Human resources will review your unemployment benefits with you. We have also hired a head hunter company to help you find a new job. I just want to say thank you for the good years, and good luck this year."

Since Howie went directly from Ithaca to China he doesn't even have a place to call his own in Manhattan. Instead of staying with his mother, Howie goes to his father's place in Port Jervis. Archie and Howie go out for dinner. Just as his 10 oz. Bourbon Street Steak arrives Howie's cell phone rings. It's Henry. Howie walks outside. Standing in the Applebee's parking lot Henry and Howie talk for 45 minutes. As expected Howie is laid-off. Henry tells Howie he is being forced to take early retirement. Henry apologizes for putting Howie through

Chapter 2: The Sons

this. Howie says the time working in Shanghai with Henry was the best experience in his life. Henry tells Howie that he will continue to get paid for the next six months. Howie says thank you. Henry then says I have a final gift for you. Bring a truck or a large van down to the main office on Monday.

Howie finds the 9 AM human resources meeting worthless. It is mainly for laid-off workers with ten or more years experience. After the meeting he walks down to the main office. He tries to get in the building but his brand new badge doesn't work anymore. He calls Henry. Henry says to pull his truck around and meet him on the north side of the building. Howie gets his dad's Escalade from the parking garage. When he pulls up Henry is standing there with two state of the art computer work-stations and five big boxes. None of the passsersby seem to care as Henry and Howie load the computers and boxes into the back of the truck. Howie takes note that with all the recent lay-offs in Manhattan it is a common site to see someone load their departing office supplies into a vehicle.

Henry gives Howie a firm handshake and says, "The four boxes marked N contain copies of all my notebooks from the last thirty years. The box marked D contains twenty external hard drives with over 10 terabytes of architectural designs. Only a fifth of those designs were ever built."

Howie asks, "Isn't this stealing from the company?"

Henry just laughs, "The company would probably sell these two workstations at a steep discount to a worthless stockbroker. My designs are only of value to someone who can apprectiate them. I feel guilty enough as it is for hiring you."

Howie says, "You don't have to feel guilty."

Henry says, "Study them all, especially the designs that were never built. Don't waste your time reinventing the wheel. There are a million geniuses out there. You have the potential to take genius to a higher level, and be one of the great architects of the 21st Century. Improve on those designs and shock the world. Good luck." And with that Henry disappears back into the building. It turns out that is the last time Howie ever sees Henry. Henry dies sixteen months later of a heartattack while taking a bath.

Big Game CEO

Burnt out, Howie decides to take the year off from school. He stays with his father, Archie, for a few weeks. During the mornings he studies Henry's notebooks and in the evenings he hangs out with his two cousins, Danny and Bobby. It is the first time in his life he hangs out with guys his own age, completely unsupervised, with no responsibilities. And for the first time in his life he feels relaxed and happy.

Danny and Bobby talk Howie into getting an apartment together. When Howie discovers his six months salary isn't going to go very far because he has to start repaying his student loans, Bobby gets him a job as a bartender working for Lucille.

Howie finds Danny's and Bobby's friendship unusual and refreshing. They honestly care about Howie, and want to see him to succeed. Unlike most people in Manhattan or at Cornell, there are no hidden motives or secret agendas. For even though Howie is a loner, there is one thing you learn growing up in Manhattan that you don't learn in the suburbs or rural America, and that is how to subtly manipulate people to get what you want. Even though he knew the black art of subtle persuasion, he had always repressed it, wanting to make it on his own ability. But the black art of subtle persuasion is always there in Howie's soul, like an ace of spades hidden in a poker player's sleeve, just waiting for the perfect hand.

Danny's childhood is the exact opposite of Howie's, and Danny's personality reflects his upbringing. He is not skilled in the social graces, he is uncomfortable around authority, he is unaware of his appearance, and his grammar is often clumsy and grating to the ear. But there are two words that summarize Danny – resourceful and resilient.

Charlie and Jordan divorce when Danny is five. His mother finds it difficult to maintain the house and the twenty acres she receives in the divorce settlement, so when Danny is six Jordan sells the property and moves to a two bedroom apartment. Danny shares a bedroom with his older half-brother, Frederic.

Jordan is terrible with money. She runs up credit card bills and is always paying interest. Her car always requires expensive repairs each year because she never bothers to service it. Once a week she gets her hair done and a pedicure. She likes to eat out every night. Frederic

Chapter 2: The Sons

and Danny both receive piano instructions from the most expensive teacher in town. Soon the money from the sale of the house and twenty acres is gone. Jordan is living from paycheck to paycheck.

Since Jordan works and Frederic always has after school activities, Danny is a latch key kid, even in first grade. This forces him to entertain himself and learn to cook. Unlike most kids his age, by the time he is seven he is comfortable riding his bicycle on busy streets. Danny often ventures more than twenty miles from his house on bike.

Living from paycheck to paycheck, Jordan's favorite hobby becomes checking out the local garage sales. Being a single mother Danny is forced to tag along. He turns their Saturday morning outings into a game. His goal is to find something broken and cheap, and then fix it. He starts out with cheap toys. By the time he is nine he knows how to take a bicycle completely apart and reassemble it in under ten minutes. By the time he is eleven he knows how to repair an electric guitar. By the time he is thirteen he can rebuild a motorcycle engine blindfolded. And starting when he is fourteen, he learns how to construct a house spending the summers with his Uncle Joe and cousin Bobby.

Danny learns a lot of his fix-it skills on his own, but he also learns a lot from his father, Charlie. As you already know, Danny spends every other weekend with Charlie, and Charlie is the den leader for Danny's scout troop. On their weekends together they work on all the extra scout achievements. Danny thinks getting all the extra achievement patches, belt loops, and beads during the ceremony at the monthly pack meeting is the coolest thing. In Danny's young mind they are military badges of honor.

Growing up Danny always looks forward to Saturday night. He and his mother always watch a movie together. Unlike Howie and Daisy, Danny and Jordan are best friends. She knows Danny isn't the smartest of kids, but he is good-natured. She loves him deeply, and encourages his musical pursuits. When Danny is ten, Frederic teaches him how to play the guitar. Not good in sports or academics, Danny's only extracurricular activity is high school band.

In high school Danny loses his virginity the traditional way, after the senior prom. His date is Missie Pross. Her nickname is Bossy Prossy. And true to form she tells Danny exactly what to do. He is to wear a black tux. Before the prom they are to have dinner at the Port Jervis

Country Club and he is to order oysters. He is to kiss her during the second slow dance of the night. After the prom they are to get a hotel room. Each will have two glasses of wine and then have sex. He is to bring a condom. Danny does as he is ordered.

In high school, with the encouragement of his father, Danny also trains to become an Eagle Scout. Everyone that knows Danny agrees they have never seen a woodsman quite like him, especially in this day and age. With only a knife and the clothes on his back, Danny can live in the woods for weeks, even in the coldest part of the winter. However, Danny never writes up his Eagle Scout Service Project and never gets his Eagle Scout badge.

Part of the reason Danny never writes up his Eagle Scout Service Project is that he is becoming disillusioned with the system. In the back of his mind he always pictured himself joining the Army after high school. But his half-brother, Frederic, returns home part way through his second extended tour of duty in Iraq with a missing right leg. However, that is not all that is missing. Frederic is no longer the easy-going person he remembers growing up who taught him how to play the guitar. He is suffering from a serious case of posttraumatic stress disorder. Almost every night Frederic wakes up in a cold sweat, screaming. During the day he curses constantly. Frederic refuses to look anyone in the eye. He has no interests in finding a job.

The spring of his senior year in high school Danny takes a part-time job at a motorcycle repair shop. He is still thinking about joining the Army in the fall when he overhears a customer talking to his boss. The customer says, "I served in the Army for twelve years. If I had to do it over again I would have just bought a motorcycle and taken off for South America."

Looking for alternatives, Danny decides to join his cousin, Bobby, and take two classes at Luzerne Community College in Scranton, Pennsylvania. Now working full-time at the motorcycle shop he manages to get a C in English 101 and an A in Automotive Electrical Systems.

In the spring Danny and Bobby move in together. Bobby convinces Danny that school will be easier if he works at Circuit City instead of the motorcycle shop. In the spring Danny gets a C in Programmable Controllers and an A in Steering and Suspension Systems.

Chapter 2: The Sons

Under financial stress and with the downturn in the economy, that April the Circuit City that Danny and Bobby are working at closes. Danny and Jordan talk about his financial situation. They agree that Danny should go on welfare. They will use the extra money to get Frederic psychological help for his posttraumatic stress disorder. Danny will find a job that pays under the table. He is to tell no one of this plan.

Being a natural grifter himself, Bobby quickly figures out what is going on. He promises Danny he won't tell anyone about the welfare fraud. In fact Bobby views this as a challenge. Soon he finds both of them a job working as waiters for Lucille McKee's catering company. Danny is happy because they are now making more money since they are no longer paying taxes.

Hanging out on his father's boat, playing in a speed metal band with Bobby, and chasing and catching girls, that carefree summer seems to fly by. Aimless, and not knowing what career to pursue, Danny starts his second fall semester at Luzerne Community College. He is thinking of pursuing a career as an auto-mechanic, but he also knows that women of his generation do not hold auto-mechanics in high esteem.

Just like Joe is the most complex character of the three brothers, his son Bobby is far and away the most complex character of the three cousins. And like his father, Bobby possesses a manic-depressive personality. In the presence of other people Bobby is the life of the party. However, when alone his dark side comes out. But unlike his father, Bobby doesn't suffer from suicidal tendencies. Instead, Bobby possesses a love for meaningless destruction.

In elementary school Bobby would occasionally get in trouble for mischievous behavior. Standard stuff like shooting spit balls at the girls or sneaking back to the classroom during lunch and dissecting all the frogs that were meant for science class. The teachers often look the other way since he is a good student and always cheerful. In fifth grade he occasionally ventures down to the railroad tracks after school and starts a small grass fire. Using a garden hose from a nearby barn he would pretend to be a firefighter. Bobby would yell things like "Wind is picking up from the north! We need more men on the south side!" One day he loses control of a small grass fire. He runs from the scene. The fire consumes three acres including the barn. He watches everything from a nearby hillside. As with most of his mischievous deeds he is never caught.

At the age of thirteen Bobby is already going through a rebellious Goth/Heavy Metal phase in his life when his parents divorce. He uses the divorce as an excuse to spend more time hanging out with his friends. He and his friends spend most of their time listening to speed metal bands like Gamma Ray, Sonata Artica, and Children of Bodom while smoking pot and playing video games. That summer he and his friends decide to form a speed metal band of their own. Walking home from band practice late one night he throws a brick through the front windshield of a brand new Mercedes-Benz SL500 just for the hell of it. Like usual he is never caught. The band breaks up nine months later.

He spends the August when he is fourteen in Lords Valley helping his father build the lodge. His cousin Danny is also there. After working on the lodge all day the two boys spend the nights camping in a large tent. Bobby introduces Danny to speed metal. Danny introduces Bobby to guns and dirt bikes. On a typical evening they take off on dirt bikes after dinner to the north end of the property and race around a small dirt track for about an hour. Just before sunset they hang out near the tent listening to speed metal from a large boom box while taking target practice with Danny's Remington Model 7400 hunting rifle. If a bird, rabbit, or squirrel wanders out onto the shooting range Bobby immediately tries to kill it. On some evenings instead of taking target practice they play guitars. Bobby is a little jealous of Danny. Danny is a much better musician.

During his teenage years Bobby and his mother have a typical mother-son relationship. She believes his son can do no wrong but hardly ever sees him. Bobby is self-absorbed, spends most of his time thinking about girls, and sees his mother as a means to borrowing the car. With his happy go-lucky personality and James Dean eyes, Bobby has more girl friends than he knows what to do with. At a New Year's Eve party when he is fifteen, he and Mona Monroe are drunk. Upstairs at the party he loses his virginity. Later that night he has sex with another girl. He doesn't even remember the second girl's name the next morning. He doesn't use a condom either time that night.

Chapter 2: The Sons

Money is never a problem for Bobby because he is a master thief. But he is not a thief in the traditional sense. During the start of his junior year in high school he cuts his hair and takes a job at K-Mart working in the electronics department. On a typical day at work he enters the store wearing a collared-shirt with no tie and slacks with no belt. On the way to his station he grabs four CDs, three candy bars, two sticks of ChapStick, and then stops by the men's clothing area. He takes a tie and belt from a display rack. Once reaching his station he opens a CD, puts it in a stereo system, turns on the music, and gets to work.

Bobby quickly becomes one of the best salesmen ever at K-Mart, single handedly doubling the amount of sales within the electronics department from a year earlier. He laughs and jokes with the customers. He quickly becomes knowledgeable about all the cameras, computers, and stereos. And if a customer is about to walk away, Bobby always says something like, "I'll throw in a CD for free if you buy that camera right now," or "I noticed you were eyeing that green jacket in lady's fashion. If you purchase this computer system right now I'll throw in that jacket for free. Go grab the jacket and I'll ring you up at my register in the electronics department." Over the Christmas season he sells so much merchandise that the store manager gives him a $1,000 bonus. When K-Mart takes storewide inventory in January, all the departments around electronics are more than $100,000 short. Bobby is so smooth the managers can't figure out why.

Within his extended family Bobby quickly develops a reputation as the salesmen of the group. At gatherings his Uncle Charlie loves to say, "That Bobby could sell snow to an Eskimo."

After nine months of working at K-Mart, Bobby's bedroom is more like a warehouse than sleeping quarters. On his nightstand is a shoebox full of ChapStick, two shoeboxes full of MP3 players, and another full of MP3 earphones. Hundreds of ties and belts fill his closet. In one corner of his room is a stack of CDs reaching to the ceiling. In another corner a stack of boxes filled with miscellaneous items such as shoes, tools, and sports equipment. In June he quits K-Mart to go live with his dad for the summer. He's happy to leave K-Mart since he has already hooked up with most of the young girls that work the cash registers. He figures that if he stays at K-Mart then his summer would be nothing more than reruns.

Bobby again spends the summer with his father, Joe, and his cousin Danny. During the day they work on building the lodge. In the evenings he and Danny ride dirt bikes, listen to speed metal music, play guitars, or take target practice. They mix their target practice time between guns and archery. That spring Danny found a compound bow at a garage sale. The boys think it is the coolest weapon ever.

In the fall of his senior year Bobby takes a job at Target. Like K-Mart he works sales in the electronics department. Things are a little different at Target compared to K-Mart. He still takes a tie, belt, two sticks of ChapStick, and a CD during each of his shifts. However, since Target is a busier store than K-Mart there are more workers. Like any good thief Bobby is hyperaware of his surroundings. He realizes he can't stimulate sales by giving away free merchandise to the customers since the odds of getting caught are too high. He decides to redirect his dark energy in a different direction.

Waverly Ashford works the service desk at Target. Bobby likes Waverly because your first impression is that she is a sweetheart but once you get to know her you discover she possesses a no-holds-barred dark side. One autumn night after work Bobby and Waverly get a pizza. Waverly tells Bobby she knows how to beat the system. Her brother picks-up the garbage for Target. If at night Bobby puts a garbage bag in the trash bin filled with merchandise then her brother can get it the next morning. After the pizza they have sex in the back of Waverly's car. That night she becomes Bobby's first serious girlfriend and first serious partner in crime.

Waverly, her brother, and Bobby each make an additional $2,000 a month fencing goods that Bobby hides in the garbage bin. They make twice as much in December because of the extra trash pick-ups during the holiday season.

Hyperaware of his surroundings, Bobby senses that management is onto his merchandise in the garbage scam just before Valentines Day. He immediately quits stealing. The following week Waverly and Bobby take jobs at Best Buy. After working at Best Buy for a month, Bobby gets a hold of a label machine. Bobby has over 300 unopened video games that he stole from Target. He peels the Target labels off the

Chapter 2: The Sons

games and puts on a Best Buy price tag. Over the next two months he returns the games to Best Buy, but only when Waverly is working the service desk. She gives him full price for each of the games. They bring in an additional $12,000 with this scam. Like usual Bobby doesn't get caught.

In early May he buys a new black 2005 Ford King Ranch F-150 Super Crew Pickup Truck. The salesman at the Ford dealership was one of Bobby's best customers when he worked at K-Mart. Bobby estimates he sold him over $4,500 in electronics equipment and video games. To repay the favor, Bobby talks the salesman into selling him the truck for $50 over invoice. Bobby pays for the truck in cash.

Waverly and Bobby go to a drive-in movie in a small town fifty miles beyond the Philadelphia suburbs the day Bobby buys the Ford F-150. The have sex four times that night, once in the front seat, once in the back seat, once in the pick-up bed under a blanket, and at 2:30 AM in the ladies bathroom next to the snack bar. They agree criminal sex is the best.

With two days of classes left in his senior year Bobby finally gets caught cheating. That is Waverly catches Bobby cheating on her with a Best Buy cashier in the back of Bobby's truck. Waverly breaks up with Bobby.

Two days later at an end of school party Bobby misses Waverly. He gets very drunk. On his way home he is pulled over by the police. Bobby tells the two officers that if they arrest him then he'll lose his athletic scholarship to Duke University playing lacrosse. The officers let him go. Bobby then talks the officers into driving his truck back to his mother's house since he is drunk.

Bobby is a good but not great student. Like his father he is an excellent writer but he is weak in math and science. To save money he decides to attend a community college for two years before transferring to a four-year university. Since his dad, Joe, teaches English at Luzerne Community College in Scranton and gets a discount on tuition for immediate family members Bobby decides to go there.

That fall he lives with his dad and commutes 20 miles to school. He takes English 101, Intro to Journalism, Western Civilization, and General Psychology. To help pay the bills he takes a job at Circuit City in Scranton. Unfortunately for Bobby, Circuit City doesn't

Big Game CEO

sell ChapStick, belts, or ties. Hyperaware of all the in-store security cameras Bobby doesn't steal a thing that fall semester, not even a CD. He finishes the semester with two A's and two B's.

Tired of living in the boondocks with his dad, Bobby wants to move to the college district in Scranton. He convinces his cousin Danny to share an apartment and join his speed metal band. He also convinces Danny to take a job at Circuit City. That April when Circuit City closes the Scranton store Bobby sees an opportunity for a big score. With Danny's help he figures they can steal $15,000 worth of merchandise during the close out sale. Danny protests, arguing that this is wrong. Bobby laughs, and replies, "Have you ever listened to Uncle Archie? Those boys at Bear Sterns are nothing but pampered rich kids. The government bailed them out. There is no difference between real money and monopoly money. It's all a game. Are you going to be a fool your whole life or are you going to be a player?" Over the next two weeks Bobby and Danny manage to steal $35,000 of electronics equipment. Over the next two months they fence the equipment, making $20,000.

For the next month, that question, 'Are you going to be a fool your whole life or are you going to be a player?' plays over and over, again and again, in Danny's head every time he sees Bobby.

Soon after Circuit City closes Bobby and a few friends are caught trying to sneak into an adult strip club in the suburbs of New York City. The bouncer at the door takes Bobby fake driver's license. With that license gone there is no easy way for Bobby and Danny to buy beer. Down, but not out, Bobby quickly moves onto his next scam.

Bobby takes a job at a local grocery store working the cash register. His initial plan is to sell Danny a few cases of beer every shift, and after a few weeks they'd have enough beer to make it through the summer. But Bobby soon realizes, why sell only beer? Every shift that Bobby works Danny comes through his checkout line with over $200 worth of groceries and beer. Every time Bobby rings up only a few items and typically charges Danny $10. After two weeks they have enough food and beer to last six months. Bobby quits the grocery store.

The following week Danny applies for welfare. Standing in line at the welfare office Danny keeps thinking, 'Are you going to be a fool your whole life or are you going to be a player?' As you already know Danny

Chapter 2: The Sons

gives the money to his mother so that his older half-brother Frederic can get psychological help for his posttraumatic stress disorder.

Bobby figures out Danny's welfare fraud scheme. He thinks it is a brilliant idea and without telling anyone applies for welfare himself the next day. A month later Bobby is visiting his mother back in the suburbs of Philadelphia when he runs into one of his former best customers when he was a salesman at K-Mart, Chester McKee. Chester mentions he is moving to northern New Jersey. Remembering that Chester's wife runs a catering business, Bobby asks, "What's your wife going to do?"

Chester replies, "Sell the business and buy an established catering business in New York City." One phone call later Danny and Bobby have new part-time jobs starting in September. Lucille agrees to pay the two boys under the table.

That summer Bobby and Danny just enjoy life. During the day they ride dirt bikes, take target practice, or borrow Danny's father's boat and go water skiing. When they ski Bobby always makes sure to invite a few girls. In the evenings they play in a speed-metal band by the name of *Zen Reaper*. Occasionally they land a gig that pays money.

In late July their speed-metal band, *Zen Reaper*, breaks-up. In late July their cousin Howie returns from China. The three cousins start hanging out together. Then they decide to move in together. Howie's father, Archie, gives them a good deal on one of his apartment units in Port Jervis. Bobby sells the lease to his old apartment to two female students, making $500 on the transaction.

That fall Bobby's schedule and Danny's schedule are classes in the morning, study in the afternoon, practice with their new band in the evening, and go bar hopping every night. Because the neighbors complain about the noise, they rent a 9'x 9' self-storage unit and hold band practice there. On weekends they wait tables for Lucille McKee.

In early October their lead singer quits the band. A week later the cousins end up at a small bar in Scranton a little after midnight with a karaoke machine. The bar is half full. There are forty drunken college students, most of them underage, talking and making fun of whoever is fool enough to sing. Bobby recognizes two girls from the community college. Bobby talks the girls into joining the cousins at their table. The one named Destiny decides to do karaoke. She asks Danny what song she should sing. Danny says *What's Up* by 4 Non Blondes.

Big Game CEO

Drunk, Destiny staggers up on stage. Danny starts laughing. Bobby asks, "What's so funny?"

Danny replies, "This is going to be a disaster. Linda Perry, the vocalist of 4 Non Blondes, is a master of the throat olympics. Every girl I've ever heard sing this song makes a fool of themselves."

Bobby whispers to Danny, "You're a genius. Girls that make a fool of themselves in public are more likely to put out."

Danny asks, "How do you know that?"

Bobby answers, "Duh, just look at any *Girls-Gone-Wild* video." Danny smiles. Bobby and Danny bump fists. Danny's words are prophecy. Sure enough Destiny falls flat on her face. Everyone in the bar is either laughing or covering their ears.

After the song Destiny returns to the table smiling, but also with an embarrassed look on her face. As she goes to sit down Bobby pulls her onto his lap. Destiny puts her arm around Bobby. Bobby pours Destiny another beer from the pitcher on the table.

At the table everyone is laughing and joking, including Howie. Then in an unusual tactic to further woo Destiny, Bobby starts laying into Howie about how he doesn't have the guts to make a fool of himself. Bobby says, "Look at you with your perfect smile, curly golden hair, and Ivy League education. You're afraid you might tarnish your reputation. It would be a shame if you couldn't get nominated to the Supreme Court because you made a fool of yourself. You are nothing but an Ivy League career planner."

Danny then adds, "You helicopter career planner. Are you afraid to take a chance because it might offend your mummy?" Danny then starts making helicopter noises, "Tu-tu-tu-tu-tu-tu-tu."

This is one of the rare nights when Howie is drunk. He decides to take Bobby up on the challenge. He turns to Bobby and says, "Let's find out if my four years of singing lessons paid-off." He walks up on stage holding a shot glass of tequila. Howie takes the shot and starts singing the same song, *What's Up*, by 4 Non Blondes.

Everyone in bar is in shock. Howie nails the song pitch perfect. Half way through the song Bobby and Danny start talking. Danny says, "Perfect boy has a perfect voice too."

Bobby says, "Song is a little gay for a guy to be singing, but he nailed it."

Chapter 2: The Sons

Bobby and Danny agree that Howie is a cross between the country singer Johnny Cash and Henry Rollins, the lead singer of the punk band *Black Flag*. However, Howie's voice has an extra octave of range. Just then Howie shows off his extra octave of range when he sings the line, "and I pray, oh my God do I pray, I pray every single day, for a revolution." Two girls at the bar with dyed blue hair, black leather pants, and each with a single diamond stud pierced through their nose stand up. Both start clapping and cheering. For the remainder of the song Howie keeps looking at the two girls with blue hair. It is clear Howie is trying to seduce the one with the knock out body.

After the song Howie sits down. Like a young man's fantasy the two girls with blue hair immediately come over carrying a pitcher of beer. The blue hair girl with the knock out body sits in Howie's lap. After some awkward introductions they finish the pitcher of beer and then order another. Bobby brings up the topic of their band. Danny convinces Howie to become their new singer. Howie agrees with one condition – the band redirects its music. Howie tells Bobby, "The main purpose of music is to woo women. You don't woo women with speed-metal." It is at that moment that Destiny kisses Bobby. Not to be out done, the blue hair girl with the knock out body kisses Howie while rubbing his crotch. After three seconds of soul searching Bobby and Danny agree to give up speed metal. Destiny's friend suggests they change the name of the band from *Zen Reaper* to *Ambivalent Swag*.

At closing time Howie goes home with the two blue hair girls, Bobby goes home with Destiny, and Danny goes home with Destiny's friend.

In summary, the three cousins are now living at the far outskirts of the suburbs of New York City in Port Jervis. On the weekends Bobby, Danny, and Howie wait tables at exclusive events in the New York City area. It gives Bobby and Danny the opportunity to press their faces up to the looking glass and peer into the world of wealthy New Yorkers that Howie already knows all too well.

Fifteen miles to the west of their apartment is Bobby's father's lodge in Lords Valley, Pennsylvania. For the three fathers it is their fortress of solitude from the world around them, and for the boys it is the base for their outdoor playground. Twenty miles further to the west is Luzerne Community College in Scranton. Bobby and Danny attend school there. Howie occasionally visits the campus. It gives Howie the opportunity to press his face up to the looking glass and peer into the system that supports wealthy New Yorkers.

Howie is taking a year off from Cornell before returning to finish his degree in architecture. Growing up in Manhattan he knows how to subtly manipulate people to get what he wants. Yet Howie doesn't even realize that the lurid depths of his soul are just waiting for the right opportunity to unleash his dark side.

Danny is quiet and likable, but doesn't know what he wants to do with his life. He wants to be deep thinker like Howie but struggles. Influencing his thoughts are all the government bailouts of large banks and watching Bobby successfully steal from the system. Lately Danny has been questioning what it means to be a moral person.

Bobby is a smooth talker and fast thinker. He views life as a game – a game to get women, a game to get as much money as possible, and a game to jump from job to job to work your way quickly up the career ladder. Staring into the looking glass of the world of wealthy New Yorkers he is growing tired of his small time suburban games. Bobby doesn't know it yet but he is about ready to step up to the big time and discover if he has what it takes to succeed.

Now that you are up to speed about the cousins' lives, back to the story. Danny is hell bent determined that one of three cousins is going to kill a wild turkey with a compound bow and arrow before sunset. He grabs Bobby's radar detector from the glove box, plugs it into the cigarette lighter, and places the detector on the dash. On I-84 Danny speeds back to Lords Valley at over 95 mph.

There is a highway patrol officer just before the Route 6 exit. The detector goes off. Danny slams on the brakes and slows down to 60 mph. Howie places the radar detector in his lap so the highway patrol officer can't see it. The officer stares intently at the truck as they drive by but the officer doesn't pull them over.

Once Danny can no longer see the highway patrol car in his rearview mirror he mumbles to himself, "I've got to show up that Uncle Archie for once in my life." Howie and Bobby don't say a word. They know that in Danny's mind he thinks Uncle Archie and Danny have a long running feud. Uncle Archie always beats him at poker, 8-ball, darts,

Chapter 2: The Sons

and last hunting season when Danny got a 10-point buck, the next day Uncle Archie shot a 14-point buck. Danny resumes his 95 mph race back to Lords Valley.

Danny runs the stop sign at the Route 739 exit, making the right turn at over 30 mph. Not wearing a seatbelt, in the back seat Bobby is tossed from the passenger's side of the truck cab to the driver's side. Bobby yells, "Hey, at least give me some warning."

Danny pulls over onto the shoulder of Valley Road near the small pond where Howie spotted several turkeys five hours earlier. They quickly unload a dirt bike from the back of the truck. Bobby grabs his camouflage equipment bag. As Danny and Howie speed away in Bobby's truck, Bobby pushes his dirt bike 100 feet and hides it from view of the road behind a large rock. He grabs his compound bow and proceeds on foot.

Two minutes later Danny makes a left into a field. He follows Bobby's five-hour old tire tracks back to where they last saw the turkeys flying over Lake Beaver. He parks the truck near the south end of Lake Beaver near the tree where he parked the dirty bike earlier that morning. The dirt bike is still there. They jump out of the truck and grab their compound bows from their equipment bags in the truck bed. Danny points north across the lake. He says to Howie, "I'll loop around the west side of the lake, you proceed up the east side. We'll meet by that groove of trees."

Howie tosses Danny three small white bags of birdseed tied with a purple bow. Howie says, "Take a few of these. If you see a good open area, bait it."

Danny replies, "Great idea. I can't believe I didn't think of this. Where'd you get the birdseed?"

"I found it in a coat closet at the Otterkill Country Club. Someone must have left it there from a wedding this past weekend."

They proceed on foot. Howie sprinkles the birdseed on some dirt in a small clearing about half way up the east side of Beaver Lake. Danny does the same thing on the west side of the lake. They rendezvous at the north side of the lake. Howie notices that since the breeze is picking up there are more and more ripples moving across the lake. Danny notices the long shadows from the trees on the west side dancing on

Big Game CEO

the ripples. The sun is low in the sky. It is just after four o'clock. Sunset is in one hour.

Howie and Danny continue north into a groove of trees, Howie staying to the east, Danny to the west. They exit the groove of trees and survey the surrounding fields. No wild turkeys. The decide to loop back around the outside of Beaver Lake except this time staying about a half mile from the edge of the small lake. Howie reaches the truck just as the sun is about to set when the cell phone in his pocket vibrates. He answers, "Danny?"

Danny replies, "Where are you?"

"Back by the truck."

"Come up the west side of the lake. I just spotted two turkeys."

Howie puts the phone back in his pocket and quietly sprints around the south side of the small lake and up the west side. In the distance he sees the two turkeys eating the birdseed Danny tossed out an hour earlier. He proceeds slowly. Danny is standing motionless against a tree at the north end of the small clearing. The turkeys sense Howie and slowly start heading north across the clearing. The turkeys are within a 100 feet of Danny but he doesn't shoot. The turkeys keep moving closer and closer to Danny. Finally when they are within 25 feet he shoots. Silently the arrow pierces the turkey's heart. It falls to the ground. For a moment the other turkey doesn't realize what is going on. As Danny steps forward the remaining turkey takes off running.

Breathing deeply from the sprint around the lake Howie stands next to Danny as he examines his kill. Danny says, "We've got to hurry back to the lodge. It is almost sunset."

Just then Howie's cell phone vibrates. He answers, "Bobby?"

Bobby replies, "I just got back to the lodge. I got one."

Howie answers, "So did Danny."

Bobby says, "I guess your nickname for the evening is turkey-less."

Howie closes the cell phone. He looks at Danny and says, "Take the truck but leave the dirt bike. I'll meet you at the lodge." Howie sprints after the other turkey.

Forty-five minutes later on the deck of the lodge Bobby and Danny are enjoying venison chili and a beer with the father's, Archie, Charlie,

Chapter 2: The Sons

and Joe. The two turkeys are hanging from a tree branch by a rope tied to their feet. The twenty-dollar bill Danny won from Uncle Archie sticks up out of his shirt pocket for all to see. Bobby is retelling the story of how he shot the turkey with the arrow and how it was almost identical to how he killed the goose earlier that day. Bobby says, "The turkey flew right past my face. I spun and shot it just after it passed by."

The sound of a dirt bike interrupts Bobby as he is about to tell how he cut off the turkey's head with his knife. Moments later Howie pulls up to the deck. He parks the bike next to the tree where the turkeys are hanging and hangs his kill next to the other two. Archie turns to Joe and says, "Get the camera."

Archie has the three boys stand next to the three turkeys. About to the take the picture, Archie says, "Say IceMan."

Holding their Diamond IceMan compound bows, the three cousins reply, "IceMan."

After Archie takes a series of photographs, Charlie walks up and slaps Archie on the back and looks at the boys. He says, "This is a story we can tell our grandkids."

Danny says, "Dad, you're embarrassing me."

Charlie asks, "How am I embarrassing you. Are you gay?"

Bobby says, "He's not gay. That twenty dollar bill has a date with a stripper's garter belt."

Archie says, "I thought we'd play some poker tonight."

Danny laughs, "There is no way you're getting that twenty dollar bill back that easily."

Chapter 3: The Anarchist

The two fathers, Charlie and Joe, have a very negative view of government and the corporate world. But they're left-wing socialists compared to Howie's father, Archie. And of the three fathers, Archie's alpha-male and anarchist view of the world finds fertile ground in the young minds of the three cousins, especially Bobby.

Six weeks before the famous turkey-hunting outing is the best example of Archie's anarchist influence. On a crisp and clear Friday in October, Archie, in his new Cadillac Escalade, is driving Howie, Danny, and Bobby to Boston. It is Boston College's homecoming weekend. Archie plans to visit his old college football teammates and reminisce about old times. On Sunday morning he plans to have breakfast with his biological daughter, Phoebe. Archie has met with Phoebe twice since reconnecting with his son, Howie. He doesn't care for Phoebe very much because he sees too much of his ex-wife, Daisy, in her eyes. But since he is in Boston he feels obliged to stop by.

Howie's main purpose for the trip is to visit Phoebe at Harvard. He hasn't seen her in nine months. Phoebe wants to discuss Howie's lay-off and make sure that he is doing fine. Howie knows Phoebe is hurting for money and wants to make sure she is good.

Bobby and Danny are simply looking for a change of pace. Bobby's main goal is to hook up with some girl for a one-night stand. Danny doesn't know what he is looking for and is just along for the ride.

Chapter 3: The Anarchist

As they drive across Connecticut on I-84 no one comments on the spectacular autumn foliage. The leaves of the Norway Maples are intense yellow, the Sugar Maples are yellow and orange, and the Amber Maples are bright red. The air is cool and crisp. Even by New England standards this is a perfect fall day.

Archie pulls over forty miles outside of Boston just before getting on the Massachusetts Turnpike. He quickly changes the license plates on his Escalade. As he starts the Escalade he turns to his nephew Bobby and says, "Politicians are crooks. There is no way I'm giving them more money than I have to. Especially the politicians in Massachusetts."

Archie rolls up the tinted windows of his Escalade and drives through the EZ-Pass lane as they take Exit 18 off of the Massachusetts Turnpike into Cambridge. Since Archie doesn't have an RF tag the light in the EZ-Pass lane remains red. Archie drives right through it. There is no highway patrol there to pull Archie over. Bobby says, "This is too sweet. All they have is a photograph of your fake license plate."

Early in the afternoon Archie drops the cousins off at Phoebe's apartment. A little later the three cousins are sitting in Phoebe's small living room talking with Phoebe and her apartment mate. The differences between the girls' apartment and cousins' bachelor pad in Port Jervis are many. The girls' apartment is uncluttered and neat; the cousins' littered with pizza boxes, video game cases, and hunting equipment. The girls' have a red designer Italian sofa from Abaco; the cousins' an old green sofa Danny found at a garage sale. Paintings by aspiring local artists neatly decorate the girls' walls; posters of speed metal bands like Gamma Ray, Sonata Artica, and Children of Bodom sloppily cover the cousins' walls. The girls' bedrooms are tidy; of all the cousins' only Danny bothers to make his bed.

Howie and Phoebe are in the kitchen discussing her credit card bills when her cell phone rings. It is their father, Archie. Earlier that day there had been a small fire at the Sheraton Newton Hotel. Health officials are not letting anyone stay there until the smoke clears out. That will be 48 hours minimum. He has already called four hotels. The hotels keep telling him that with the changing of the leaves this is the height of tourist season. There are no vacancies. Phoebe says, "You can stay here. I'm house sitting for the apartment next door. We have room."

Big Game CEO

Phoebe's apartment mate is very attractive, and Bobby is very disappointed when she has to leave to catch an evening flight to Las Vegas. Carrying a leather Tommy Bahama designer suitcase she turns to Phoebe as she walks out the door and says, "Time to make some sugar from daddy."

Danny, unaware like usual, is oblivious to the comment. Howie is in the bathroom and doesn't hear it. But Bobby's eyes light up. Phoebe walks over to the kitchen and asks, "Do you want a campari and soda or a daiquiri?"

Bobby just stares at Phoebe for a few seconds. He finally says, "Forget the drinks. What the hell was that about sugar from daddy?"

Phoebe matter-of-factly says, "She has a 43 year-old sugar daddy who lives in Charlotte, North Carolina. He made millions selling medical supplies. He pays for her tuition and the rent for this apartment. He bought the sofa Danny is sitting on."

Danny's jaw drops. Bobby says, "Tell us more."

"There isn't much to say. She sees him a couple times a month to satisfy his needs. You know, you'd think all these older rich guys would have their act together but they are all so emotionally immature."

Bobby asks, "What do you mean by emotionally immature?"

"Rule number one: never tell a sugar daddy you have a boyfriend. These rich old guys tell you they just want companionship. But they got rich by wanting to own everything. What they really want is a commitment. If you tell them you have a boyfriend then they become more jealous than some insecure high school boy with a silly crush."

Just then Howie walks out of the bathroom and asks, "Who's jealous?"

Bobby interrupts, "How many older rich guys do you know?"

Phoebe plainly states, "You know the apartment next door that I'm apartment sitting for and you are staying in tonight? Both Helen and Brittany are in New York City this weekend with their sugars."

Bobby says, "Hear that Danny, tonight were sleeping in a house of ill repute."

Phoebe says, "You're so behind the times. Half the gals I know have a sugar. Right now I'm between sugars."

Howie asks, "You never told me you had a sugar?"

"It never came up."

Chapter 3: The Anarchist

Bobby asks, "Why'd you break up?"

Phoebe answers, "He started calling me twice a day once I told him I had a boyfriend."

Danny says, "Hence your rule number one."

Phoebe replies, "Exactly."

Bobby asks, "What's your rule number two?"

"I'm not supposed to tell guys the rules, but you're such a nice guy Bobby."

"So what's your rule number two?"

"Own a stock portfolio, even if it is just a few stocks. It helps attract a better breed of man."

Bobby asks, "Rule three?"

"Always take stock tips from your boss or sugar because if the stock goes down they feel guilty and will make-up for your loss."

"Rule four?"

"Never shop at Wal-Mart. Better to own a few nice things than all the necessities."

"Rule five?"

"To save money wear no clothes in your apartment and forget some of your lingerie."

Danny says, "I like rule five."

Bobby continues, "Rule six?"

"Never lend money to a boyfriend."

"Rule seven?"

"I can't remember. I'd have to get the list."

Bobby asks, "Can I see it?"

The four of them talk about sugar daddies and SeekingArrangement.com for the next half hour. Howie doesn't say much. By the look on his face it is easy to tell that he is stunned by the revelation his sister had a sugar daddy and is looking for a new one. He is waiting for the chance to talk to his sister alone. Danny doesn't say much either. He quickly assumes young coeds with sugar daddies are the norm at big universities. How else can they pay for tuition? Bobby does most of the talking. He is like a hardcore voyeur who just discovered the peep show in the seedy part of town. He asks question after question. 'How easy is it to find a sugar daddy online?' 'What's the etiquette for exchanging

85

money?' 'How often do you have to see them?' His list goes on and on.

Around four o'clock Phoebe leaves with a girlfriend to go exercise at the campus gym. Howie gives Bobby an annoyed 'please quit talking about sugar daddies' look, but Howie doesn't say anything. The annoyed look doesn't register with Bobby. The three cousins decide to checkout Harvard's campus. Bobby and Danny invent a new game, 'Guess which coeds have a sugar daddy?' as they walk across Harvard Yard. At first Howie keeps silent. After a few minutes he forgets about the revelation of Phoebe's ex-sugar daddy and gets caught up in the game. Soon they invent numerous variations such as 'Guess which coeds are so rich they don't need a sugar daddy?' 'Guess which coeds could get over $10,000 per month from a sugar daddy?' and 'Guess which coeds are too ugly to have a sugar daddy?'

At 8:00 PM the cousins meet-up with Phoebe and two of her friends at the India Pavilion for a late dinner. The two friends share an apartment down the hall from Phoebe's. As they enter the restaurant Danny asks Bobby, "I wonder why there are so many India-style restaurants around Harvard?"

Bobby quickly replies, "Because the students that go here all want to be Slumdog Millionaires."

Crowded, the wait for a table is 45 minutes. Phoebe tells Howie the wait will be worth it. They decide to stay.

Standing outside the restaurant the six of them begin to talk. Like Phoebe, her two friends, Marie Cardona and Ruth Joad, are seniors and plan to attend law school after graduating. Howie mentions he is an architect. Phoebe tells her friends that Howie is being humble. She goes on and on about Howie's awards, about his job in China before the lay-off, and how he is taking the year off to refocus and come up with new ideas. Howie smiles and just shrugs his shoulders. Self-conscious about only attending a community college, Bobby and Danny tell Marie and Ruth their names, but skip the detailed introduction.

Bobby and Danny immediately know they are in over their heads when the next topic of conversation is the difference in food from Northern and Southern India. For Bobby and Danny this is their first trip through the looking glass of well-educated upper class America. They are very uncomfortable.

Chapter 3: The Anarchist

Soon the topic of conversation changes to which writer was the first existentialist. One of the girls argues that Albert Camus is the first to fully develop the idea of existentialism in the book *The Stranger*. Another argues the first existentialist was Nietzsche. Now that Howie is back with a group of peers that can challenge him intellectually his eyes light up. Not to be out done by three young women Howie says, "Thomas Jefferson was the first existentialist."

Phoebe, Marie, and Ruth look at him in disbelief. Phoebe says, "You've got to be kidding!"

Howie replies, "Jefferson studied the philosopher John Locke, and understood Locke's ideas of life, liberty, and property. So why did Jefferson instead write, '*Life, Liberty, and the Pursuit of Happiness*' in the Declaration of Independence? Because Jefferson knew there is more to life than property. He understood that it is up to each individual to find meaning in his or her life. Bottom line is that America was founded on the idea of existentialism. Existentialism is an American creation." Marie and Ruth flash Howie a big smile. At that moment the young women know they are in the presence of an intellectual alpha-male and tonight is going to be a fun evening.

Soon the group is discussing how Sigmund Freud influenced the art of Picasso. Bobby and Danny excuse themselves to purchase a bottle of water at a convenience store across the street.

Standing across the street, each drinking a bottle of Avyaz water, Bobby and Danny slowly scan the crowd in front of the India Pavilion restaurant, taking in all the details. Almost all of the people in front of the restaurant are wearing Barack Obama for President buttons. There is a group of seven young Japanese women all wearing black boots, white designer jeans, and trendy leather jackets with Obama buttons. There is a group of six medical students with Obama buttons. There is a group of two caucasian women, a caucasian man, a black man, and two men from India with Obama buttons. There is a group of three unshaved physic students wearing beige dockers and white sneakers with Obama buttons. There are some hippie throwbacks wearing tie-dyed shirts, old jeans, and wool socks with leather sandals with Obama buttons. There is a group of well-dressed MBA students, another group of well-dressed students from Brazil, and another from Saudi Arabia with Obama buttons. Bobby says, "Think this Avyaz bottled water is sophisticated enough for the Harvard crowd?"

Danny answers, "The label says that the water is from a natural spring near the village of Avyaz, Turkey."

Bobby replies, "Right now I'd rather be hunting turkey."

Danny says, "I feel like a turkey."

Bobby asks, "Who do you think is going to hook-up with Howie tonight?"

Danny answers, "That's obvious. Ruth is too fat. Even if Howie gets drunk she is totally out of his league. That leaves Marie."

Bobby says, "Ruth isn't that fat. You know, I bet Ruth is out for a quick one-night stand with no strings attached. Look at her. I bet she doesn't have a boyfriend because she spends most of her time studying and planning her career. But she has needs. Life at Harvard is a lonely existential existence. She just needs some affection for a night. And I'm just the guy to give her the affection she is looking for."

Danny asks, "What does existential mean?"

Bobby answers, "Hell if I know. But you sound smart when you say it. You know, like other pretentious Swedish sounding words such as forsvunnen, kvinnlig, pinsamt, and methodology."

Danny laughs then asks, "So you think Ruth is looking for a one night stand?"

"She said she's from Philly."

Danny again laughs and says, "Yeah, all girls from Philly put out."

"Ruth would be a slam dunk if Phoebe weren't here."

Danny asks, "Why?"

"All college women get hot and wet if they think you have earnings potential. We could lie and say we're business majors."

"Yeah, too bad Phoebe is here."

Bobby looks over the diverse crowd of individuals and says, "An older Harvard woman would be a nice change of pace from our steady diet of teenage cashiers in the suburbs."

"Think the Harvard crowd thinks we are losers?"

Bobby answers, "Ever listen to Uncle Archie talk about Harvard. He hates this place. Says it breeds an obnoxious sense of entitlement."

Chapter 3: The Anarchist

"I remember Uncle Archie saying that they have the incoming freshmen heckle the movie *Love Story* so the students become numb to pain and suffering. It helps turn them into ruthless businessmen."

"Or ruthless businesswomen." Bobby takes a sip of water then says, "I have a hard time believing anyone would heckle a woman dying of cancer. Even for me that seems twisted. Plus *Love Story* sounds like a boring movie, but who knows. All I know is graduate from this place and the corporate world hands you the keys to the money vault."

Danny asks, "Harvard's not like Luzerne Community College, is it?"

"Guys like us have to fight for everything we get." Bobby takes another sip of water and then says, "I can't get this sugar daddy thing out of my head."

"I know, it sucks. All these old guys are stealing all our young women."

"That doesn't bother me. We'll be old someday chasing younger women. Look at our dads. The only thing sexier than a rich old guy is a rich young guy. There has to be a way to make money on this."

Danny asks, "Why do you think the girls do it?"

Bobby answers, "Would you sleep with an older woman if she paid for your tuition?" Danny just smiles. Bobby takes another sip of water then says, "Look at them. They all pretend to care about society, but as soon as they get a chance to upgrade to a better set of friends, boom, their gone."

"Is Howie just slumming with us until he goes back to Cornell next year?"

"Howie's not a Slumdog Millionaire. Howie is blood. Blood matters." Bobby finishes his water and wipes his mouth with his sleeve. He leaves the empty bottle on the window ledge in front of a Barack Obama for President poster as silly act of protest against the politically correct crowd, and walks across the street to rejoin Howie, Phoebe, Marie, and Ruth. After hesitating Danny also leaves his water bottle on the window ledge instead of throwing it in the trash can three feet away. He follows Bobby.

At 9:03 PM the six are seated for dinner. Topics of conversation between Howie and the three girls include 'whether Malcolm Gladwell is a good writer or a pop phenomena', 'whether the Scot-Irish who

Big Game CEO

settled the Appalachian Mountains are aggressive because they descended from herdsmen and not farmers', 'whether an underlying reason that lesbianism is becoming more trendy is because young men are having more difficultly making a living and supporting a family', and 'whether Barack Obama can maintain his lead against John McCain in the presidential election'.

During the discussion about the presidential election Bobby tries to defend John McCain and Sarah Palin. The three girls are all Obama supporters and quickly gang up on Bobby. Howie has been flirting with Marie all night and knows to keep his mouth shut. Feeling out of place, Danny hasn't said a word all night. He sees no reason to defend Bobby.

The girls blame George Bush for all the lax regulation that led to the current economic crisis. Bobby argues that the corporate bailouts are wrong, and that the Democrats will start handing out even more money to losers for no good reason. He tries using some of Uncle Archie's arguments like that the entire purpose of the government, taxes, and the judicial system is to let the weak survive in the world through game playing, networking, and conniving. The girls laugh with each other as they win handily. Bobby raises his voice as he goes down in flames. Danny sits there with a blank expression on his face. Howie just laughs to himself.

Howie agrees with Bobby that the Democrats will weaken the idea of individual responsibility, and individual responsibility is the highest sense of morality. But Howie also understands that you have to convince people slowly, especially women. During dessert Howie brings up a new topic of conversation. He mentions that a recent study finds that lawyers at big law firms advance more quickly if they assign blame for losing a case to other lawyers. These fast advancers realize that if you know you are going to lose a case, instead of working harder to win, you immediately start planning how you are going to assign the blame. Since all three girls plan to attend law school next year they feel embarrassed they hadn't heard about the study.

Howie points out again and again that back stabbing lawyers are the most successful. Then Danny opens his mouth for the first time all evening and blurts out his blue-collar manifesto, "This is why the Senate and Congress are so dysfunctional. Most Senators and Congressmen are

Chapter 3: The Anarchist

lawyers, and they rose to the top by blaming others for their mistakes. Blaming others is all politicians know how to do. Who cares about Republican policies or Democratic policies anyway? I don't know why my taxes should go to pay the salary of lawyers in such a screwed up system." Danny sounds just like his father, Charlie. The table is silent. The girls feel guilty. They clearly understand Danny is implying that he and people like him are tired of paying for the corporate jet-set lifestyle of Harvard graduates.

A few minutes later Ruth orders her third glass of wine. She starts playing footsy with Danny under the table. Danny's eyes light up with the unexpected advance. Danny starts rubbing his foot against her left leg. Ruth leans over and whispers in Danny's ear, "I like the strong, silent types." At that instant Marie and Howie are talking about Hollywood and China, and Marie uses the phrase 'imagination economy'.

Danny looks at Ruth, and while pretending to shoot himself in the head, he says, "Imagination economy, pacific rim economy, European economy, U. S. economy, health care economy, porn economy. If I hear the word economy one more time I'm going to blow the economy out of my brains."

Ruth smiles and says, "Your funny. I don't know why people have to add the word economy to the end of their sentences just to make ideas sound legitimate."

Danny smiles back. He knows he's on a roll. He asks, "What's existentialist mean?"

After dinner they walk a few blocks to a dance club where they meet Phoebe's boyfriend. Just after midnight Ruth and Danny are anxious to get back to her apartment. Howie is in the midst of another failed attempt to kick his Dexedrine habit and is feeling tired. He wants to head back with Marie and make an early night of it. Bobby isn't into dance clubs. He is more comfortable meeting girls where he works, or in his community college classes. The seven of them head back to Phoebe's apartment.

On the way back Danny whispers to Ruth that Howie's favorite place to make-out is on the roof. After they enter the apartment building Danny and Ruth disappear without saying a word to anyone.

Big Game CEO

The remaining five go to Phoebe's apartment for another round of drinks. After a few minutes of small talk Howie and Marie leave. Only Bobby, Phoebe, and Phoebe's boyfriend remain. After a few minutes of awkward conversation, Bobby asks, "Am I sleeping in the apartment next door tonight?"

Phoebe says, "Here's the key."

Next door Bobby plops himself on the sofa and puts his feet up on the coffee table. Bored, he turns on the TV. Every channel is showing ads for online dating services, Viagara, or tampons. He turns off the TV and opens the laptop sitting on the coffee table. Browsing through the website SeekingArrangement.com he keeps muttering to himself, "Young good looking coeds, rich old guys, there has to be a way to make money on this."

There is a knock at the door. He opens it. There stands Uncle Archie wearing a Boston College baseball cap, Boston College jacket, and the smell of Scotch on his breath. In his standard alpha-male tone Uncle Archie loudly says, "I couldn't remember Phoebe's number and I left my cell phone in the Escalade. Damn doorman made me walk all the way back to my Escalade just to get my damn cell phone."

Bobby says, "No doorman around here is going to trust someone wearing a Boston College jacket."

Uncle Archie asks, "Where's Howie and Danny?"

Bobby answers, "Got lucky."

"Good for them." Uncle Archie then glances over at the laptop on the coffee table and says, "Left surfing porn on the Internet. Don't feel bad. We've all been there before."

Bobby replies, "It's not what it looks like. I'm checking out the website SeekingArrangement.com. Did you know the two girls that share this apartment are both visiting sugar daddies this weekend in New York City?"

In his typical alpha-male tone Uncle Archie replies, "Rich, poor, young, old. The sooner you realize all women are whores the sooner you can start enjoying sex. Seniority gets the bedroom. Be a good guest and don't leave any stains on the sofa."

Bobby sarcastically laughs, "Ha, ha." Uncle Archie disappears into the bedroom. A few seconds later Bobby hears him fall on the bed. It is clear Uncle Archie didn't even bother to take off his clothes.

Chapter 3: The Anarchist

Bobby goes back to scrutinizing the website SeekingArrangement.com. Twenty minutes later Latino dance music starts blaring from the street below. Bobby walks over to the balcony to investigate. Uncle Archie comes out and yells, "What the hell is that?"

Bobby says, "I don't know. Looks like a dance party. There is a band and about seventy people."

Uncle Archie immediately goes to Phoebe's apartment and bangs on the door. After a delay Phoebe answers the door wearing a robe. It is clear she's been having sex with her boyfriend. Not knowing how to address him, she stutters, "Archie, dad, father."

Archie replies, "What the hell is going on?" Phoebe just shrugs her shoulders.

Phoebe, Bobby, and Archie walk over to Phoebe's balcony and stare down at the street. Phoebe's boyfriend walks out from the bedroom, barefoot, wearing only a pair of jeans and a t-shirt. He says, "I know what's going on. They want to get arrested for disturbing the peace. This way they get free front page publicity and everyone hears about the band."

Phoebe says, "Just let it go. I'm sure the doorman already called the cops."

Bobby says, "Check out their tour bus. It's an old school bus with a pimped-out paint job."

Uncle Archie looks at the cyan, yellow, and magenta school bus and says, "My God, the band is some sick cross between Menudo and the Partridge Family." He then looks at a large planter on the balcony with a dying fig tree, and says to Phoebe, "Looks like you don't have much of a green thumb."

Phoebe responds, "It's my apartment mates."

Archie says, "I'm sure she won't miss it." Archie looks up at the roof and then showing off his strength easily picks up the hundred and twenty-pound planter.

Phoebe asks, "What are you doing?"

Archie answers, "Men don't call the police."

Phoebe's boyfriend says, "Are you going to do something stupid?"

Uncle Archie stops, looks at him for a second, and growls, "You Harvard boys have no idea what it means to be a man. All you know how to do is strut around with an obnoxious sense of entitlement." He then says, "Bobby, get the door." Archie, wearing his Boston College jacket and lugging the hundred and twenty-pound planter with a dead fig tree disappears into the stairwell at the end of the hall.

Bobby runs back to the balcony in Phoebe's apartment and says, "I've got to see this."

Uncle Archie exits the stairwell onto the roof of the six-story apartment building. Not looking down he stumbles over Danny and Ruth. They are making out on a large blanket. Uncle Archie looks down and says, "Ignore me. Just go back about your business."

Uncle Archie walks over to the edge of the building and looks down at the street. With the bus as his target Archie walks forty feet to the south, tosses the planter off the roof, and says, "This is what I should have done to Meyer Wolfsheim fifteen years ago."

There is a loud bang. The sound of shattered glass fills the air. The planter lands directly in the center of the roof of the bus, crushing the roof, and breaking almost all of the bus's windows. The music immediately stops. The crowd scatters. Uncle Archie doesn't bother to look down at the chaotic scene below. He turns and immediately walks back down the stairwell.

Bobby, Phoebe, and Phoebe's boyfriend run out to the hall and just look at the stairwell. Howie and Marie come out of Marie's apartment and join them. Archie exits the stairwell and marches down the hall. Howie asks, "What happened up there?"

Archie looks at his son and says, "Dan is making-out with some voluptuous young coed. Looks like he's rounding third base. Good for him. I'm going to bed." Archie disappears in the apartment and closes the door.

Standing in the hall, no one says a word. Bobby finally breaks the silence. He looks at Howie and says, "Your dad is the coolest old guy on the planet. I wish my dad had spent six-months behind bars." Howie just laughs. Phoebe, Marie, and Phoebe's boyfriend look at Bobby and Howie with disgust.

On Saturday, Archie goes to the Boston College football game. Howie, Bobby, and Danny walk around Faneuil Hall Market Place for a while then over to Bunker Hill. On more than one occasion their fathers have said that their great-great-great-great-great-great-great-

Chapter 3: The Anarchist

grandfather died at Bunker Hill. Howie wonders if the story is true. In the evening the cousins hang out at a sports bar and watch the Ultimate Fighting Championship on the big screen. Bobby hits on a waitress but she rebuffs his advances. Danny wonders if he should call Ruth. Howie and Bobby both tell him to give it a rest.

Sunday morning Archie takes Phoebe, Howie, Bobby, and Danny out for brunch. Phoebe picks Café of India, a trendy restaurant in Harvard Square. Archie finds the place too trendy and artificial, but he doesn't say anything to Phoebe since he is trying to establish a friendship with his long lost daughter. Over breakfast Bobby and Danny call him Uncle Archie while Howie calls him dad. Phoebe carefully words her sentences to avoid using his name.

Aware of the surrounding tables, none of the five mention the planter incident from Friday night. Instead they spend the first part of breakfast talking about Danny and Ruth, and Howie and Marie. Howie and Phoebe feel funny talking about sex in front of their father. It doesn't bother Bobby. He jokes over and over again that Ruth and Marie were just using Danny and Howie to relieve the stress of midterms. Uncle Archie laughs at his jokes. Danny, not knowing what to think, starts laughing along. Soon Bobby brings up the topic of SeekingArrangement.com. Uncle Archie, Bobby, and Danny then start joking about coeds and sugar daddies.

Seeing that Phoebe is uncomfortable, Howie changes the topic to politics. Phoebe mentions she is working for the Obama campaign. Archie tells Phoebe she is wasting her time, that voting and politics are a waste of time, and that her generation spends too much time blogging and making contacts and not enough time living. Phoebe calls Archie an anarchist. Archie, in his standard alpha-male tone, replies, "Thank you."

After Archie pays the bill, the five of them walk back to Phoebe's apartment. Phoebe and Howie walk slowly so they can talk alone. They psychoanalyze their father. Both agree that he tossed the planter off the roof Friday night because he wasn't there to see the two of them grow-up, and that he is subconsciously mad that he will never be able to get back that missing part of his life. Phoebe then says that their father needs to back-off with is alpha-male attitude or he is going to end up in jail again. My God, he could have killed someone. Howie defends his father. He says that after jail Archie somehow managed to get back on his feet without anyone's help. How many people are capable of doing that?

Howie then brings up the topic of Phoebe's credit card bills. Phoebe tells Howie that over the summer she did an internship with a law firm in Washington, DC. They expected her to wear a new $1000 outfit everyday. Howie replies that looking at your credit card bills you must have spent more on clothes than vice-presidential candidate Sarah Palin. Howie then tells Phoebe that they've changed the law. You can't file bankruptcy on your student loans. The bank is garnishing 60% of his paycheck from Symanski and Nowicki. She defends herself, saying lawyers make more than architects. I'll be fine once I get a job. Howie tells Phoebe she's living in a dream word. The banks are falling apart. Good paying corporate jobs are a thing of the past.

Then a light goes off in Phoebe's head. She realizes Howie is upset about her sugar daddy that she saw for three weekends in September. They discuss the sugar daddy. Phoebe tells Howie that she liked it when he bought her expensive gifts. It made her feel special. Howie asks her about the sex. She says it's no big deal. Her boyfriend is cool with it. Next week she is starting a new relationship with a rich businessman from Chicago. He's flying in for the weekend. He has luxury box tickets for the Patriots / Bears game.

Concerned, Howie asks if she is going to be OK. Phoebe says, "I'll be fine. I don't feel like I'm being used. If anything, I feel like I'm taking advantage of him. The girls in my apartment have an informal support group. We stick together and exchange notes."

Howie accepts the fact that his younger sister is going to be OK. But he is also starting to agree with his father. Rich, poor, young, and old – that all women are whores. The sooner you realize this the sooner you can start enjoying being a man.

Phoebe then changes the subject. She asks, "Are you concerned about my financial future because subconsciously you are concerned about your financial future?" Howie tells Phoebe that the last few months have been difficult, much more difficult than he's led on.

Howie then tells Phoebe about Henry Cameron giving Howie his lifetime collection of notebooks. Howie says, "It was like Henry was saying no one in America cares about architecture any longer. Why

Chapter 3: The Anarchist

should I be an architect? I'm not sure what I want to do with my life anymore."

Later Phoebe asks Howie about Marie Cardona. They both agree she is nothing but a one-night stand. Phoebe then asks Howie about Dominique Francon. Howie says he hasn't talked to Dominique since she graduated from Cornell five months ago.

After saying their good-byes, Archie and the three cousins make the four-hour drive back to Port Jervis. Along the way they joke about the planter incident. Bobby calls Uncle Archie an American hero. Archie congratulates his son and Danny for getting laid. He then makes the comment that girls today are a lot easier than when he was young.

About half way back to Port Jervis, Howie starts giving Bobby a hard time about losing the Obama versus McCain argument to the girls over dinner. At one point Howie says, "If you want to win arguments then you have to be subtle. Like when my dad wanted me to go out for the football team my senior year in high school. Instead of saying leave me alone, I said, what's more harmful to my body, football or marijuana? That shut him up."

Archie says, "You conniving little brat."

Howie replies, "I'm six foot four and take after you in almost every way." Archie laughs.

Bobby asks, "So what should I have done?"

Howie answers, "Winning arguments with smart women is tough. But if you do it right then it becomes a big turn on. Your big mistake was when Marie said, 'prayer is the lottery for fools.' That is a code phrase meaning that white trash from Pennsylvania has nothing in their lives other than guns and God. You fell for that code phrase hook, line, and sinker. You immediately raised your voice and brought up the issue of Obama's racist pastor Reverend Jeremiah Wright."

Bobby asks, "What should I have done?"

Howie answers, "Rule one: never raise your voice, it is a sign of weakness."

"Cable news commentators yell at each other all the time."

"Cable news commentators are unsophisticated idiots. That is why they work for the cable news. Rule two: laugh at yourself but always with a twist. If it was me, I would have said 'I play the lottery because

I know it pays for the college education of people like you. I guess that makes me a fool.' That line subtly tells them that because the girls go to Harvard they have an obnoxious sense of entitlement. But you don't want to say they have an obnoxious sense of entitlement directly to their face."

"Archie said that directly to their face."

"My dad's crazy. He doesn't care about winning arguments."

Archie says, "That's because I know I'm right. Everyone else can go to hell."

Howie looks at Bobby and says, "Rule number three: when arguing with women let them win most of the battles. Your goal is to win the war. The only point of getting into a heated argument with a woman is to get laid. Most woman find it a turn-on if you show them the world from a different point of view."

Archie interjects, "You should call rule number three the Sam and Diane strategy."

With a confused look on his face Howie asks, "Who are Sam and Diane?"

Archie answers, "God, do I feel old. The television show *Cheers?*"

Howie says, "I don't know what you are talking about."

Bobby asks Howie, "Are these rules for debate what they teach you in architecture school?"

Howie says, "This is what they teach in prep school. My debate instructor made us study Sun Tzu's *The Art of War*. He said Sun Tzu holistic approach to life and war would make us better debaters."

Bobby asks, "Are there any more rules."

Howie glances at Danny and says, "Last rule: it's always best if you can get someone else to make your argument for you. At dinner Danny was brilliant with his blue-collar manifesto. He implied that he and people like him are tired of supporting the corporate jet-set lifestyle of the Harvard crowd. Being born and raised in Manhattan, if I would have said that then I would have sounded like a hypocrite."

There is a moment of silence as Archie speeds past a line of four cars. Danny stares at a woman talking on a cell phone, driving slowly in a Toyota Prius, and holding up traffic. Archie breaks the silence after passing the Prius and says, "You know, that Marie is right."

Bobby asks, "Right about what?"

Chapter 3: The Anarchist

"Prayer is the lottery for fools."

During the entire discussion Danny doesn't say a word. He just listens intently. For the remainder of the drive Danny daydreams. He reminisces about going to church every Sunday with his mother and wondering if that was a total waste of time. He thinks about Bobby's comment when they worked at Circuit City, "Those boys at Bear-Sterns are nothing but pampered rich kids. The government bailed them out. It's all a game. Are you going to be a fool your whole life or are you going to be a player?" Danny thinks about Howie's comment "It's always best if you can get someone else to make your argument for you." Danny thinks about Uncle Archie's comment about prayer and ponders, "If prayer is the lottery for fools then what does it mean to be a good citizen?"

Chapter 4: The Ayn Rand Society

For most of us, our friends and peers have a bigger influence on our beliefs than our parents. Howie is no exception.

Two weeks after the famed turkey-hunting outing, Lucille McKee lands an exclusive catering affair in the center of the universe, commonly known as Manhattan. The event is the keynote dinner for the Ayn Rand Society.

Crossing the George Washington Bridge in Bobby's F-150 Pickup Truck, the first snow of the season begins to fall. Danny and Bobby talk about how they are glad they don't live in Manhattan. It cost too much, life is too confining, and you can't go snowmobiling. Howie quietly looks down at the Hudson River then up at the Manhattan skyline. Studying the swirling snow around each of the tall buildings he makes notes of the wind patterns and files the results into the architectural regions of his brain. Howie then wonders if one of his building designs shall every grace the Manhattan skyline.

As the three cousins set-up for the dinner, Lucille is torn on whether to tuck the bar away in a quiet corner or put it front and center in order to show off Howie's eye-candy to the females in the audience. Lucille decides on front and center. She places the bar along the back wall, overlooking the dining hall, and opposite the podium. Hustling, the cousins set-up the white linen table clothes, white linen napkins, and silverware with gold trim. Lucille personally arranges the blue rose centerpieces.

Chapter 4: The Ayn Rand Society

For Howie the dinner seems like a typical dinner. The smell of prime rib fills the dining hall. The older women fill his tip jar. After serving dinner there is the standard lull. During the break Bobby and Danny hangout at the bar and make small talk with Howie. Danny whispers, "What the hell is the Ayn Rand Society?"

Bobby answers, "It sounds like a German fascist society that's into sadomasochism."

Danny replies, "That stuff is weird. I could never get into sex and pain. However, I wouldn't mind hooking up with a girl that's into those kinky black leather outfits. That would be fun."

Bobby says, "If you wear black leather you have to toss in a little suffering. I wouldn't mind getting my butt spanked by some hot German barmaid."

Just then the head of the Ayn Rand Society announces the after dinner keynote speaker. It is Dominique Francon. Danny is oblivious to the ghost-like look on Howie's face, but not Bobby. Bobby studies Howie expression, and then studies Dominique as she gracefully glides across the front of the room to the podium. Her pale skin, black lipstick, and large circles of dark purple eye shadow give the appearance she is tired and emaciated. However, it is clear the painted on bags under her eyes are a subtle protest against the overwhelming dominance of the sports industrial complex in America. Dominique's firm gaze, confident posture, and large black belt accessorizing her low-cut bronze evening dress leave no doubt this is a strong and self-assured woman. Her hair is purposefully wild and perfectly unkempt in a manner that is the envy of even the trendiest of hairstylists. Dominique's look immediately tells the audience she is a new type of power player that plans to take the 21st century by storm.

Bobby asks Howie, "Is this the famous Dominique from Cornell?"

Howie just mutters, "Oh God."

Danny asks Howie, "Is she into black leather and sadomasochism?"

Howie again mutters, "Of God."

Standing at the podium Dominique radiates confidence. No one would guess she is only 22 years old. With a strong voice she addresses the dining hall, "Even though Ayn Rand was a woman, most analyze her writings and philosophy from a man's point of view. Tonight I want to analyze Ayn Rand from a woman's point of view. First let's ask a few questions. Is Ayn Rand still relevant? Is Dagny Taggart, the heroine from Rand's most famous novel, *Atlas Shrug*, a heroine of the Cold War era who is still relevant today? The answers are simple. Ayn Rand is more relevant today than ever. Dagny Taggart is a heroine who was ahead of her time. She is the role model of what a woman should be in the 21st Century!" A few older men and women applaud.

Danny looks at Howie and whispers, "Who is Dagny Taggart?" Howie signals to Danny to be quiet.

At that moment Dominique looks towards the back of the room and makes eye contact with Howie for the first time. She stumbles for a moment. She repeats herself in order to collect her thoughts, "Dagny Taggart is a role model of what a woman should be in the 21st Century. She effectively ran the Taggart Transcontinental Railroad. She fought to change the misguided social policies of the government. And more importantly, but often overlooked, she had sexual relationships with three men of ability: Fancisco d'Anconia, Hank Rearden, and John Galt." After Dominique's last sentence, everyone in the audience looks confused.

Dominique pauses and looks directly at Howie. Next she looks at a wealthy older man in the audience sitting next to her mother. Dominique continues, "You may ask, why is having sexual relations with three men of ability so important? To answer that question you have to ask another. Over the last several thousand years how did the human race come to dominate the planet? It is because smart women like Dagny Taggart, acting in their own selfish interests, decided to have sex with men of ability. Imagine what the human race would be like if over the last thousand years women decided to have sex with lazy and incompetent men. Humans would be slow, fat, ugly, and dim-witted. We would all be manatees." A few people in the audience laugh under their breath.

Dominique looks at the few people who are laughing and says, "Being slow, fat, and ugly is funny in a sick and twisted sort of way." She pauses for dramatic effect and slowly looks over the room. In a commanding voice she says, "And our government is making us lazy and weak in a sick and twisted sort of way! Welfare, Medicaid, Social

Chapter 4: The Ayn Rand Society

Security, and Sarbanes-Oxley allow the weak to survive! And the weak are like termites. Once they find a foothold they want more and more and more. They take and take until destroying the foundation of society. I ask you this – In America is there a man alive today that is willing to take responsibility for his own actions?"

Dominique glances again at the rich man in the audience sitting next to her mother and says, "Critics of Ayn Rand say that selfishness is evil and that sacrifice for the needs of others is good. Her critics are misguided fools. Ayn Rand was a visionary. She is the first woman to clearly state how a woman needs to live to make the world a better place. To help build a prosperous society, a virtuous woman will do what she must to find the best man available: an ambitious man; a man who can build her a castle; a man who can build a prosperous business so that society can thrive; and a man who can produce wealth she can pass on to her children. Complex societies did not spontaneously form out of nothingness. They are the product of many women acting in their own selfish interests. Ayn Rand is the first to clearly understand this." The audience applauds.

Dominique looks towards the back of the room and stares directly at Howie, "Acting in her own selfish interests, a virtuous woman will seek out an ambitious man with the best genes available; genes that she can pass on to her children. Language, art, math, humor, music, resourcefulness, ingenuity, strength, and dexterity are not an accident. For thousands of years, women have been acting in their own selfish interests. Human DNA didn't spontaneously form out of nothingness. Human DNA is the product of thousands and thousands of mothers acting in their own selfish interests. Thank God for selfish mothers. Thank God for Ayn Rand's enlightment." The crowd applauds.

Dominique again looks at the rich man sitting next to her mother, and continues, "Today capitalism is under attack. The agents of mediocrity who control the guilt industrial complex are constantly tainting all the fruits of self-interests. It is absurd to blame corporations for poverty in third world countries. It is counter-productive to associate corporate jets with greed. It is ridiculous to blame American foreign policy for the creation of the Taliban. Yet they do. These agents of guilt and mediocrity want you to believe that wealth is evil. But what's more evil, to cut enterprise off at the knees so the average amongst us can feel good about themselves, or for the leaders of enterprise to lift the community to a higher level on the back of rational self-interests? Is it moral to wallow in government regulation and the self-pity of the social welfare state? Or is it moral that a community prospers by trading and producing goods by self-interested individuals?" The audience applauds.

Dominique pauses, studies the room again, looks at her mother, and continues, "And these agents of guilt and mediocrity want you to believe that women who chase wealthy and talented men are conniving bitches. But Rand understood that conniving bitches are the oil that greases the wheels of free enterprise." The audience laughs. Dominique smiles and continues, "I'm just stating the obvious. Everyone knows that conniving bitches are the oil that greases the wheels of free enterprise. Everyone is just afraid to admit it. Everyone that is except for Ayn Rand." A few people in the audience applaud.

Dominique clears her throat and continues, "Instead of rambling on and on, let me conclude with a power question and answer session. I'll ask the questions and I'll provide the answers."

Dominique pauses, studies the room yet again, looks directly at Howie, and rapidly rattles off, "Why, on average, does a taller man father more children than a shorter man? Because most women believe height is a desirable trait. Why do boys want to be rock stars? To woo women. Why are some women groupies? Wealth and musical ability are desirable traits. Why do some women chase doctors? Because wealth and intelligence are desirable traits. Why do soldiers fight? To woo women. If you don't believe me there are seventy-two virgins you can ask. Why do men create great works of art? To impress women. Why do rich older men marry younger women? So they can pass on more of their genes to the next generation. Why do men design and build castles? To honor the good life." Howie catches Dominique's eye. He shakes his head and smiles.

Dominique looks at everyone in the audience and concludes, "Why is the welfare state harmful for the community? Because it helps lazy men and lazy women propagate their genes. It makes us all weaker. And one last question: Is Ayn Rand still relevant? The answer is more so than ever!" Everyone gives Dominique a standing ovation, everyone that is except her mother. Her mother just sits there proudly with a

Chapter 4: The Ayn Rand Society

wide smile. Finally her mother stands and walks over to Dominique. They hug in front of everyone. There is another round of applause from the audience.

Back at the bar Bobby and Danny don't know what to think. Danny looks confused. Bobby's face has a surreal look, as if he just found himself on another planet. Bobby turns to Howie and says, "Dominique is one freaky woman."

Danny looks at Bobby and says, "I'd do her."

Bobby replies, "I'd do her eight ways on Sunday. So Howie, I bet Dominique knows more than eight positions. She must be a freak in the sack?"

Howie says, "Just button it."

Danny says, "Hey Bobby, did you know that a female eagle will mate with a male eagle for life, unless the female eagle is unhappy with her mate. Then she'll kill it and find a new mate."

Bobby replies, "I did not know that female eagles live in Manhattan."

Danny says, "They like to nest at the top of tall buildings."

Bobby says, "Thanks for pointing that out to me."

Danny replies, "You're welcome."

Bobby says, "I think Howie's in freaky love."

Danny adds, "With a freaky eagle woman."

Danny and Bobby start singing Rick James most famous song, "She's a super freak, a super freak, she's super freaky."

Howie says, "Don't you have to serve dessert?"

Bobby and Danny head into the kitchen, laughing together and still singing, "She's a super freak, a super freak, she's super freaky."

The standard crowd of older men and older women make their way to the bar for another round of scotch and water. Howie keeps looking at Dominique. She never looks up, focusing all her attention on the older rich man sitting next to her mother. After dessert most of the audience stays around and mingles for another thirty minutes. Slowly everyone starts to leave. A trendy thirty-something year old French man with platinum white hair joins Dominique, her mother, and the wealthy older man. The four leave together. Howie is heart-broken.

A few minutes later a familiar voice asks, "Bartender, I'll have a screaming orgasm."

Startled, Howie replies, "Ah, ah, were out of Bailey's Irish Cream."

"Cat got your tongue?"

"More like a tiger's got my tongue."

Dominique replies, "Roar."

"How are you doing Dominique?"

"Doing well. I'm working two days a week at Christie's Auction House. I can get you a really good deal on a Claude Monet. With the economic downturn you find out just how many seemingly wealthy families are hopelessly in hock when working at Christie's."

"You're Dominique. That can't be all you're doing."

"You know me too well. I'm just waiting for a few geezers to retire so I can get a seat on the board of directors. I'm also putting together plans for a new business."

"And what business might that be."

"Top secret."

"Good to see you're keeping busy. Who's that French guy with neon white hair?"

"That's my assistant Stephan Mallory. Don't feel threatened. He's flaming. So how are things with Howie?"

"Killing time until I go back to school next year. Got laid-off from my job in China."

"That architecture gig didn't last long."

"Two months."

"So you're a bartender now."

"Tips are good. Have to pay back my student loans."

"Looks like you've gone native."

"Funny."

"Seriously. Working for tips. You're a great artist. Your buildings are genius. This has to be some kind of sick joke."

"To be honest I've never been happier."

"You really have gone native."

"Quit saying that. I'm losing respect for you. Are you turning into Paris Hilton?"

"Please. You know I'm not some kind of Paris Hilton-like tramp. Paris Hilton does what men want her to do. Men do what I want them to do. That's why all men respect me."

"You haven't changed a bit. So how'd you land this gig?"

Chapter 4: The Ayn Rand Society

"Mother thought it would be a good idea for me to impress Gail."

"That was Gail Wynand, the billionaire?"

"Yes, the billionaire."

"So your family's billion isn't enough?"

"With the recession our wealth is only eight-hundred million now."

"Only eight-hundred million."

"That's not much split three ways."

"Three ways?"

"Between mother, brother, and me. Father passed away a few months ago."

"Sorry to hear that."

"His time had come."

"So your mother is already back in the saddle."

"Please, Gail isn't going to chase a woman my mother's age. Even one of my mother's caliber. She knows that and I know that."

"Don't tell me."

"We've been talking about getting married."

"What is this, thirteenth century Europe? Are you negotiating the merger of two empires?"

"Pretty much."

"Jesus Dominique, he's fifty years older than you."

"Power is beauty. Look, I told him I had to go to the bathroom. Gail doesn't like to wait. His helicopter is on the roof. We are flying to a hedge fund managers' conference in the Virgin Islands. Give me your cell number. I'll call you when I get back. Oh, if you want I can pay off your student loans."

"That's OK."

"You really have gone native."

Howie writes his cell number on a napkin. Just as he finishes Dominique's mother approaches the bar. She says, "Let's go."

Dominique replies, "This is Howie Roark."

"The Howie Roark. He's even more handsome than you described." She then gives Howie a stay away from my daughter look and puts a thousand dollars in the tip jar. Dominique secretly slips the napkin into her pocket. Dominique's mother grabs her hand. In a flash they are gone.

Five days later Dominique calls. Howie wants to say no but he can't. They secretly rendezvous at her penthouse apartment on the Eastside of Manhattan. At midnight, with the lights off and the windows open, they look over the Manhattan skyline. Dominique knows that for Howie there is no bigger turn-on than the skyline of Manhattan at night. They have sex. Dominique lights up her customary after sex cigarette. Howie says those cancer sticks are going to kill her. Dominique laughs, and says she only smokes during and after sex. Howie laughs, and asks, "During?"

They have sex again. This time she leans against her bedroom desk, casually smoking a cigarette while Howie gets her from behind. With the cigarette in her mouth, Dominique moans, "Now this is good sex!" Howie just stares at the Manhattan skyline and doesn't say a word.

Afterwards Dominique says, "I've got a secret, but you can't share it with anyone, not even your sister."

"You can trust me."

"My dad wasn't my biological father."

"What?"

"A month after he passed away, my mother told me she conceived me with a more desirable man. She said she did it because she loved me. She didn't want me to be short, ugly, and gruff like my father."

"Your family has an unusual take on the word love."

"My mother is a great woman. She is a woman ahead of her time."

"So who's your father?"

"I'll just tell you this. He was a quarterback in the NFL."

"Really. Who?"

"I'm not telling."

"Phil Simms. No wait. Your mother likes older men. Joe Namath. You have Joe Namath's eyes."

"Please, it wasn't Joe Namath. I'm not telling you anymore about my real father. Do you know why I brought this up?"

"No. Wait. Oh, God."

"You figured it out, didn't you?"

"You want me to be the father of your children."

Chapter 4: The Ayn Rand Society

"You're the most talented man I know. Just think that your son will have the wealth to build all of your dreams."

Howie doesn't say a word. He just silently stares over the night skyline of Manhattan and sighs.

Chapter 5: The Rose of Scranton

Howie hopes Dominique will call his cell phone on New Year's Eve. The call never comes. For Howie the New Year arrives with a whimper as he watches Bobby and Danny hook-up. Depressed, Howie makes zero New Year's resolutions the next day. He considers spending January and February in Tahiti working as a bartender but he is tired of traveling overseas. As a rich kid growing up in Manhattan, he's already traveled to the Caribbean, South America, Moscow, Tokyo, India, Turkey, Egypt, South Africa, Chile, Spain, and Morocco. Spending time with his cousins in Port Jervis just feels more exotic.

Bobby teases Howie for most of January that for someone not in school he studies way too much and never sleeps. Howie's answer is always the same, "Television bores me."

Howie is now taking four Dexedrine a day. He sleeps only three and a half hours a night. On a typical weekday Howie wakes at 5 AM and works at the computer for six hours. Between 11 AM and 12 AM he eats brunch and reads the New York Times, The Wall Street Journal, every architectural magazine imaginable, and occasionally one of Danny's survivalist magazines. Howie works out at the gym for two hours after brunch. In the late afternoon he either works at the computer and tries to improve one of Henry Cameron's architectural designs or hangs out with his cousins and plays video games. After dinner there is band practice for a few hours. Between 10 PM and 1 AM the cousins hit the local clubs.

Chapter 5: The Rose of Scranton

Before hitting the local clubs the cousins go through their standard ritual. Bobby fast-forwards to the end of the movie *Bride Wars*. They watch the scene where Olivia is about to marry. Her friend and nemesis, Emma, mad and determined, races down the aisle. Bobby always heckles, "Here comes the nut job."

In the movie Emma tackles Olivia to the ground. The two wrestle in front of friends and family. Howie always says, "If I produced this movie I would have somehow dumped water on them. Women wrestling in wet wedding dresses always increases the size of your target demographic."

During the fight scene Emma and Olivia have a revelation that their feuding is silly and they should be friends again. Danny always heckles, "Isn't that sweet."

Next Emma's fiancé, Fletcher, arrives. Bobby yells, "Do it! Be a man and dump the bimbo." Fletcher breaks up with Emma. The three cousins cheer.

Howie turns off the DVD before Emma gets in the last word. Danny always says, "Fletcher is the only normal character in the whole damn movie. For his sake I hope Fletcher somehow escapes that psycho-ward known as Manhattan."

Bobby always replies, "Yeah, look at what Manhattan did to Kramer and George Costanza."

Danny says, "Yeah, Howie is the only guy we know from Manhattan who isn't uptight and psycho." Howie knows Bobby and Danny do this routine every night because they want him to become one of their own. At this point in his life Howie is confused and doesn't know which side of the Hudson he wants to live his life.

One January day Howie stumbles upon an article in The Wall Street Journal summarizing a study of the two recessions of the early 1980s. The study followed the careers of college students who graduated during those recessions. Starting out during a recession, the students obviously had a hard time finding a good job. However, the study also finds that twenty years later many of these graduates still have a hard time getting their careers back on track. The study estimates that graduating during a recession costs an average college graduate several hundred thousand dollars in lost salary. The article concludes that things will probably be even worse for the unfortunate graduates of this Great Recession. Howie cuts out the article and tapes it on the wall next to his computer.

For Howie none of the local girls compares to Dominique. In January he realizes it's not her money that he is attracted. It's Dominique's intelligence, style, flair, and taste for life that he misses. It never dawns on Howie until now that he loves Dominique. He realizes they are soul mates. He wonders if there is any way they will end up together.

On the weekends he hangs out with Bobby and Danny at Uncle Joe's lodge. They spend most of their time snowmobiling or taking target practice with their compound bows. Danny and Bobby invent of new game. Riding double on the snowmobile, the driver tries to run down rabbits, squirrels, and other small animals while the other tries to shoot the animal with an arrow. Howie takes part in their game to take his mind off of Dominique. On his second time out he kills a rabbit with Bobby driving. It is the only time in January that Howie feels alive.

February comes. For Howie the grayness of winter is mind numbing. With Dominique gone there is a void in Howie's existence. Bored of the local clubs and bored of his January routine he is looking for a change.

One evening Bobby and Danny are talking about Bobby's 'Literature of the Western World' class. Danny tells Bobby that having your dad as a teacher is a bad idea. Bobby agrees but then says the downside is worth it since Catherine Halsey is in the class. Danny agrees that Catherine Halsey gives you something to look at during all those boring lectures about literature. Plus she's smart. It is the first time Howie hears the name Catherine Halsey. He's curious.

Howie asks Bobby, "So is your dad's literature course that boring?"

Bobby answers, "Actually it's not too bad. The theme of the course is '*What does it mean to be a man in the modern world?*'"

Howie replies, "That sounds interesting. Mind if I tag along with you tomorrow morning? Don't tell Uncle Joe I'm sitting in on the course. I'll go incognito."

Later Howie asks Bobby for a copy of the reading list. Howie doesn't say anything to Bobby and Danny but notes to himself that

Chapter 5: The Rose of Scranton

he has already read almost every book on the list by the time he was a sophomore in prep school. The only books on the reading list he hadn't read are Hawthorne's *A Scarlet Letter* and Lewis's *Liar's Poker*.

The next day Howie catches a ride with Bobby in his F-150 Pickup Truck. As they approach Luzerne Community College it strikes Howie just how spartan a community college campus is compared to Harvard or Cornell. Wearing sunglasses and a baseball hat Howie sits in the back row. He counts sixty-two students, forty-seven females and fourteen males. Howie quickly figures out that Bobby is taking this class not because his father is teaching it but because of the female-to-male ratio.

For Howie the visit to Uncle Joe's class quickly turns into an anthropological expedition. He mumbles under his breath, "Now I know how Margaret Mead must have felt like when she visited Samoa in the 1920s." During Uncle Joe's lecture Howie quietly takes mental notes of the similarities and differences between this class and his classroom experiences at Cornell. At Cornell over half the students brought tape-recorders to class to record the professor's lecture while at Luzerne there isn't a single tape-recorder in the room. At Cornell almost every student took detailed notes while at Luzerne only about half the students do. At Cornell the professor would lecture, and then later the students would break up into smaller discussion groups led by a teaching assistant while at Luzerne Uncle Joe is the lecturer and discussion leader. Most of Uncle Joe's class is simply a question and answer session. From the student's answers it is clear to Howie that most haven't read the material.

Just like at Cornell, at Luzerne both female and male students have carefully engineered the seating arrangement to maximize the number of dating opportunities. Bobby has taken a seat in the third row, just in front of a group of vivacious young women, and just behind a group of five women sitting in the first two rows. Among the group of five is by far the most beautiful young woman in the class. Howie mumbles under his breath, "That has to be Catherine Halsey. From Bobby's seating position he is clearly on the hunt."

During Uncle Joe's question and answer session Catherine Halsey and her friends ask the most intelligent questions and have the most insightful answers. Howie mumbles under his breath, "I wonder how those five ended up at Luzerne Community College?" Occasionally Bobby says something funny, insightful, and something you didn't have to read the book to already know. Howie mumbles under his breath, "Bobby is smart, but he works too hard at being lazy and clever."

After class Bobby rushes to his next class. Howie has an hour to kill waiting for his ride. He walks over to the coffee shop at the campus center. He gets a coffee, sits down, and starts reading one of his architectural magazines when he sees Catherine Halsey. She is with a big, good-looking young man. Howie can hear Catherine say something about wedding plans in June. She then says, "Peter, I'll meet you here in an hour." Before she can turn around Howie quickly slips into the bathroom, throws his ¾ full coffee cup in the trash, and checks himself out in the mirror to make sure everything is in order. He quickly exits the bathroom and stands in line behind Catherine.

She orders a gingersnap latte. As she stands there waiting for her order Howie asks, "You just came from Literature of the Western World, didn't you?"

Warily she responds, "I'm in that class."

"I enjoyed your comments on the *Scarlet Letter*. The theme of original sin, and that once Adam and Eve were expelled from the Garden of Eden that God forced them to labor and procreate – two labors that seem to define the human condition. That was dead on the money."

"What's your point?"

"It's clear that you and your four friends are the smartest group in the class. Do you mind if I look at your notes. I'm thinking about sitting in on the class."

"Fine."

Howie orders a large black coffee and joins Catherine at a small table in the corner. He purposefully takes off his baseball cap and sunglasses. Catherine takes note of his curly blonde hair and steel blue eyes. She is surprised by his male model good looks and wonders if he has been sent by God or by the Devil. Catherine asks, "What's your name?"

From that moment on, Howie decides to tell Catherine the truth. He tells her that he is from Manhattan, that he went to Cornell for four

Chapter 5: The Rose of Scranton

years, that he plans to return for a fifth year this fall, that he took a job as an architect last May, spent time in China last summer, was laid-off, lives with his cousins in Port Jervis, and works part-time as a bartender. He tells Catherine that Professor Joseph Roark is his uncle. The time off from school has been a good change of pace, but he is starting to get bored. He thinks that sitting in on a literature class with the theme '*What does it mean to be a man in the modern world?*' might be a good way for him to figure out what to do with his life. Telling his life story to a beautiful young woman is like therapy for Howie.

Catherine doesn't say a word during Howie's self-analysis. She finally says, "You were the last thing I was expecting this morning. Here are my notes. You can look them over for a few minutes."

Howie glances at the first few pages. He thinks about saying that she has beautiful handwriting but catches himself. He can tell she is not interested in him and he doesn't want to use any obvious pick-up lines. So instead he reads the first few pages of her notes in detail and starts asking all types of questions. "What do you plan to do for your term paper? I see that on the last day of class Uncle Joe also expects a 250-word idea for a new novel on what it means to be a man in the modern world. He wants to use these ideas as inspiration for his new book this summer. What idea for a novel do you plan to submit?"

Catherine opens up a little bit. She says that if she were to write a book on what it means to be a man in the modern world she would keep it simple. Heroes are for losers. The James Dean bad boy theme is old. Get rich quick schemes are over-played. Someone who is willing to go the distance in life is what matters. Life is simple. Those who haven't figured this out yet are the ones who make love so complicated.

Howie is stunned by her answer. He stumbles then says, "I guess you have thought about what you're going to write."

"A little. I don't plan on sharing my best ideas with the teacher."

"You are a smart woman. I never share my best designs for a new building with anyone until it matters. You never know who might steal your idea."

"So how many of these books did you read while you were at Cornell?"

"Not many. That's because I read most of them in prep school. At Cornell I just read the Cliff Notes to refresh my memory. I'm not

Big Game CEO

taking the class to learn about literature. I'm taking the class to figure out what it means to be a man in the modern world. Why do you think Uncle Joe selected these books for his reading list?"

"With *Bonfire of the Vanities*, *The Great Gatsby*, *Liar's Poker*, and *The Grapes of Wrath*, money is clearly a main theme."

"Do you think money is the most important part of being a man in the modern world?"

With that question Catherine opens up. She answers, "In this day and age, money is too important. The other major themes from the books on the reading list are war, glory, and power. To be honest, war, glory, money, and power all bore me." They talk intently for the next half hour. She loses track of time. After glancing at her watch she says, "I have to run."

Howie asks, "One question before you leave. Why all the rose stickers on your notebook?"

"My middle name is Rose."

"Rose is a nice name."

"I enjoyed our conversation." Catherine bites her lip, knowing she shouldn't have said that. Howie smiles. She quickly leaves.

Howie watches as she walks away with her fiancé, Peter. He sighs. From their hour-long conversation Howie is highly aware she is very different from all the other young women he's met in his young life. In today's jaded world her outlook on life is healthy and fresh. Even though she initially gave Howie the cold shoulder, he knows she is a sweet girl – authentic and caring. In a more innocent time Catherine would be the type of girl every young boy would want to marry.

There is no one in line at the coffee shop counter. Howie walks up, slips the cashier a five-dollar bill, and asks, "Who is that guy with Catherine Halsey?"

The cashier replies, "His name is Peter Keating. That's all I know."

From that day on Howie sits in the back row of every single one of Uncle Joe's lectures wearing a baseball cap and sunglasses. And everyday after class he and Catherine secretly rendezvous. They share a coffee in a secluded table in the corner of the coffee shop at the campus center. She always makes sure to leave early. It is clear to Howie she doesn't want Peter Keating to know of Howie's existence.

Chapter 5: The Rose of Scranton

Howie and Catherine spend most of their time discussing the reading material for that week. Often they talk about what it means to be a man in the modern world, but Catherine also likes to discuss what it means to be a woman in the modern world. Occasionally they discuss Catherine's dream to become a writer. Howie listens carefully and provides advice. He tells Catherine about his mentor, Henry Cameron. Howie recalls Henry's parting words of advice, "Don't waste your time reinventing the wheel". He then mentions that she could use a mentor. Catherine asks, "What other advice do you have for aspiring writers?"

Howie makes the mistake of answering honestly, "One time I overheard Uncle Joe talking with my father. Joe said most women have a hard time writing anything original for the same reason they make lousy stand-up comics and scientists. Women have a hard time objectively observing people from an outsiders' point of view. Women always want to write about themselves and how they feel. You know how boring that is."

Catherine is furious. She replies, "That's not true!"

"You asked for my advice. I'm just telling you what my Uncle Joe said." Catherine is still mad. Howie looks deep into her eyes. She turns away. He says, "Look, we're very similar people. You want to be a renown writer and I want to be a great architect. So do thousands of other people. The world is highly competitive, more so now than ever. If either of us is going to make it big then we are going to have to do things differently."

Catherine looks at Howie and smiles. She asks, "Do you have any other advice?"

As spring approaches Howie watches his rose blossom. During Uncle Joe's question and answer sessions Catherine shines. Her answers are concise, to the point, and in Howie's opinion occasionally brilliant. Her questions are insightful. Howie smiles every time she starts a question, 'If I were a man I would ...', or 'His point of view is completely different than ...'.

With spring comes spring break. Bobby and Danny are planning on heading to Jamaica with a large group from Luzerne. They ask

Howie if he wants to come along. Howie replies, "Give me a few days." It is at that moment that Bobby knows something is up.

Bobby asks, "Who is she?"

"What do you mean?"

"Don't play dumb. There is no reason for you not to come on spring break with us unless there is a girl involved. So who is she?"

At that instant Howie's cell phone rings. Like the cat that keeps coming back, it is Dominique. Howie tells Bobby, "Excuse me." He then locks himself in the bathroom and takes the call.

Dominique tells Howie she wants to fly him first class to Melbourne, Australia for the launch of her new company. Howie wants to say no. He wants to tell Dominique about Catherine. But he can't. He looks in the mirror, smiles, and says, "What about Gail Wynand?"

Dominique replies, "He'll be thousands of miles away."

Howie shakes his head and asks, "So how is the weather in Melbourne this time of year?"

During their secret rendezvous the next day Howie asks Catherine, "What are you doing over spring break?" She dodges the questions. After a little prodding Howie gets Catherine to admit she is staying with some friends at a condo in Pensacola. Howie quickly deduces the 'some friends' is Peter Keating. Howie spitefully jokes, "You mean Pensacola, Florida, the Redneck Riviera?" Catherine gets up and quickly walks to the bathroom. Howie can hear Catherine crying.

After a few minutes she exits the bathroom and walks past Howie without saying a word. Howie says one word, "Soul mate."

Catherine stops. She sighs and says, "Let's talk about this after spring break. I think it would be a good idea if we don't see each other until then. I don't want to do anything stupid."

Up until that moment Howie was having second thoughts about flying to Australia to see Dominique. Immediately after Catherine leaves Howie calls Dominique's assistant, Stephan. He asks for assistance with the plane reservations. Stephan asks if Howie would like to share a hotel room. Howie replies, "I don't think so. I'm not bisexual. I'm not even curious."

Chapter 6: The Tasmanian Producers Festival

Howie can't miss Stephan's platinum blonde hair when the limousine drops him off at The Hotel Windsor in Melbourne. Howie looks around the lobby for Dominique but she is nowhere to be found. Stephan walks up to Howie and with his slight gay affectation asks, "How was the flight?"

"Even flying first class that's an exhausting trip.'"

"Take these melatonin pills. They'll help with the jet lag. And before bed take this Valerian."

"What's Valerian?"

"A herb. It's a natural sleep aid."

"Thanks. So where is Dominique?"

"She had some business to attend to in Buenos Aires. She'll be here tomorrow."

"Oh, Gail Wynand?"

"Don't worry about it. Just get some sleep. We're only staying here tonight. We need to get up early before heading to the yacht."

"Yacht?"

"Please, you didn't think we'd entertain clients at a stuffy old hotel, did you?"

"I didn't know I was entertaining clients."

"Didn't she tell you? Dominique wants to sprinkle a few good looking people on the yacht to improve the ambiance and raise our clients interests. But I know you're here only because Dominique likes you."

"So now I'm one of the good looking people?"

"Don't act stupid. You really should make more of an effort to show Dominique that you love her."

"You know as well as I do that Dominique only loves things she can't have."

"You're wise beyond your years. Speaking of Dominique, she told me to buy you some new clothes."

"Really?"

"You can see right through me. Truth is, I want you to get a new wardrobe. Look at you with those Levi jeans and that L.L.Bean shirt. You look like some hick from Pennsylvania. Maybe Dominique was on to something when she said you are starting to go native."

"Jesus, she told you that."

"You know Dominique is always right. She sees the world clearly." Stephan pauses and puts his hand on his hips. He looks Howie over from head-to-toe and says, "Look Howie, I like you. I'm buying you a new wardrobe first thing in the morning. But don't expect any more favors. It's hard enough managing the empire she is building. I don't need a man who can't dress himself holding us back."

"If you weren't gay I'd consider that last line an insult."

"You should feel lucky. The only reason we are here and not Sydney is a few of our most important clients were interested in visiting Melbourne during fashion week. Hopefully one of the top designers has something in your size."

In the morning Howie is still wiped-out from the jet lag. He takes a Dexedrine to help focus. After shopping for a new wardrobe, Stephan and Howie head down to the docks in Port Phillip Bay. Howie is stunned by the size of the yacht. The Alexandra is 400 feet long and can handle 60 guests. Howie ask Stephan, "How much does it costs to rent the Alexandra for the week?"

"More than a typical architect makes in three years."

With forty clients and crew on board they set sail for Tasmania. Howie walks around the ship. Dominique is nowhere to be found. Howie takes note that almost all the clients onboard are wealthy women

Chapter 6: The Tasmanian Producers Festival

in their forties, fifties, or sixties. Many of them flirt with Howie as he walks by.

At 3:04 PM a helicopter appears on the horizon. A minute later it lands on the deck. All the clients are directed to the rear of the yacht. Waiters serve caviar and champagne. Wearing a dark blue dress with gold trim Dominique exits the helicopter, walks across the deck, and starts talking with a few of the clients. The helicopter takes off and heads for the Tasmanian coastline on the horizon. Stephan hands Dominique a wireless microphone.

Dominique takes a deep breath of the salty ocean air and addresses the crowd, "I hope you are all having a good time. As you know, you are here because you understand 21st Century art. Paintings, sculptures, and other art from the past are losing value. That's because paintings are old and static. But movies, television, and video games are new and dynamic."

Dominique pauses, looks at Howie, and continues, "If we are going to construct a better world then those with money and perspective have to provide the masses with a better set of shows and video games. Besides, at a dinner party would you rather tell your friends that you just purchased a Picasso, or that you just produced a new movie?" The crowd laughs in agreement.

She points to the coastline on the horizon and continues, "Tomorrow in Tasmania will be the first annual Producers Festival. We are here to connect you, the ones with money and vision, with directors, writers, and actors that can bring new ideas to the screen. You will meet with these directors, writers, and actors. They will promote what they believe to be their best ideas. There will be seminars on how to maximize your entertainment investment, on how to promote your movie, television show or video game, and how to navigate copyright laws."

For dramatic effect Dominique slowly scans the audience then continues, "But as you know investing in art is not the only reason to produce new media. In America, President Reagan and Governor Schwarzenegger were not anomalies. In Italy, media titan and two-time Prime Minister Silvio Berlusconi was not an accident. In India more and more Bollywood stars are running for political office. It should be apparent that as entertainment becomes a bigger and bigger part of our lives that those who successfully navigate the inner workings of the

Big Game CEO

media industrial complex have a political advantage. And in my opinion masters of the media industrial complex make better politicians. That is because there is no line of business that is more competitive than new media. To succeed you must be talented and politically savvy."

Dominique looks at Howie and says, "Building a better world means building a better political system. And as the recent economic downturn has taught us, it is not the system, but the people that run the system that matters. It is up to people like you to inspire the next generation. Cynicism is like a virus. So is optimism. Enjoy the first annual Tasmanian Producers Festival. Several directors, writers, and actors will be joining us shortly at this pre-festival party." The forty clients give Dominique a generous round of applause.

Leaning against a rail, Howie watches as Dominique and Stephan work the crowd. Stephan talks fashion, friends, and family with the clients. Dominique talks business. The helicopter returns and lands on the deck. Out march a group of seven men and five women. He recognizes one Bollywood actor from a poster he once saw at Cornell. He has no idea who the other eleven are. Dominique turns on the microphone again and introduces the dozen guests to the clients. There are two Academy Award winning screen writers, directors from Britain, Italy, Japan, and India, two video game creators from America, and a handful of actors and actress from around the world.

She then introduces the clients. It is an introduction of alpha female dominance. There is the wife of the CEO of the largest steel company in the world who is from India. There is the wife of the CEO of the largest semiconductor foundry in the world who is from Taiwan. There is the wife of the CEO of the largest shipping company in the world who is from Greece. The list goes on and on. Howie notes that Dominique never uses the word wife. She always uses the word partner. It is immediately obvious to Howie that Dominique is trying to change the game. Collecting art is passé; producing new media is today's expression of alpha female dominance. And Dominique wants these wealthy women to go on a buying binge at the Producers Festival.

As Howie leans against the rail looking at the Tasmanian coastline a client from Norway who has had three glasses of champagne walks up from behind. She squeezes his firm butt. He quickly straightens up and turns. From a quick glance at her blonde hair, radiant stare,

Chapter 6: The Tasmanian Producers Festival

and tight evening dress he initially estimates she is in her late thirties. But upon further study he deduces that her younger look is the result of plastic surgery, and that she is really in her fifties. Not knowing how to respond he looks over at Dominique, but she is busy talking with a woman from Dubai. Not knowing what to say Howie drops his champagne glass into the ocean. Howie then says, "I need a refill."

As Howie starts to walk away the lady from Norway snaps her fingers. A waiter immediately arrives and hands Howie another champagne glass. Howie smiles and shakes his head for he knows that tonight he is the one being hunted. Howie starts planning his strategy for how he is going to end up with Dominique at the end of the evening. The lady from Norway introduces herself, "I'm Therese Defarge." She then starts making small talk. Next she walks over and tips a waiter $5,000 to make sure Howie is seated at her table for dinner. Howie whips out his cell phone and tries to text Dominique but there is no reception. So instead Howie scribbles a note on a napkin and asks a different waiter to hand it to Dominique. Dominique reads the note – 'Blondie from Norway wants you and me to join her in a three way'. Dominique looks over at Howie and smiles.

A few minutes later Dominique walks over and says, "Therese Defarge, so how are the taxes in Norway?"

"Still horrendous. That's why I spend most of my time on my yacht in the Mediterranean. Speaking of yachts, this one is quaint."

"With the economic downturn I felt funny renting something overly ostentatious. So I see you discovered my personal architect."

"So that's what they are calling them these days."

"You should see his portfolio."

"I'm sure I would enjoy it."

Howie stands there speechless as the two ladies bicker back and forth, mixing architectural lingo with sexual innuendo.

Howie finally interrupts, "Seriously Madame Defarge, I am an architect. I worked with Henry Cameron before the economic downturn."

Therese replies, "I know Henry Cameron. He designed the StatoilHydro Eco-office."

Howie says, "I was studying the plans of that building just last week."

"I'm thinking of building a new vacation home. Let's talk later." Therese saunters away.

Dominique looks at Howie and says, "I wasn't thinking. I should have known a number of my clients would be hitting on you."

"I wasn't thinking. I should be using this time to promote myself as an architect."

"I like your outfit. Did Stephan pick it out for you?"

"He told you didn't he?"

"No. I'm not stupid. I was able to infer."

"How are you doing?"

"Small talk later. I'm still at work. Well get together after dinner."

As Dominique walks away, Howie says, "This is damn impressive. I knew you were talented. I didn't think you were this talented."

Dominique smiles and says, "Thanks."

Dominique talks with Stephan. They make some minor tweaks to the seating arrangement. Howie sits at Stephan's table. The best looking of the six male models on board is seated next to Therese Defarge."

There are thirteen people at each table. Howie is seated between a rich heiress from Spain and a soap opera writer from Brazil. He tries to talk architectural design but no one is interested. Tonight the only topic of conversation is new media. After the main course Howie watches the sunset in silence. Finishing dessert he looks over at the bartender and mutters to himself, "Jesus, just last weekend I was bartending an event at the Crystal Springs Country Club. I wonder what I'll be doing next weekend."

After dinner Stephan leads Howie to Dominique's bedroom. A few minutes later Dominique joins him. Howie asks, "Why all the secrecy?"

"Howie, do you know why I love you?"

"I didn't know you loved me until now."

"I love you because we are of the same mold. At Cornell it was obvious to my friends and me that you would make a lousy husband because you would be married to your work. Everyone could see that except you."

"Did you really talk about me like that?"

Chapter 6: The Tasmanian Producers Festival

"Yes, and then some. You know damn well you're tall, strong, and handsome. Women love talking about good-looking men. That's because they all want to have good looking children."

"Were you serious that one time when you said you wanted me to be the father of your children?"

"Dead serious. I have this all planned out. I'm going to marry Gail Wynand. I'm going to have two children from you before I'm twenty-seven because I don't want to be some old mother. You'll marry you're job and become a famous architect. Gail will die in few years. We'll get married in our early forties, maybe have another child or two, and rule our empire together. You'll have the wealth to build anything you want and I'll be empress of the media."

"What if I find somebody else?"

"From your architectural designs it is clear you expect perfection from yourself. I can tell you'll also expect perfection from your wife. You'll never settle."

"What if I found somebody else that is perfect?"

Dominique pauses for a moment. It never dawned on her that there might be somebody else. She says, "That's I'm a chance I'm willing to take. My only concern is that living in the boondocks you might go native."

"Quit saying that."

"You haven't looked in the mirror lately, have you. Your demeanor is not as polished as it used to be."

"Speaking of polishing mirrors, why do you need Gail Wynand anyway?"

"Because he's financing this business venture."

"Don't you have enough money to finance this yourself?"

"No. I need two billion minimum to get me through the first five years. At that point we'll start turning a profit. After that the sky is the limit."

"Why don't you do a stock offering?"

"Please, look at the banking and auto industries. The stock market is the 'we cash checks here' part of the financial world. With private equity you stay rich by keeping all of the profits."

"You sound like my Uncle Charlie."

"Why is that?"

"One of his favorite lines is 'we cash checks here'."

"I need to update my catch phrases. The last thing I want is to sound like some fifty year old maintenance man."

"So what is your business model?"

"I connect clients and new media artist for a very small fee. The fee isn't enough to pay the bills. The fee is just large enough to keep out the riff raff. Besides, anyone with any common sense knows that minus the popular hits, producing new media is a money losing operation. I make my money by having everyone agree to sell their television shows, movies, and games through our websites, theater chains, and distribution network."

"You're a smart business woman. So during your speech what was all that about new media and building a better political system?"

"All these rich clients want to believe they are the invisible hand that controls the political system. But in the end it is the new media gatekeeper that is the ultimate invisible hand."

"You would make Kurt Lewin proud."

"Who is Kurt Lewin?"

"In 1947, just before he died, Lewin coined the term 'gatekeeper' when describing who controls what media should be admitted to the public arena and what news should be withheld."

"That's why I love you. Besides being hung like an elephant you have the memory of one too. I want to make love right now." Dominique walks over and opens the curtains.

Howie asks, "What are you doing?"

"No one can see us out here on the high seas. I'm going to get on top and you're going to tell me what buildings you would construct to blend into the natural beauty of the Tasmanian coastline."

The next day Dominique informs Howie she rented the Alexandra because of him. Her mother gets seasick easily and Dominique knew she wouldn't visit the yacht. However, her mother is at the Producers Festival and she doesn't want mother to know she is seeing Howie. Howie is not happy but there's not much he can do since he is Dominique's guest.

Stephan arranges a deep sea fishing charter to occupy Howie's time. That day he hits the jackpot, catching a pinkie, snapper, elephant fish,

Chapter 6: The Tasmanian Producers Festival

rock cod, and two gummy sharks. At four in the afternoon the group of three men on the tour barbeque his rock cod on the deck of the boat. Howie pays to have the snapper butchered, packaged, and shipped to Uncle Joe's lodge in Lords Valley, Pennsylvania. At six o'clock a helicopter picks up Howie and returns him to the yacht. Dominique arrives a half hour later.

Sitting at separate tables Dominique and Howie have dinner aboard the deck of the Alexandra along with forty of Dominique's most select clients, and some writers and directors. Howie tries to talk architecture hoping to land some business. No one is interested.

During dessert Dominique studies Howie. She notices Howie intently watching the older writers and directors trying to sell their ideas to any of the rich clients who are willing to listen. She can tell that Howie understands the writers and directors are desperate, and the rich clients are enjoying the thrill that only the power of money brings. Dominique studies further the growing fear in Howie's eyes as he realizes that he is a lot like these writers and directors, an artist without much money. She understands he fears becoming a middle-aged artistic beggar. Dominique can sense a change in Howie – he is starting to plan how he is going to attain a position of power so he never has to beg. Dominique catches Howie eye and flashes him a smile. After dinner Howie and Dominique adjourn to the yacht's master bedroom.

The next day Howie catches a helicopter ride with Dominique to Devonport, Tasmania. There he rents a motorcycle and spends the day touring the island. He almost gets killed when he forgets they drive on the left side of the road in Australia. In the evening he catches a helicopter ride back to the yacht with Dominique. Again they have dinner at separate tables. Again after dinner they adjourn to the yacht's master bedroom.

Sensing that Howie is not happy, Dominique decides to miss the morning sessions on the third and final day of the Producers Festival. She and Howie take a private helicopter tour of Tasmania. After lunch she drops Howie off on the Alexandra and returns to festival for the afternoon auction and to make her closing remarks. After the festival she flies back to the Alexandra, picks up Howie, and flies to The Hotel Windsor in Melbourne. There they spend the night together.

The next day Dominique and Howie kiss good-bye at the airport. After the kiss Dominique asks, "You'd never settle, would you?"

"Sometimes I hate you because you are always right. I'd never settle."

Dominique says, "I love you."

Howie says, "Wait!" as she turns and starts to walk away.

"Yes."

"I have met someone else that is in your league."

"You're bluffing just because you don't want me to marry Wynand."

"Her name is Catherine Halsey." Howie bites his lip because he knows he should have kept his mouth shut.

"You just made that up. Who in our generation goes by the name of Catherine?"

"Like usual, you are right. I just don't want you to marry Wynand."

"Marrying Wynand is for the best. But I'll always love you."

With that Dominique and Stephan board her private jet. They are off for Hong Kong to meet up with Dominique's fiancé and business partner, Gail Wynand. Howie boards a 747 and begins the 24-hour flight back to New York. As Howie looks down at the Australian coastline from his first class seat aboard the 747, he mumbles under his breath, *"What does it mean to be a man in the modern world?"*

Chapter 7: The Last Lecture

Howie is in a daze. After tasting the sweet ambiance of Dominique's jet set lifestyle he views the walls of his apartment as a prison. For the next week all Howie does in Port Jervis is work out at the gym six hours a day, practice with the band in the evenings, and drink only strawberry-banana smoothies. He quits taking Dexedrine and sleeps over eleven hours at night.

Seven days after his return from Australia his sister calls. Phoebe asks if he is going to visit Harvard for her graduation. Howie unenthusiastically says yes. Sensing something is wrong Phoebe begins to probe. Howie admits he is a little jealous. She is graduating and moving on with her life while he is heading back to Cornell in the fall. Phoebe can tell that is not the only reason he feels depressed.

Howie didn't want to discuss Dominique again with his sister, but he finally breaks down. He tells Phoebe about his trip to Australia. They talk for over an hour about his unusual relationship with his rich girlfriend. As he turns off his cell phone Howie realizes that his depression is not because of Dominique but because of Catherine Halsey.

The second Monday after spring break Howie catches a ride with Bobby to Luzerne Community College. Wearing sunglasses and a baseball hat he takes his familiar seat in the back row. At the start of class he and Catherine make eye contact. She smiles. But for the rest of class she never turns around. Howie finds Uncle Joe's lecture about

Albert Camus's *The Stranger* boring, and the subsequent discussion on manhood and existentialism shallow.

After Uncle Joe's class Howie makes the familiar walk over to the coffee shop at the campus center. Catherine is already sitting at their secluded corner table. Howie asks, "May I join you?"

Catherine responds, "Feel free."

They sit there quietly like an old couple. Catherine reads Nietzsche's *Thus Spoke Zarathustra* while Howie reads today's edition of *The Wall Street Journal*. After fifteen minutes Howie breaks the silence, "I've missed our conversations."

"I have too. So where have you been?"

Howie hesitates. He can't decide what to tell Catherine. Deep in his subconscious he decides it is best to tell her the truth. He discusses spending spring break in Australia visiting his rich, on again, off again, girlfriend from Cornell. He tells Catherine that for the last week he's been depressed. At first he thought it was because Dominique is marrying Gail Wynand. Then he realized the true cause of his depression is because she is marrying Peter Keating.

At the end of Howie's confession Catherine is speechless. Confused and emotionally conflicted, and just wanting everything to go back to the way it was before spring break, she says, "I don't get Nietzsche."

Visibly upset, Howie loudly asks, "You want to talk about the reading list?"

"I want things to go back to the way they were."

"That's never going to happen."

"All I want out of life is to get married, raise a family, live near my sisters so our kids can grow-up together, and find work as a writer. Everything was going according to plan until you came along. If I run off with you then what kind of life do you have planned for me?"

"I don't know."

"You're an architect. Architects always have plans."

"I don't know."

"Are you willing to settle down around here so I can live near my family?"

"Why do you want to live near your extended family?"

"Because I love them."

"Do you love me?"

Chapter 7: The Last Lecture

"Look, we only have a few weeks left in class. Can we just go back to talking about the reading list?"

"Forget the reading list. These are the moments that define what it means to be a man in the modern world. Do you love Peter Keating more than me?"

"Can we just go back to how things were? We both knew this was going to end once the semester was over. I'm getting married and you're heading back to Cornell."

"Answer the question."

"You'll never settle down will you? You're the type of man who will always be married to his work."

"Answer the question. Do you love Peter Keating more than me?"

"I don't like it when you raise your voice."

"The reason I've been depressed for the last week is because I finally realized I love you more than I love Dominique. Peter's a lucky man."

Howie stands and starts to walk away. Catherine says, "Wait. To be honest I don't know who I love more."

"You're going to marry Peter, aren't you?"

Catherine looks down at the table and answers, "Yes."

Howie points at the book *Thus Spoke Zarathustra* resting on the table. He says, "You know, Nietzsche isn't very complicated. He believed people are dung of the Earth. You do or say what you must to get them to do what you want. He also had a very low opinion of women."

"Sounds like a jerk."

"I'm sure Nietzsche had a low opinion of women because he never met a woman like you. That's why we are going to have to end this. I have to figure out how to move on." Catherine sits there speechless. Howie looks up at the ceiling and condescendingly asks, "Do you mind if I sit in on the rest of Uncle Joe's lectures. I find his lectures on what it means to be a man in the modern world light entertainment."

"I don't mind."

And with that Howie leaves the coffee shop.

Still disguised by sunglasses and a baseball hat, for the next two weeks Howie continues to take his familiar seat in the back row. After class Catherine continues to visit the coffee shop at the campus center. She sits at their secluded table. But for the last two weeks of class Howie is nowhere to be seen. She wonders where he is hiding on campus as he waits for his ride home with Bobby. It is during these lonely two weeks that she realizes she loves Howie more than Peter Keating.

On the last day of class Howie is again seated in the last row, slouched over to disguise his height. On this day Uncle Joe enters through the rear door instead of entering from the front of the lecture hall. He stops next to Howie, flips off his baseball hat, and says, "Do you think you can hide from your Uncle Joe disguised as the Unabomber? I know you've been in here since February."

"I was just bored and looking for a change of pace."

Uncle Joe whispers, "What's her name?"

"Excuse me."

"I'm not stupid. I was young once too."

"I just wanted to study the differences and similarities between your class here at Luzerne and my classes at Cornell."

"A lover, an architect, and an anthropologist. Interesting. Why don't we all get together tonight and finish the rest of those snapper filets you had shipped back from Australia. A few are still in my freezer."

"Sounds like a plan."

Uncle Joe walks to the front of the room. He begins his lecture. Since it is the last day of class he summarizes the remaining tasks. Next week there will be a two-hour in class final. Term papers are due at the start of the final. Students must also turn in their 250-word idea for a new novel on what it means to be a man in the modern world. For the lucky student with the best idea he'll raise their final grade ten-percentage points.

Uncle Joe then looks up at Howie and says, "Let's review the different visions of manhood within each of the novels that you should have read during the semester." A few of the students laugh at Uncle Joe's 'should have read' comment.

Over the next few minutes the class changes from lecture into a discussion session. Howie notes that Catherine is oddly quiet. She doesn't ask or answer a single question. Twenty minutes into the discussion Uncle Joe asks, "In the *Scarlet Letter* how does the evolution of Reverend Arthur Dimmesdale's character tell us about what it means to be a man?"

Chapter 7: The Last Lecture

From the back of the room Howie blurts out, "You're asking the wrong question."

You could hear a pen drop. For the students the mysterious stranger from the back of the room finally speaks. And the first words out of his mouth are a challenge to their professor. The students sense the coming of a dual. All the students, especially the women in the class, anxiously await the tall mysterious stranger's opinions about manhood.

After a long pause Uncle Joe responds to Howie's challenge, "What question should I be asking?"

"What does the evolution of the character of Hester Prynne tell us about what it means to be a woman? See, in my opinion manhood is boring. Men are simple creatures. They are driven by money, power, glory, and war, with an eye on the ultimate prize, women. And once they get the ultimate prize, they father a few children. As their life moves on, they wonder why they are hanging around the house. A mid-life crisis follows. They try to rediscover the sweet smell of youth by finding more money, power, glory, and war. If they get lucky, these mid-life crisis men celebrate victory with a new group of women. Then these men enter their golden years. Unable to compete, these older men try to relive their youth through their sons and grandsons. As they approach death, men create stories of how they will relive their glory days in the after life. Men are simple creatures."

Uncle Joe chimes out, "Men are not that simple."

Howie responds, "Please, of all the people in this room you must clearly know that I speak the truth. You have more life experience. How many men do you know that got divorced in their thirties and forties because of a mid-life crisis?"

Uncle Joe knows Howie is referring to his divorce and the divorce of his two brothers. Visibly annoyed Uncle Joe answers, "This is a literature class not a psychology class."

"Good literature is deeply psychological."

Uncle Joe chimes out again, "Men are not that simple. Men are artists. Men are engineers. Men are architects. Men are politicians."

"Professions and careers are just a means to an end, and that end is women. You could have covered everything in this class in two weeks. Let's examine my thesis of money, power, glory, and war in reverse order. First war. Shane is your standard Lancelot character. He is a lost soldier suffering a mid-life crisis, in search of an honorable war so he can find a beautiful princess. In the end he sleeps with his friends wife before saving the town. Cowboys are just lonely, wandering soldiers, in search of love."

Uncle Joe says, "But a soldier's life is more complicated than war and women. For honor is what gives a soldier's life purpose."

Howie asks, "Honor? Honor? What century are you living in, the 20th? Honor is imaginary. Glory is real. And glory's wine is the sweet taste of a woman's kiss. Foolish soldiers mindlessly chase honor. But the wise soldier evolves from war to glory. Captain Ahab from *Moby Dick* falls into the glory category. I'm positive that in his sailor's mind he initially wanted to kill Moby Dick so he could sail back into town, show off his prize, spin a few tales of life on the high seas, and then bang a few of the local women. Nineteenth Century adventurers were simply the rock stars of their day. That's why today's adolescent boys don't want to be soldiers. Instead they want to be superheroes because they dream of fame and glory. Deep down in their DNA they know fame and glory makes them more attractive to the opposite sex."

Uncle Joe says, "But fame and glory are so immature."

Howie stands up and plans his next move. He looks around the room, making sure not to make eye contact with Catherine. He continues, "Immature? Immature? Is not an adolescent man's life defined by the discovery of women? And maybe that is why young glory seekers evolve into wise power seekers. *Hamlet* is Shakespeare's best effort to look at power. In the beginning, Uncle Claudius murders Hamlet's father, the King, to ascend to the throne and marry Hamlet's mother, the Queen. The ultimate expression of power is to lay with the Queen. We could waste an hour discussing Freud's model of the human mind, and that Hamlet's Oedipal desire to sleep with his mother, the Queen, stems from his id, and Hamlet's desire to avenge his father's death stems from his superego. The male mind is not that complicated. Men want power because power brings unto man the highest quality women."

Uncle Joe asks, "Is that the point of a man's life? To obtain the highest quality women through power? Rousseau believed women deserve romance."

Howie steps into the aisle and takes two steps forward so Catherine, the object of his oratory outburst, can get a better look at his muscular

Chapter 7: The Last Lecture

build. Howie continues, "Romance? Romance? What's more romantic than to sit on a throne and be queen? This should be obvious since the word romance comes from the word Roman, the greatest empire to rule Europe. You know Rousseau died just before the French Revolution, and the French Revolution changed everything."

Uncle Joe asks, "How so?"

"Part of *The Tale of Two Cities* is about the king's hated salt tax. For what is a king's power without a king's money? And the French Revolution marks the rise of democracy and the fall of aristocracy. And it is at this moment in history that a king's power evolves into common man's money. For kings and princes define manhood from a time of lore. To be a man in the modern world has nothing to do with romance. To be a man in the modern world requires cold hard cash. Almost all stories from the modern era are about money. Money has been so engrained into our democratic societies that we think it is an end unto itself. Marketers ram this modern idea of the money-romance connection down our throats. Show her you really love her with the gift of a diamond necklace."

Uncle Joe says, "I sense both sarcasm and anger in that last sentence. Is this because you wish you were a man of more money?"

Howie begins to look at Catherine but suddenly looks to the other side of the class in order to mask his intentions. He continues, "So you want to psychoanalyze me? Instead let's psychoanalyze the modern world. Money, money, oh where to begin? *Liar's Poker, Bonfire of the Vanities, The Grapes of Wrath*, or *The Great Gatsby*? Ah, *The Great Gatsby, The Great Gatsby*. James Gatsby is your standard man of money in the modern world. He is your typical Horatio Alger story. Young and poor, he was unable to win the heart of Daisy, the one true love in his life. So he takes up bootlegging to become rich. Armed with money he tries to win back his flower, only to die from a case of mistaken identity at the gun of a jealous man."

Howie takes a few steps forward and turns toward Catherine. But instead of looking at Catherine, he looks at Bobby who is sitting directly behind her. Howie smiles at Bobby and says, "Both Voltaire's *Candide* and Camus's *The Stranger* are the antithesis of the money, power, glory, and war thesis of manhood. I find it interesting that both Voltaire and Camus are French. For maybe the great minds from the land of the French Revolution were the first to clearly see faults in democracy, and the mindless pursuit of money. These writers attempt to find meaning in an existential existence. Candide spends his life chasing his true love, his lady, only to find misery and misfortune. In *The Stranger* there is an unfaithful girlfriend. The main character, Meursault, accidentally shoots the brother of this unfaithful girlfriend once, then three more times. These extra shots are not for revenge, but just to experience some kind of sensation in his meaningless life. Convicted, and awaiting execution, Meursault finds no remorse. There is no such thing as empathy in the modern world."

Uncle Joe stands there in awe, completely blown away by Howie's powerful interpretation on what it means to be a man in the modern world. Awestruck, Uncle Joe simply says, "I never looked at *Candide* and *The Stranger* like that before. Excellent interpretation."

Howie glances at Uncle Joe, politely acknowledging his complement. He then turns his attention to the object of his oratory outburst. Howie stares deep into Catherine's eyes. In a heart-felt voice he says, "You know what I find interesting. I find interesting that writers like Voltaire, Camus, Fitzgerald, and Shakespeare always associate tragedy with the pursuit of women. Maybe all great writers are simply men that loved and lost. For would a woman by any other name smell just as sweet? Shakespeare understood full well that there are Violets, Lilies, and Daisies. But there are few Roses that inspire a man to build a better world. Those that lose at love become emotionally numb like Meursault. But those that win at love live life to the fullest everyday." A bead of sweat forms on Catherine's forehead. Her heart pounds. She understands when Howie said the word Rose he was referring to her middle name. At that moment if Howie asked Catherine to marry him she would have definitely said yes.

Uncle Joe startles Howie when he asks, "Money, power, glory, and war equals women. Interesting thesis. But reading between the lines of your thesis you believe that manhood is defined by taking these pursuits to an extreme, don't you?"

Howie looks at Uncle Joe, then Catherine, and then Uncle Joe again. He answers, "Maybe it is. I never looked at it from that angle. Maybe the male peacock's tail is man's ultimate destiny. History is filled with examples of men who pursue money, glory, power, and war to

Chapter 7: The Last Lecture

an extreme. Maybe they go to extremes so they can forget about the women that they loved and lost. Look at Alexander the Great. His Greek soldiers fought not for political and strategic gain, but for the sake of glory and war. Once his soldiers realized Alexander's campaign into the Indian subcontinent was a suicide mission they came to their senses and headed back home to get laid." The class laughs at the laid comment.

Howie looks up at the flag in the southeast corner of the room, "Or look at America today. We've taken money to an extreme. We have CEO's and businessmen who pursue money for the sake of pursuing money. In my opinion, Warren Buffet is a fool. Who in their right mind worth more than $100 billion continues to pursue more money? At that point in your life you give back to society. You spend your money to create art and architecture. Art and architecture lead to a higher culture. And higher culture leads to a better breed of woman. And a better breed of women gives the next generation of men a higher level of inspiration."

Uncle Joe asks, "So you believe the modern world is about creating a better breed of women that will create a better breed of men?"

"Would men build cities if the women that lived in them were ugly and unsophisticated? I think not. Like I said, men are simple creatures. Money, glory, power, and war are our aphrodisiac, and women are our desire. But women are complex and interesting." Howie stops, walks back to his desk, and sits down.

Uncle Joe says, "You can't leave us hanging like that."

Howie says, "Why not?"

Uncle Joe says, "Because you never answered your own question. What does the evolution of the character of Hester Prynne tell us about being a woman?"

Howie looks at the ceiling, "Women, women, women. Women are complicated. Look around the room. In raw form, steel, glass, wood, and concrete are useless. But architects use these materials to create modern buildings. In raw form money, power, glory, and war are society's demise. But women use these to create a better man. See, women give birth to the children of victorious men. Women, through their daughters, and using all the tricks in their playbook, then set out to create the culture that will define the next generation of civilized men.

A deconstructionists reading of the *Tale of Two Cities* tells us that it was women that pulled all the strings during the French Revolution."

Howie again looks at the American flag and continues, "And it is when women play games to build a better society that life becomes interesting. These games are about compromises. Architects make compromises because there is no such thing as a perfect building; and women make compromises because there is no such thing as a perfect man. However a good architect works hard at minimizing the compromises he has to make to satisfy his clients so he can remain pure of spirit; and a good woman minimizes the compromises she must make to men in order to remain pure of heart."

Howie looks at Catherine and continues, "But compromises come with risks. Male characteristics that are an asset during times of peace are liabilities during times of war. Women have to play this delicate balancing act. If all women pursue only men of war then society collapses under the weight of violence. If all women pursue only men of money then society becomes corrupt and collapses under the weight of greed. To strike a balance women must find a man who is ambitious, but not too greedy; a soldier who will protect against aggression but not destroy society; self-confident enough to succeed, but not so vain that he leaves her to spread his seed with the other ladies in the community."

Uncle Joe says, "You are losing me. What does this have to do with Hester Prynne?"

Howie says, "It is simple. Everyone in this room is half man and half woman. That is because our DNA is the product of the love stories of our parents, grandparents, and great-grandparents. This chain of love stories goes back beyond the beginning of mankind. We breed ourselves for success or failure. All the good characteristics that are in our DNA, such as ambition, strength, endurance, humor, empathy, and intelligence, are the result of our descendents love stories. These love stories are often complicated. That is because motherhood is the second oldest profession. We all hate to admit this but before our descendents were mothers they were all good whores just like Hester Prynne."

Uncle Joe asks, "What do you mean by good whore?"

Still looking at the ceiling as if trying to contact God, Howie answers question with question, "Women have to make compromises,

Chapter 7: The Last Lecture

and compromises lead to questions of morality. Was Hester Prynne's act of adultery moral or immoral?"

Uncle Joe asks, "And what's your opinion?"

Howie looks at Uncle Joe, and then Catherine, and answers, "Her act of adultery was not only moral – it was honorable! In fact I would consider her a savior of society. Why was she a savior? Because her husband, Chillingworth, was a loser. This is why she seduces the Reverend Arthur Dimmesdale. She didn't want Chillingworth's genes being passed along to the next generation. Was she a whore? Yes. Did she do the right thing? Yes. As they grow older, Reverend Dimmesdale life spirals downward as he is tormented by the guilt of his so called sin. On the other hand, Hester Prynne survives the shame and scorn. She rises in stature within the community because in youth she made the right decision of being the good whore. The scarlet letter A stands for ascendance – the ascendance of mankind. And the ascendance of man is all because of the guidance of women. Women are complicated because society has to live with the consequences of their decisions. Men are simple creatures because they don't."

Uncle Joe says, "There are a lot of holes in your analysis."

Howie replies, "True. But always remember, the victors create history, the losers spend their lives trying to rewrite herstory."

Uncle Joe says, "Clever play on words. I would love to discuss this further but we are running out of time."

Howie says, "In conclusion may I say that in one semester you can learn all there is about being a man in the modern world. But no one will understand what it means to be a woman in the modern world because the modern world is always changing."

With that Howie stands and leaves. For the next fifteen seconds no one says a word. Uncle Joe breaks the silence and says, "Final is Wednesday at nine. Class dismissed."

After class Catherine quickly walks to the coffee shop at the campus center. Howie is nowhere to be seen. She wonders where he is. Patiently she waits at their secluded table hoping for one more conversation on what it means to be a man in the modern world. She has no idea what she is going to say. Catherine just wants the opportunity to say something, anything. Love makes you do strange things. After forty-five minutes of no Howie, Catherine leaves their table and breaks the mirror in the woman's bathroom.

An hour after class Howie meets Bobby in the parking lot for the ride back to their apartment. Bobby starts his truck then looks at Howie and says, "You're such an ass."

"What did I do?"

"How the hell am I supposed to write a term paper after you give that noble prize winning speech?"

"Sorry, I wasn't thinking."

"I wanted to title my term paper *Modern Men Think with Their Third Leg*. Thanks for stealing my idea and then blowing it away."

"Sorry, I wasn't thinking."

"And man's ultimate prize is a woman. Well duh! You don't have to have an Ivy League education to see that. So how long have you been chasing Catherine Halsey?"

"Was it that obvious?"

"It was obvious to me. You know she is marrying Peter Keating in July."

"I know."

Chapter 8: The Road Trip

The day after his last final Bobby again takes a job at a local grocery store as a cashier. Bobby and Danny work their old scam where Danny puts over $200 worth of groceries in a shopping cart and brings it through Bobby's check-out line. Bobby then charges Danny only $10. Within two weeks they have enough beer and food to make it for another six months. Bobby quits the week before Memorial Day.

Over the Memorial Day weekend Howie attends Phoebe's graduation from Harvard. There he sees his mother, Daisy, for the first time since Christmas. Daisy is completely stressed out because of the collapse of the wealth fund of her husband, and Howie's stepfather, Meyer Wolfsheim. It turns out Meyer had invested 60% of their savings in the ponzi scheme of Bernie Madoff. Constantly talking about their wealth fund, Daisy doesn't even ask Howie about how he is doing. She does ask about how his father, Archie Roark, is doing. It is clear to Howie that she is starting to formulate a back-up plan incase Meyer becomes bankrupt.

A few days later Bobby convinces Danny and Howie they need to take a road trip. He knows a girl in Rochester, NY and she can get them tickets to the *Coldplay* concert at the Performing Arts Center in Canandaigua. Howie asks why she has extra tickets. Bobby answers because her best friends had to go out of town for some reason. Danny suggests they camp out along the lake after the concert. He also suggests that instead of taking Bobby's truck, he can borrow three

Kawasaki Ninja ZX-6R super sports from the motorcycle shop where he is currently working.

With only a small pack on their backs, and the Ninja ZX-6R between them and the road, the three cousins ride to Rochester during the first weekend in June. Along portions of I-390 they race each other. One cousin rides ahead to make sure the highway patrol isn't around. The other two cousins then race for two to three miles. Bobby always wins these mini-races since he is the only one willing to push the motorcycle over 160 mph.

Along the I-390 corridor Howie notes the large windmills that line the hilltops on either side of the highway. Bobby and Danny could care less about the new wind generators.

In Rochester they arrive at the George Eastman House as it is closing. Pearl, one of Bobby's many girlfriends, meets them at the door. She is working as a tour guide for the summer. Bobby convinces Pearl to give them a private after-hours tour. Danny is amazed by George Eastman's huge living area. There are trophy-animals from Africa everywhere, even an elephant head mounted on the wall. Howie starts talking about all the problems with the room's layout and flow. Bobby constantly talks about George Eastman's money. Danny is sick of both of them. He tells Howie and Bobby that he is sick of architecture and money. He then starts asking Pearl about all the big game trophies. Pearl describes to Danny in detail George Eastman's trips to Europe and Africa. George would bring over 600 people as guests. He even brought his own private band.

Bobby says, "His own private band with him? That sounds a little gay."

Pearl responds, "George Eastman wasn't a little gay. He was very gay. His business associates spent much money making sure his homosexuality never became public."

Bobby replies, "You know, that means this house has never been properly broken in."

Pearl just looks at Bobby. Bobby heads upstairs to George Eastman's old bedroom. Pearl follows. As they listen to Bobby and Pearl have sex, Danny looks at Howie and says, "Now I know why Bobby was in such a hurry to get up here."

Howie responds, "Bobby is the ultimate opportunist."

Chapter 8: The Road Trip

Staring at the elephant head mounted on the wall, Danny doesn't paying attention to Howie's comment. Danny asks, "Do you think I could kill an elephant with my IceMan compound bow?"

Howie answers, "From close range you could get the arrow to penetrate maybe one foot into his flesh."

Danny counters, "With a direct hit at full force, I bet I could penetrate two to three feet into his flesh."

"You couldn't penetrate two to three feet."

"I bet I could."

"To kill it you'd have to hit the heart or the brain."

"If he didn't die immediately, I bet I could chase him down."

"If he didn't chase you down first. Why the questions? Are you thinking of going on an African Safari?"

"Why not? It would be manlier than hunting deer and turkey in Pennsylvania. Look at George Eastman. He lived a hundred years ago, he was gay, and he'll be manlier than we'll ever be."

Howie sarcastically says, "You forgot that he also invented the film camera."

"Are you saying we should go to Africa and take pictures of elephants on the Serengeti like some female photojournalist?"

"That would be really gay."

Pearl loudly moans from George Eastman's bedroom. Danny says, "That's not gay."

"I bet a picture of Pearl and Bobby right now would make a perfect Kodak moment."

Danny whips out his cell phone and quickly turns on the camera. "I've got to get a picture of this."

"That would be uncool."

"Bobby would take a picture of me even if you said it was uncool."

"Bobby doesn't listen to anyone."

"I know."

Pearl moans again. Danny turns off his cell phone and puts it back in his pocket. Howie asks Danny, "I wonder what was the topic of Bobby's term paper on what it means to be a man in the modern world?" Danny doesn't answer, he just laughs.

Big Game CEO

That night the four of them hit the local clubs in Rochester. Danny and Howie have to play the field since Pearl's best friends are out of town. Neither Danny nor Howie find anyone that interests them. After hours Bobby and Pearl disappear to have sex on the Ninja ZX-6R. Danny says, "Once we return these bikes back to the shop I feel sorry for the guy that buys Bobby's motorcycle. He'll never get the stink off that leather seat."

The next day the four of them make the short trip down to Canandaigua for the *Coldplay* concert. During the concert all Bobby and Danny talk about is how great life would be if *Ambivalent Swag* makes it big. Imagine all the money and all the women. Howie doesn't say a word – instead he just enjoys the concert, trying to forget Catherine and Dominique. That night Pearl and the three cousins camp along the shores of Canandaigua Lake.

After dropping Pearl off the next day the three cousins head down to Ithaca. Howie wants to stop by the Cornell admissions office and take care of some paperwork. Howie also figures it is a good time to take his mind off of Catherine and Dominique. He calls up a few of his old Ithaca flames. The first four no longer live in Ithaca. He finally gets a hold of Lois Cook. Lois and two of her friends agree to meet the cousins at the Moosewood Restaurant for a late dinner. Afterwards they will head over to The Haunt to listen to the band *Dog Soldier*.

Sitting in the center of the Ithaca Commons the three cousins wait for Lois and her friends. Howie looks up towards South Hill at Ithaca College then East Hill at Cornell University. He studies the skyline of the campus, and then studies the skyline of the hodge-podge of five and six story apartment buildings that make up college town. His old apartment reminds him of Dominique. Next he looks around the Ithaca Commons at all the townies going about their business. He points to his old apartment and says to Bobby and Danny, "You know, looking out the window of my old apartment I often wondered what the people downtown thought about the architecture up on the hill. But until now it never occurred to me what they were most likely thinking about were the people who attended the university."

Bobby answers, "You think too much. They're just busting their butts trying to make it in the world. And when they have time to think

Chapter 8: The Road Trip

about Cornell, they probably say that if I could graduate from Cornell, that would be my ticket to the money train."

Danny asks, "So are you going to remember us once you become a famous architect?"

"I promise we will always get together every Thanksgiving."

Danny says, "So you can rub our face with your fancy cars and supermodel girlfriends. Bobby and I are going to have to fight for everything we get."

Bobby looks at Danny and says, "There has to be a way we can make millions off of SeekingArrangement.com."

Howie responds, "Don't tell me you are still obsessing over SeekingArrangement.com. The idea has already been taken."

"Yeah, but when there are rich old guys and young beautiful women involved, there is more than one way to make a buck. I just haven't figured it out yet."

Howie says, "Quit wasting your time."

Danny says, "Yeah Bobby, quit wasting your time. Our best chance at winning a ticket to the good life is to win the Battle of the Bands in two weeks."

Bobby looks at Danny and says, "It doesn't matter. Even if we win Howie will break his promise and go back to Cornell in the fall."

Howie doesn't say a thing. Danny asks, "Is it true?"

"If we win a good music contract I'll go on tour."

Bobby looks at Danny and says, "See, he is already waffling."

Howie responds, "Don't make me out to be the bad guy. I promised to go on tour if it looked like we had a promising music career."

Danny says, "We won the first two rounds of the Battle of the Bands competition."

Howie replies, "Yeah, and you know how many band members in their thirties end up playing weddings. I'm only going on tour if it looks like we have a legit shot at making it big."

Bobby says, "You promised us a new song by the end of the week. It better be good."

Howie says, "I know what I promised. I'm still working on it. Watching all the townies walk by is giving me some inspiration."

Danny says, "Regardless of whether we win or lose, we should do something big this summer."

Big Game CEO

Bobby replies, "Don't tell me you still want to go camping in northern Canada."

Danny says, "Howie and I were talking about a big game hunting trip."

Bobby asks, "When were you talking about that?"

Howie answers, "When you were banging Pearl in George Eastman's bedroom."

Danny says, "I've been thinking."

Bobby sarcastically quips, "Thinking is always your first mistake. That's why you hardly bang anyone."

Danny replies, "Seriously, we could go to northern Canada and bow hunt a polar bear."

Bobby says, "Isn't there some stupid endangered species law about that."

Danny says, "Seriously, this is the one chance in our lives to be men before life passes us by. I don't want some gay, George Eastman, guy to out man me. I want to go hunting, and I want to kill something big."

Howie says, "If you want to go after the biggest game on the planet, why don't you bow hunt the masters of the universe."

Danny asks, "What the hell are you talking about?"

Howie says, "Take down a few CEOs."

Bobby pretends to aim and shoot an arrow with an imaginary compound bow, "Now that would be fun. The richer the better."

Danny asks, "Isn't there some stupid endangered species law about killing CEOs?"

Bobby answers question with cynical question, "When's the last time a CEO paid attention to the law? Why should we?"

Danny says, "Image the thrill of taking down a ten billion-point buck. No wait, how much is Bill Gates worth?"

Howie says, "I think a hundred billion."

Danny corrects himself, "A hundred billion-point buck. Now that's big game hunting." He then shocks Howie when he says with all sincerity, "Let's do it."

Howie asks, "You're joking?"

Danny answers, "No, I'm totally serious."

Chapter 8: The Road Trip

Bobby adds, "I'd do it. Look at all the government bailouts. Do you think those CEOs give a damn about us? Think we'll ever get a bail out? It's time someone knock them down a notch or two."

Howie says, "Wait until you sober up tomorrow morning."

Danny replies, "We haven't had anything to drink all day."

Howie says, "That's what's scaring me."

Bobby looks at Danny and says, "See, I told you Howie was going to leave the band by the end of summer, and I told you we were going to have to fight for everything we are ever going to get out of life."

Howie says, "Don't try to lay a guilt trip on me. That's so girlie. You won't be happy until I get an eating disorder."

Bobby says, "Then prove to me you are one of us. Let's bow-hunt a CEO."

"You're totally joking?"

"I'm totally serious. Danny is right. This is our one chance to be men. Let's be men."

Howie looks up to see if anyone is listening. At the far end of the Ithaca Commons he sees Lois Cook and her two friends walking their way. Howie says, "There's Lois."

Danny asks, "Are you with us?"

"You guys are nuts. Why did I have to suggest the idea?"

Danny asks again, "Are you with us?"

Howie ignores Danny and says, "Oh great, it looks like Lois has gone Ithaca native."

Bobby asks, "What's that mean?"

"She's dressed like a vegan."

"I hope she doesn't start preaching about saving the planet over dinner."

Danny says, "Her being a vegan is a good thing."

Bobby asks, "And why is that?"

"Because vegans always put out on the first date because they are dying for the protein." Howie and Bobby laugh. Howie waves to get Lois's attention. She walks up to Howie, gives him a big hug, and kisses him on the cheek.

Chapter 9: The Glory Seekers

It is the third Friday in June. The final for the Battle of the Bands is at The Roseland Ballroom in Manhattan. Seven of the New York City area's best bands are there, including *Ambivalent Swag*. The three cousins are backstage getting ready with their drummer, Gus Webb, and the newest addition to *Ambivalent Swag*, Kent Lansing. Kent is a sixty-two year old clarinet player that Howie personally recruited after returning from the *Coldplay* concert. He chose Kent because of his great look. With his long white beard, shaved head, double-breasted pinstriped suit, and wide brim hat with falcon feather, Kent is a cross between Merlin the Wizard and Al Capone.

Danny returns from the bar carrying four shots of tequila and one shot of Jack Daniels. They toast to success. The younger members finish the shot of tequila in one gulp. Kent takes two sips of the Jack to savor the aroma before finishing the shot. Danny then says to Howie, "What was the name of your ex-billionaire girlfriend that spoke at that Ayn Rand thingy?"

"You mean Dominique Francon?"

"Yeah, yeah. She's in the audience."

"What the hell is she doing here?"

Bobby says, "You're going to find out anyway. I invited her."

"Why?"

"Because she is someone that can get us a big music contract."

"I don't want Dominique getting us a big music contract."

Chapter 9: The Glory Seekers

Bobby yells, "Why the hell not? In the music industry it is all about whom you know!"

"You're such a dick."

"Why am I such a dick? You're the one holding us back. You went to the fancy schools. You have all the big shot connections. When the hell are you ever going to use them?"

From behind the backstage curtain Howie scans the audience. He says to Danny, "Dominique is here with her posse, including her assistant Stephan."

Danny asks, "Which one is Stephan?"

"The one with the bright white hair."

"He's gay, right?"

"Yes he's gay."

Bobby asks, "Are you going to talk to her?"

"I'll wait till after we play. Oh, great. Catherine Halsey is here too."

Bobby says, "No way."

Howie yells, "Bobby, you really are a dick! You spend all your time obsessing over money, then this. Why the hell did you have to invite Dominique and Catherine?"

"You're the one being a dick! I didn't invite Catherine! And what was with the obsessing over money comment? You're the one always obsessing about the perfect woman. I should punch you out right now."

Howie laughs, "Like you could."

Kent grabs Bobby and says, "Kids, save the energy for the stage."

Danny says, "Howie, you really are a dick. I'm the one that indirectly invited Catherine yesterday."

"When?"

"I ran into her at the store. She asked about *Ambivalent Swag*. I told her we were playing tonight."

Bobby says, "Remember when I told you that Howie loves Catherine Halsey."

"I'm not an idiot. I remember. I thought I was doing Howie a favor."

Bobby says, "Maybe Catherine is here to get some pre-bachelorette party action. You know she is getting married over the 4th of July weekend."

Danny replies, "I didn't know that."

Howie says, "Catherine is getting married the weekend after the 4th. And Dominique is getting married in August."

Bobby says, "This is classic. If you play your cards right you can get a pre-bachelorette party three way with Catherine Halsey and eagle super freak. You'll be a living legend."

Danny says, "Now that would be a Kodak moment."

Howie says, "I just want to forget about both of them."

Danny says, "Then let's get out there and woo some new women. There is more than two fish in the sea."

Bobby says, "Come on Howie, we've got a whole audience of little mermaids out there."

Howie looks at Bobby and says, "You shouldn't have called Dominique without telling me. I'm still going to kick you ass tomorrow."

Bobby laughs, "Sure you are."

Ambivalent Swag is the last group to perform. The band waits backstage for another two hours. In the bathroom Howie takes two Dexedrine to stay awake and help focus. By midnight the audience is loud and drunk. There is a mixture of cheers and boos when *Ambivalent Swag* walks on stage. This is because the crowd doesn't know what to make of their costumes. Gus Webb, the drummer, is dressed in a green Mandarin Collar Cheongsam with gold trim. He looks like a cross between a kung fu master and Chinese business executive. Bobby, on back-up guitar, is wearing a white tuxedo that has been tie-dyed bright green, yellow, orange, and red. He looks like a best man at a Grateful Dead wedding. Danny, on lead guitar, is dressed as a McDonald's fry cook.

Howie is dressed as a convenience store cashier. He scans the audience. He sees Dominique sitting near the back. She stands and starts making her way towards the stage. Howie then sees Catherine. They make eye contact. Catherine starts pressing her way through the crowd towards Howie.

Chapter 9: The Glory Seekers

Kent, dressed as the wizard-gangster, walks up to the microphone and says, "*The Ballad of Bonnie and Clyde.*" Kent then starts playing a Benny Goodman-like tune with his clarinet. Danny mixes in a speed metal riff with his electric guitar. The sound is completely original. The crowd doesn't know what to make of it. Then Howie, dressed like a cashier, walks up to the center microphone, and looks directly at Catherine. With a young Johnny Cash-like voice, he sings,

Working at the Kwikie Mart, life is such a bore
Another dreary Friday, nothing on the radio

Just a people watching, a fat woman pumping gas
Stoners feed their munchies, play the lotto, get rich fast

Door then opens, in walks a long legged honey
She pulls a 44, says give me all your money

I say take me with you, I'll make it worth your while
We'll travel around the country and we'll do it in style

So we blow the safe, with her dynamite
Scored twenty thousand, hit the road that night

By this point Catherine is now in the first row. Howie is still making eye contact with Catherine. He winks then moves to stage left while Danny lays down a mean guitar riff and Kent is jamming on his clarinet. Howie scans the crowd. Dominique is pressing her way to the front. Howie makes eye contact with Dominique and sings,

Cruisin' south on I-95, she says let's get it done
She pulls over, fugitive sex is so much fun

Sometime the next morning, I ask what's your name
She replies Bonnie, danger is my game

Her name's even sexier and all because she lied
So I lie right back and say my name's Clyde

Big Game CEO

Outside Atlanta, we steal a Cadillac
Then we hold up a bank, I know there's no pulling back

Somewhere near New Orleans, we rob three more
Then off to Mexico, for the cops declare war

After pressing her way to the front Dominique is standing directly behind Catherine. Howie is on stage directly in front of them. He looks down. Dominique points and lips, "Is this Catherine Halsey?" Catherine turns her head and looks at Dominique for the first time. Howie looks up, purposefully ignoring both of them. He walks to stage right and scans the other women in the crowd. With his bright white hair Howie notices Dominique's assistant Stephan standing in the middle of the crowd checking him out. Howie walks to stage left and continues,

After six months, the excitement seems to fade
She says let's head north, time for another raid

First we hit Vegas, then Hollywood
Out in Death Valley, fugitive sex never felt so good

We make Canada, enjoy Niagara Falls
Money on the bed, we dance the fugitive ball

Dominique and Catherine are standing in the front row, shoulder to shoulder. During a short drum solo Howie shows off his vocal range with a low to high pitch, "Ahhh". Catherine cheers. Dominique looks bored. Howie walks back over to center stage. He looks at Dominique, then Catherine, and sings,

Canadian Mounties surround us, things are looking bad
She says, kiss me, kiss me, and don't be sad

All of a sudden, in comes the metal rain
My Bonnie returns fire, and yells, I feel no pain

Chapter 9: The Glory Seekers

I think of the Kwikie Mart, blood surrounds my friend
I'm going out shooting, this is the end

The music stops. Gus, the drummer, lays down four quick beats that sound like gunfire. Howie repeats himself.

This is the end.

The crowd goes crazy. Everyone is cheering. The younger band members take a bow. The crowd roars. Then Kent tips his wide brim hat to the audience. There is an even louder roar. Kent walks across the stage. Standing between Danny and Howie he says, "It's been an honor playing with the two of you."

Danny replies, "Likewise."

Fifteen minutes later the judges announce the winners of the Battle of the Bands competition. *Ambivalent Swag* finishes third. With the announcement there is a mixture of boos and cheers from the crowd. Someone throws a beer bottle at one of the judges. Bouncers immediately wrestler the bottle thrower to the ground and kick him out of the club. Bobby is visibly pissed. He looks intently at Howie. Howie looks at Bobby and says, "Fine, I'll do it."

Howie jumps down from the stage. He looks at Catherine and then across to the other side of the room towards Dominique. Catherine stands and starts walking towards Howie. He meets Catherine halfway. She says, "I don't know what the judges were thinking. You should have won."

"Thanks. So what brings you into Manhattan?"

"Just studying what it means to be a man in the modern world."

"That's the sexiest thing anyone ever told me. Are you still planning on marrying Keating?"

She hesitates then says, "Maybe."

Howie turns around and looks at Bobby. Bobby is visibly annoyed that he is talking with Catherine. Howie says, "Look, I have some business to attend to. Will you stick around? Maybe we can talk some more."

Catherine smiles and says, "Sure."

Howie walks over to Dominique. Her posse steps back to give Howie and Dominique space. However, Stephan stays close enough so he can hear his boss's words. She says to Howie, "Have you gone totally native?"

"I was wondering what you were going to say. Have you gone totally native was third on my list."

"And what was first on your list?"

"Up for robbing a Kwikie Mart?"

"Give your pistol a rest for a few minutes Clyde. You're not the rock star type. You are destined to be a great architect. You know how stupid old rock stars look on stage?"

"It's hard to look stupid when you're filthy rich."

"Mick Jagger and Bono look stupid."

"No they don't."

"Trust me as a woman, they look stupid. And you look stupid right now, dressed as a cashier."

"So what did you think of the performance?"

"You know the contest was rigged. The drummer of *Dante's Inferno* is the grandson of the owner of The Roseland Ballroom."

"Figures."

"I have no idea why *The Flaming Androgyny* won second place." She looks over at Stephan and says, "Must have been the gay vote."

Stephan says, "Howie could have taken the gay vote if he would have worn something a little tighter. You know, something to show off his firm butt."

Dominique cuts Stephan off by saying, "That's enough."

Howie asks, "Speaking of enough, do you think we are good enough to make it?"

"Your voice is very good but still needs some work. Your lead guitarist can play."

"Danny is something else."

"I loved your clarinet player. The Gandalf-Al Capone look is mint."

"Hiring Kent was my idea."

"Your excellent taste ceases to amaze me."

"Thanks."

Chapter 9: The Glory Seekers

"You'll have to find a new bass player and drummer."

"I thought you would say that."

"I don't know if you have what it takes to compete with some of those bands in Los Angeles. Those boys and girls in Hollywood know the music industry inside and out."

"I know."

"If you really want it then I can get you a music contract. You know this will take three years away from your career as an architect."

"I know."

"Chances are ten years from now you'll be playing a county fair somewhere."

"I know."

"Let me convince you that architecture is your future. I have access to the board room at the top of the Chrysler Building."

Howie looks over at bar. Catherine is talking to his cousin Danny. Howie jokes, "I didn't think they still called it the Chrysler Building now that Chrysler is bankrupt."

Dominique follows Howie's line-of-sight to the bar. She asks, "So is that Catherine Halsey? I thought you were just making her up to make me jealous. So how many times have you two had sex?"

"We haven't."

"I can't believe that. But who in this day and age goes by the name of Catherine and wears those kind of clothes."

Stephan adds, "Does your Catherine have any self-awareness? She'd might look hip in the age of Nancy Drew."

Howie ignores Stephan's comment. He says to Dominique, "She's getting married in a few weeks to someone named Peter Keating."

"This is too, too much. I'm marrying Gail Wynand in August and your Catherine is marrying a Peter Keating in July. This would be a tragedy if marriage actually meant something these days."

"You can be a bitch sometimes."

"I'm only a bitch when someone doesn't like to face the truth. You know as well as I do that you were planning on marrying your career."

"I hate it when you're right."

"So do you want to go to the top of the Chrysler Building and consummate your marriage to your career in architecture? Or are you still thinking about becoming a rock star?"

"Give me a few minutes. I need to talk to my cousin and to Catherine."

"Don't take too long."

Howie walks over to the bar. He says to Catherine, "Excuse us for a minute. I need to talk with my cousin."

"Sure."

Danny and Howie step away from the bar. Howie asks, "Where's Bobby?"

"He's still pissed that we lost. He's taking out his frustration backstage banging some drunk bimbo."

"Figures. Even when he's mad everyone loves Bobby."

"So what did Dominique say?"

"She can get us a contract but we have to get rid of Bobby and Gus."

"But Bobby's blood."

"I know."

"So what are you going to do?"

"This is your decision. To be honest I could care less one way or the other about the music industry. I know what I like and I like designing buildings. However the fame and money would be nice. Making it big is still a long shot. If you want to go for it I'm with you for three years."

"What happens at the end of three years?"

"What is going to happen at the end of this summer? We each go our separate ways."

"What do you want me to say?"

"Just tell me what you really want. Why don't you sleep on it."

"Fine."

"I got one favor to ask. Can you take Catherine home tonight?"

"Are you going with Dominique?"

"Unfortunately you have to keep the money happy. Can you give Catherine and me a few minutes?"

"Sure."

Danny heads down to the other end of the bar. Howie walks up to Catherine and says, "You were right."

"Right about what?"

Chapter 9: The Glory Seekers

"That I would marry my career. I want to build buildings. I want to see the world. This past year in Port Jervis and Scranton has been a nice break but I'm not the type that could ever settle down there."

"I'll go with you."

"That's not what you want. After a few years you'd want to move back to be close to your family."

"I want to be with you."

"No you don't. You wouldn't be happy. You love your family too much. I envy you because of that."

"You don't love your family?"

"Not like you do." Howie looks down at Catherine's feet. He feels guilty. Catherine can see it in his face. She grabs his right hand. Howie says, "I've got to go."

As Howie turns around Catherine says, "Wait."

"Yes?"

"Do you love me?"

"I love you more than any woman I've ever known."

"More than Dominique."

Howie sighs, "More than Dominique." And with that Howie turns and walks back to his billionaire mistress.

Danny watches the break-up from a distance. After Howie leaves he walks over to Catherine and says, "I'll drive you home."

A tear trickles down Catherine's cheek. She says, "I have to go to the bathroom first." She quickly walks away. She is gone for thirty minutes, crying in a bathroom stall, not satisfied with the man she is about to marry.

Danny waits patiently at the bar. Kent walks over. He buys Danny a beer and a whiskey for himself. Running his fingers through his long white beard he says, "Howie seems to have a lot of women in his life."

"I don't know if it is Howie or if it is all the women that makes his life so complicated."

"So did Howie land *Ambivalent Swag* a music contract?"

"No."

"What are you going to do now?"

"Have you enjoyed your career as a freelance musician?"

"I wouldn't sell my clarinet for the world."

Big Game CEO

In the parking garage Howie takes Danny's motorcycle out of the back of Bobby's truck. With Dominique straddling the motorcycle seat and holding on tight from behind, Howie races over to the Chrysler Building. They take the elevator to the top floor. Dominique unlocks the door to the boardroom. She quickly undresses and sits down in the large leather seat at the head of the table. Howie looks at Dominique then out the window. He can't decide which is more beautiful, Dominique's naked body, or the New York skyline at night.

Howie walks over, grabs Dominique with his left arm, and tosses her on the boardroom table. They have sex. Dominique moans, immediately having an orgasm. But Howie isn't finished. He pumps harder and harder. Finally he grabs Dominique like a rag doll and tosses her to the edge of the table. He lays her face down with her legs dangling off the edge of the table. He stands firmly on the floor, looks over the New York skyline, and mounts Dominique from behind. He pumps harder and harder.

Laying facedown on the table, Dominique stretches out her left arm and grabs her purse. Pulling out a pack of cigarettes and lighter she moans again, having another orgasm. She lights up, takes a puff, and blows a smoke ring over the boardroom table. She says, "You seem frustrated tonight."

"Must be the damn Dexedrine. Is my frustration bothering you?"

"I'm enjoying your frustration thoroughly."

Again Howie looks out over the New York skyline. He pumps harder and harder. He let's out a billowing moan. The consummation of his marriage to his career is complete.

Thirty minutes later Howie drops Dominique off at her apartment. She asks if he wants to stay the night. Howie says he feels like being alone. On Danny's motorcycle he races through the streets of Manhattan back towards Port Jervis. Half way across the George Washington Bridge he pulls over to the side. Howie looks down at the Hudson River and then up at the New York skyline. He whispers to himself, "I never realized it until now. The skyline to this city looks so old. It's time for a change."

Still wired from the Dexedrine, Howie pulls over at an all night Internet coffee shop in Clifton, New Jersey. He spends the last few

Chapter 9: The Glory Seekers

hours before dawn researching the lives and lifestyles of the most powerful corporate executives in America.

Chapter 10: The War Seekers

It is a warm and muggy June morning in Port Jervis. At 8:37 AM Howie pulls up to their apartment. He parks Danny's motorcycle and looks in the direction of New York City towards the rising sun. Howie saunters up to the apartment and quietly opens the door. Standing in the kitchen he looks around. Three of Danny's survival magazines and an open pizza box with two slices lay on the counter. The sink is full of dirty dishes. In the living room the television is on and Bobby is sleeping face down on the sofa wearing only a pair of red shorts. Competing with the background noise of the Saturday morning cartoons is snoring from Danny's bedroom.

Howie decides to make a strawberry-banana smoothie for breakfast. Without thinking he turns on the blender. Bobby groggily yells, "You and that damn blender could wake up Rip Van Winkle! Why the hell did you do that?"

Howie turns off the blender and says, "Sorry." He then asks, "Are you awake?"

Bobby groggily yells, "I'm awake now!" Howie turns the blender back on and finishes mixing the smoothie. Bobby yells, "Jesus!" He stands up and turns off the television.

Howie asks, "Do you want some strawberry-banana smoothie?"

"Hell no! Smoothies are the food of the cubical crowd." Bobby grabs a slice of sausage and onion pizza from the box on the counter and takes a big bite. With his mouth half full he says, "So Danny told

Chapter 10: The War Seekers

me you were busy last night trying to convince Dominique to give us a music contract."

"That's where I was."

"Well I hope you convinced her brains out."

Howie doesn't say a word. He is trying to decide how to break the news to Bobby when Danny walks out of his bedroom wearing only a pair of old blue jeans. Danny mumbles, "Can you keep it down."

Howie asks, "Did Catherine get home OK?"

"Yeah."

Howie looks into Danny's eyes. He can tell Danny has already made up his mind not to accept the music contract since that would force Bobby out of the band. Howie looks at Bobby and says, "We're not going to get a music contract."

Bobby yells, "Damn it!"

Howie says, "It is probably for the best. If we got the contract then ten years from now we'd probably be playing a county fair somewhere."

Bobby asks, "I bet that's what eagle super freak said."

Howie laughs, "Nothing gets by you."

"So what was her real reason for not giving us the music contract?"

Howie hesitates then answers, "She wouldn't say."

Danny says, "Let's not worry about it. What's done is done."

Still upset Bobby takes another big bite of pizza. Howie looks at Danny and says, "You know, we are all going our separate ways at the end of the summer. We should do something big to celebrate."

"Like what?"

"Like what you were talking about in Ithaca."

"Hunting polar bears?"

"No, the other thing."

"Big Game CEO?"

"Big Game CEO."

Bobby asks, "I thought you said killing is immoral."

"What I meant to say is killing a moral man is immoral."

"Like morality has anything to do with anything anymore."

"Socrates said that morality is being able to reap the rewards of your own labors."

Big Game CEO

"Who cares, Socrates is dead."

"It's time to raise Socrates spirit from the grave. I did some research last night. I've identified three men that got rich by stealing from the system and taking from the labor of others. Now they're so rich they think they are above of the law. It's time to bring God's country to their country clubs."

Danny asks, "Are you sure we should do this?"

"You're the one that wanted to prove you're a man by killing a polar bear. If you really want to prove you're a man then take down something that will make society a better place."

Danny replies, "Then let's do it."

"Let's do it, but only if you do exactly as I say. I've got the whole thing planned out. But we've got to do it next week. I'm going last and I have to take my target out on the Fourth of July. The Fourth is the only time I'll have access to him."

Bobby asks, "Who's your target?"

"Boomer Mapple, former CEO of the Axton Oil Company."

Danny asks, "Why him?"

"On top of everything else that he did, Mapple loaded the board of Axton with all his buddies, and his buddies gave him a $500 million golden parachute when he retired at the age of 54."

Bobby asks, "Howie, when you become powerful will you put me on the board of your company?"

"Will you give me a $500 million dollar golden parachute?"

"How much of a kickback do I get?"

Howie laughs and says, "Always angling aren't you."

Danny says, "This Boomer Mapple guy sounds like a fat cat."

Howie responds, "He is. Weighs over 300 pounds."

Danny jokes, "Why not just feed him another biscuit? He'd keel over of a heart attack."

Bobby jokes, "So I guess Howie's code name is Captain Ahab." Howie laughs.

Danny asks, "Why's that funny?"

Howie answers, "Because Captain Ahab's quest in life was to slay the great white whale Moby Dick."

"Oh."

Chapter 10: The War Seekers

Howie says, "If we are going to do this we've got to get moving. I want you and Bobby to travel down to South Carolina and get everything on this list. Wear sunglasses and a hat. Only pay cash. Make sure not to get your fingerprints on anything. Also fill a small plastic bag with the red clay soil from down there."

Danny asks, "Why do you want a small plastic bag full of red dirt."

"You'll see when the time comes."

Bobby looks at the list and says, "It says here we have to steal a Honda Gold Wing motorcycle with South Carolina plates. Golden Wings are for old, fat people. Why can't we steal a Kawasaki Ninja?"

"Your personality and your ride go together. None of us would be caught dead on a Honda Gold Wing, that's why we are going to use one. Besides, we need a big bike with a large storage compartment. How else are we going to carry our Iceman compound bows? After we're finished we are going to dismantle the Gold Wing and destroy it."

Danny asks, "Are we going to destroy every piece of evidence when we're done?"

"Every piece. One more thing, when you get back from South Carolina, park the Gold Wing in our ministorage unit up the street where the band used to practice. I don't want anyone seeing the Gold Wing."

Bobby sighs and repeats Howie, "Where the band used to practice. I guess *Ambivalent Swag* is dead."

Danny says, "It's dead. Happy graduation."

Four days later the cousins are in the kitchen of their apartment. Danny asks, "So Howie, why did you want us to get both white and black full-face motorcycle helmets?"

Howie answers, "You wear the white helmet up to the target site. Then within a mile of the site you switch to the black helmet."

Bobby puts on the black full-face motorcycle helmet. He breathes deeply and says, "This black helmet reminds me of Darth Vader's favorite pick-up line."

Howie asks, "And what's that?"

"Once you go black you never go back." Howie and Danny laugh.

Big Game CEO

Howie places six arrows, a diamond tip stylists, and a plastic bag filled with clay soil from South Carolina on the kitchen table. He puts on a pair of surgical gloves, sits down, and says, "We need to make this look like the work of a lone serial killer. So what name should we give this serial killer?"

Bobby says, "*The Zen Reaper.*"

Danny replies, "Are you an idiot? That was the name of our old speed metal band."

Howie looks at the plastic bag of clay soil and says, "Where did you find this clay soil? It's more scarlet than red."

Danny answers, "Just south of Greenville."

"Since the clay is deep red we should pick something that starts with the letter A in honor of *The Scarlet Letter.*"

Danny asks, "Why not Aardvark?"

Bobby says, "What the hell are you talking about?"

"Aardvarks are cool."

"If you have a long nose and you like to eat ants."

Howie says, "I've got the perfect name for a serial killer of billionaires. The Antagonist."

Bobby says, "The Antagonist, I like it."

Danny asks, "What's an antagonist?"

Howie answers, "Villain to a stories hero."

Bobby adds, "Villains and heroes always depend on the narrators point of view."

Danny asks, "And what story are we writing?"

Howie answers, "We've just entered the era of free form jazz." With that Howie puts on a surgical mask and takes the arrows out of their package. With the diamond tipped stylist he lightly carves 'The Antagonist' on the shaft of each arrow. Next he takes a little scarlet red South Carolina clay and rubs it over the carved letters. For Howie the red clay filler serves three purposes: First, to help rebalance the arrow's weight; second, to reestablish the arrow's aerodynamic form; and third, to make the FBI think the killer is from the Southern United States.

Eight days before the Fourth of July the three cousins begin Operation Big Game CEO. Howie has purposely selected Bobby to go first. Going first gives Bobby the element of surprise to hide any

Chapter 10: The War Seekers

mistakes that might result from his lack of discipline. Also, Bobby's lack of moral character means he will have no hesitation firing the arrow. Once Bobby has killed someone Danny's sense of duty will takeover eliminating his moral hesitation.

In their apartment Bobby gives Howie his credit cards and cell phone. Howie gives Bobby a Magellan GPS. Howie then double-checks that Bobby has memorized the time, latitude and longitudinal coordinates for his kill, and the time, latitude and longitudinal coordinates for their rendezvous.

On the Honda Gold Wing motorcycle Bobby drives fourteen hours to Charlevoix, Michigan. Stopping to buy gas is his only contact with other people. He never takes off his white motorcycle helmet and always pays with cash. Five miles south of Charlevoix he pulls over on a quiet dirt road. He changes out of his size nine boots and into Howie's size fourteen boots, and changes from the white helmet into the black helmet. Finally he takes the stolen Pennsylvania license plates off the motorcycle and puts on the original South Carolina plates. A mile up the road he finds a quiet spot to camp for the night.

While Bobby is traveling to Charlevoix, Danny and Howie drive Bobby's Ford King Ranch F-150 Super Crew Pickup north on Interstate 87 toward the Adirondack Mountains. They pay for gas with Bobby's credit card, dinner with Howie's credit card, and supplies with Danny's credit card. Along the way Howie makes phone calls between all three of their cell phones. All the credit card and cell phone activity is to make it appear that all three cousins are traveling together.

Charlevoix is a northern Michigan community perched on an isthmus between Lake Michigan and Round Lake. It has the look and feel of an 18th century resort community. On the last Saturday in June it is also the location of the Run Charlevoix Marathon. And for the last seven years Gerald Steiner, Bobby's target, has competed in this marathon.

At 4:05 AM the next morning Bobby packs up his tent. He checks the campsite making sure no clues are left behind other than his footprints. In the early dawn Bobby travels north on Highway 31 through Charlevoix scouting the marathon route. Just north of town he turns right on See Road then immediately left on an abandoned railroad track. A hundred and fifty feet up the tracks he pulls over.

He studies the grove of trees between Highway 31 and the abandoned tracks. He has reached the GPS coordinates – he just has to wait for the time.

At 7:00 AM the marathon begins. At the same time Bobby quietly paces back and forth wearing Howie's size fourteen boots, making sure to leave footprints in the dirt. At 8:19 AM the first group of runners pass Bobby's position. He walks up to the Honda Gold Wing and opens the rear storage compartment. Silently he lifts out his Iceman compound bow and takes two arrows out of their sealed plastic bags.

Bobby pulls a recent picture of Gerald Steiner from his pocket. He studies Steiner's face and thinks of Howie's words from three days earlier, "Gerald Steiner is the CEO of the insurance company AGG. He also sits on the board of nine other companies. He and his board buddies scratch each other's backs. AGG got billions in government bailout money. Just think that all that money went to pay the salaries of lawyers, government administrators, his buddies, and not much else."

Bobby stares more intently at the picture then whispers to himself, "Why does Howie have to justify everything. Gerald's rich and greedy. In this winner-take-all economy he is just someone standing in my way. Game on."

Howie estimates that Gerald will reach the fifteen-mile mark of the marathon at 8:57 AM. Hidden in the bushes Bobby watches with binoculars as the steady stream of marathoner runners make the slight bend on Highway 31. At 9:10 AM Bobby is getting anxious. He considers killing a random marathon runner when he spots Steiner. Bobby mumbles to himself, "He's in perfect position."

Gerald is running ten feet behind two other runners. The next group of runners is three hundred feet back. Bobby waits until Gerald makes the slight bend. At 9:12 AM, and without hesitation, Bobby shoots with full force. Silently the arrow penetrates Gerald's right temple and the tip exits just behind the left ear. A narrow cylinder of bone, blood, flesh, and brain spurts out and lands fifteen feet away on the shoulder of the road. Gerald begins to fall. Bobby steps out from the bushes to get a better angle and fires a second arrow through his heart. Gerald falls silently to the ground. The two runners in front of Gerald don't realize something has happened and keep on running.

Chapter 10: The War Seekers

Bobby studies his kill for a few seconds. There is no movement and no sound. The smile on Bobby's face is covered by the faceshield of the black motorcycle helmet. The next group of runners rounds the corner. Bobby disappears into the bushes but not before one of the runners gets a glimpse of Bobby's shadow.

The runners stop. Gerald's motionless body lay in a pool of blood. They look down at the arrows through his head and heart. The chirps from the birds in the trees sound eerie, like something from an Alfred Hitchcock movie. It takes a few moments for the runners to comprehend Gerald Steiner's murder. Then from the trees they hear a motorcycle engine start. One of the runners sprints into the woods. By then it is too late. Bobby is gone.

Sunday evening Bobby makes the rendezvous with Danny and Howie just outside the Fish Creek Pond campsite in the Adirondack Mountains. They hide the motorcycle in the woods, eat dinner in town, pay for the bill with Bobby's credit card, then all three make fools of themselves at a local bar during the karaoke hour. They drive back to camp. Tents and RV's crowd the sites of the Fish Creek Pond campground. Howie plays cards with an elderly couple from Canada while Danny and Bobby play their guitars around the campfire.

Monday the three cousins head south to Six Flags Great Escape in Lake George with Bobby and Howie in the truck and Danny following on the Honda Gold Wing. At the theme park each cousin uses his credit card numerous times. After riding the Sasquatch, a ride with a 200-foot drop, in the souvenir shop Howie buys the picture of all three cousins. Howie turns to Bobby and says, "I'll be back in a few minutes. I want to put this picture in the truck."

Bobby says, "Can we go? This place is boring."

Howie answers, "I know. It's like the whole damn country is nothing but one big boring theme park with lots and lots of souvenir stands. However, I want us to stick around here for another few hours." That night the cousins stay in a motel in Lake George.

Tuesday morning the three cousins eat breakfast at Denny's. Danny uses his credit card to pay for the meal. In the parking lot Danny gives Howie his credit cards and cell phone. He then puts on the white motorcycle helmet, gets on the Honda Gold Wing, and heads for the world famous 'Black' Golf Course at Bethpage State Park on Long Island. At 1:15 PM, three miles away from the golf course, Danny pulls over. He looks up and watches a corporate helicopter fly overhead. He whispers to himself, "That must be Roger Cly flying in for his 1:30 PM tee time. I don't know how Howie figures these things out. The Internet is an amazing thing. After today I bet a CEO will never post his golf scores on the Internet."

Danny opens the right side storage compartment and switches from the white motorcycle helmet and into the black one. Next he changes into Howie's size fourteen boots. Finally he changes the motorcycle tags from the stolen Pennsylvania plates to the South Carolina plates.

At 1:25 PM he parks the Honda Gold Wing on a quiet side street. Silently he opens the rear storage compartment and lifts out a large black leather bag. At 1:28 PM he takes a position in the bushes on a hill overlooking the second green. He opens the leather bag, puts on a pair of gloves, pulls out his Iceman compound bow, and takes two arrows out of their sealed plastic bags.

Danny pulls a recent picture of Roger Cly from his pocket. He studies Cly's face and thinks of Howie's words from a few days earlier, "Roger Cly is the worse kind of hypocrite. He says it is patriotism that inspires all his business dealings but he is in it just to make money. His investment bank has financed much of the transfer in technology to the Chinese. He sits on the board of five companies. He and his board buddies scratch each other's backs, making sure management keeps all the money. And most of that money resides in overseas bank accounts."

Danny stares more intently at the picture then whispers to himself, "In, out, without a trace other than the footprints."

At 1:42 PM a golf ball lands behind the second green. Danny whispers to himself, "This is beyond perfect. Let the game come to you Danny boy. Let the game come to you." At 1:43 PM Roger walks over the green carrying a putter and pitching wedge. He drops the putter at the back of the green and keeps walking towards his ball. Thirty feet behind the green he positions his feet for a chip shot. Danny steps out from behind a tree and with full force launches an arrow. It silently strikes just above Roger's right ear and the tip exits just above his left ear. A narrow cylinder of bone, blood, flesh, and brain spurts out and

Chapter 10: The War Seekers

lands in a nearby sand trap. Roger begins to fall. Danny takes a step forward to get a better angle and fires a second arrow through his heart. Roger Cly falls silently to the ground.

At 1:45 PM one of Roger's golf partners walks over the ridge on the back of the green and yells, "Are you having a problem finding your ball?" By then Danny is over a mile away. Danny doesn't take the South Carolina plates off the motorcycle or change out of the black helmet until he is thirty miles north of New York City.

At 2:15 PM Howie and Bobby drive into town, purchase gas and supplies using all three of their credit cards, and make calls using all three of their cell phones.

That evening Danny makes the rendezvous with Howie and Bobby just outside the Fish Creek Pond campsite. They hide the motorcycle in the woods. The three cousins drive back to the mini-city of tents and RV's that make up the Fish Creek Pond campground. Howie plays cards with the same elderly couple from Canada while Danny and Bobby again play their guitars around the campfire.

Tuesday night news is leaked from the FBI to the press that 'The Antagonist' is carved on the arrows that killed Gerald Steiner and Roger Cly. By Wednesday morning 'The Antagonist' is on the front page of every newspaper. It is also the lead story of every cable news show. Even in the remote location of Fish Creek Pond campground 'The Antagonist' is the primary topic of conversation. Some people think 'The Antagonist' is a hero, others a menace to society.

At lunch Danny says, "Howie, this is getting too dangerous. The whole nation is on their guard."

Howie replies, "Don't worry about me. From the paper it is clear no one has spotted the Honda Gold Wing yet."

Bobby says, "I'm more worried about Danny and me."

"If I get caught I'll take the fall for all three of us."

Bobby sarcastically says, "Sure you will."

"I will."

Bobby responds, "Even if you take the fall we are accomplices. The FBI will nail Danny and me for using your credit card and making calls on your cell phone."

"Then I better not get caught."

"You'd better not."

Wednesday, Thursday, and Friday the three cousins enjoy some quiet canoeing and fishing.

Early Saturday, on the Fourth of July, Howie gives Bobby his cell phone and credit cards. He then heads off for Massachusetts on the Honda Gold Wing. At 4:45 PM he arrives the port city of Gloucester and pulls over. While taking off the white helmet he flips open the right side storage compartment with his foot. He changes into the black helmet with facemask and a black leather-riding suit. He disguises his appearance further by putting a few towels inside the leather jacket to give the appearance of a beer belly. He changes the stolen Pennsylvania plates to the South Carolina plates that came with the stolen motorcycle. Lastly he takes a Dexedrine and washes it down with a Red Bull energy drink.

For the next twenty minutes he rides around the back streets and alleys of Gloucester looking for quiet side streets and a good hiding place. At 5:05 PM he pulls up to Inner Harbor. He turns off Rogers Street onto Harbor Loop. Howie parks the Gold Wing behind a van. The motorcycle is mostly hidden from view by the van and a shed. To get a better vantage point Howie walks out onto the only nearby vacant lot. Looking down he checks to make sure he is leaving footprints in the dirt.

From the vacant lot he scans the nearby buildings. As an architect he considers the jumble of arbitrary lines disgusting, and the lack of planning in this old port city nauseating. Howie can't understand how some people find old New England towns like this quaint.

Next he scans Inner Harbor. A whale watching boat is returning to port. He studies the many fishing boats. All the roads that loop around Inner Harbor are congested with holiday traffic. Numerous tourists are walking the piers. Local artists are selling their paintings. The intermittent sound of firecrackers fills the air. Howie takes a deep breath of the salty ocean air and studies the destination of his target, the S.S. Odyssey. With its modern sleek design, bright white hull, and two levels of dark windows, it looks like an alien spacecraft among the weather beaten fishing boats.

Chapter 10: The War Seekers

For the Fourth of July the S.S. Odyssey is leased to Boomer Mapple. He has invited 500 guests to dinner on the high seas. At 6:00 PM the guests are to set sail for Boston Harbor to watch the Boston fireworks celebration. Howie has other plans for tonight's entertainment. He studies the aerodynamic lines of the S.S. Odyssey and says to himself, "Time to hunt the great white whale."

At 5:16 PM a corporate helicopter appears on the horizon. It lands in a small open area a few hundred feet from where Howie is standing. Dominique, Dominique's mother, and Gail Wynand exit the helicopter and start making the quarter mile walk to the S.S. Odyssey. Howie says to himself, "I didn't know they were going to be here. I could take Wynand out instead. No Howie, remember Sun Tzu and *The Art of War*. There is no strategic gain in killing Wynand. He's not on the right board of directors."

Howie silently watches as Dominique, her mother, and her much older fiancé walk across a parking lot to the pier. As soon as they board the S.S. Odyssey a waiter offers each a mixed drink of champagne, gin, and tangerine schnapps appropriately named Fireworks.

At 5:19 PM he walks back over to the Gold Wing. Hidden from the general field of view Howie opens the rear luggage compartment and pulls out a black leather bag. He takes his seat on the Gold Wing, adjusts his riding gloves, places the leather bag between his legs, unzips the bag, and prepares the compound bow and two arrows. Through the small opening between the van and storage shed he silently watches the line of limos pull up to the S.S. Odyssey, and the wealthy passengers climb on board.

At 5:27 PM a white stretch limo pulls up. Eight people climb out including Boomer Mapple. Howie starts the motorcycle. Boomer Mapple slowly walks towards the S.S. Odyssey. His 320-pound body struggles with every step. Howie sarcastically says to himself, "How majestic."

Quickly yet casually he pulls forward. Howie stops twenty-five feet behind Boomer Mapple. Howie lifts the compound bow and arrows from the black leather bag. Mapple turns and looks. He sees his own reflection in the mirrored facemask on Howie's black motorcycle helmet. With full force Howie shoots. The arrow strikes between Boomer's eyes. The tip of the arrow exits the back of his head a few inches. A narrow cylinder of bone, blood, flesh, and brain spurts out and land on the back of a lady's sequin evening dress. Howie quickly fires a second arrow full force into his heart. The arrow penetrates the layers and layers of fat but never exits Boomer's body.

The lady in the sequin evening dress screams as Boomer Mapple falls silently to the ground. Howie is now half a block away. A few tourists snap pictures of the mysterious masked assassin wearing a black leather-riding outfit. Boomer Mapple's limo driver tries to give chase but the streets are filled with holiday traffic. Howie quickly makes his getaway east along the shoulder of Rogers Street. He turns left on Manuel F Lewis Street, left on Main Street, and right on Pleasant Street. He rides across a parking lot and turns up an alley between an old warehouse and abandoned railroad track. He parks the motorcycle between the warehouse and a storage shed. A large garbage dumpster, bushes, and trees also surround his hiding location.

At 5:31 PM he pulls a tarp from the left storage compartment and tosses it over the Gold Wing motorcycle. Underneath the tarp Howie changes out of the black leather-riding outfit. With the towel that was stuffed into his jacket to make him look fat he wipes the sweat off his arms and upper body. He takes the South Carolina plates off the Gold Wing and puts on the Pennsylvania plates. Howie changes into a t-shirt, jeans, tennis shoes, baseball hat, and sunglasses. He grabs this month's edition of *Architectural Design* out of the right storage bin and starts walking south, back towards the scene of the crime. Howie knows that by now all the roads into and out of Gloucester are sealed off. He is just buying his time.

At 5:46 PM Howie casually returns to the scene. Paramedics are wheeling a cart with a white sheet covering Mapple's body into the back of an ambulance. Police officers are interviewing tourists. One officer is downloading pictures from a tourist's digital camera onto a computer in the trunk of his police car. Howie says to himself, "I didn't know they could move information that quickly."

Boomer Mapple's guests are standing shoulder-to-shoulder along the rail, on the top deck of the S.S. Odyssey, looking down at the scene. Dominique's mother is talking to Gail Wynand. Dominique is talking to her assistant, Stephan.

Chapter 10: The War Seekers

A pack of nine boys between the ages of twelve and thirteen ride up on BMX bikes to check out the commotion. One of the boys is wearing a yellow baseball hat with the phrase 'The Antagonist' written in black ink across the front. At 5:51 PM two cars of FBI agents arrive. The first agent out of the lead car immediately interrogates the boy in the yellow hat. Howie laughs at the irony. At 5:53 PM he starts a long walk around Inner Harbor. At 6:02 PM the first news helicopter arrives.

At 6:37 PM Howie walks out onto a pier on the other side of Inner Harbor. Among the gawking tourists Howie watches the growing circus across the water. FBI agents are everywhere. Police are holding back reporters. Howie turns and casually strolls among the painters selling their works. He thinks to himself, "So this is what artistic types do when they get old."

At 7:06 PM Howie finds a hill off of Eastern Point Boulevard, sits down under a tree, and stares out over the Atlantic. He wonders what it would have been like two hundred years ago working on a whaling ship. After a while he starts to read the latest copy of *Architectural Design*. Soon bored, he puts down the magazine and continues to stare out over the Atlantic.

At 7:44 PM he notices the S.S. Odyssey sailing out of Inner Harbor. Howie says to himself, "That's cold. I bet those rich people came up with the excuse that they didn't want to deal with the press."

Between 7:55 PM and 8:46 PM Danny and Bobby eat dinner, get gas, and purchase supplies in the town of Saranac, NY. They use all three of their credit cards. They also make calls using all three of their cell phones.

At 9:55 PM Howie sees the first large firework go off in the night sky. He starts his long walk back. At 11:05 PM he returns to the motorcycle. Howie removes the tarp, takes a Dexedrine, and washes it down with a Red Bull energy drink. He begins the long ride back.

Howie meets up with Danny and Bobby early the next day near Port Henry. That Sunday morning they dismantle the Honda Golden Wing with wrenches, a sledgehammer, and a chain saw. They cut the black leather riding outfit and both motorcycle helmets in two. At a local dump they dispose of the evidence. They keep their three compound bows, but that is it. That afternoon they return to Fish Creek Ponds.

Big Game CEO

For the next three days they canoe, fish, and camp the inlets in and around Saranac Lake.

On the final night of their camping trip Bobby breaks open a bottle of tequila. Even Howie gets drunk on this most perfect of camping nights. Sitting around the campfire Howie asks, "You understand we're under an oath of silence?"

Danny answers, "Of course we are. Do we look stupid?"

"I wasn't going to tell anybody this, but do you remember the two days you drove down to South Carolina."

Bobby sarcastically says, "Yes, we remember. It was only two weeks ago."

"Well the morning after you left Catherine Halsey showed up at the apartment."

Bobby exclaims, "No way!"

"She was only wearing a trench coat. She opened it up and said, 'Take me. Take me now. I want you.'"

Bobby exclaims again, "No way!"

Danny asks, "What did you do?"

Bobby hits Danny in the back of the head and says, "Does Howie look stupid? Does Howie look gay?"

Danny replies, "His curly hair makes him look a little gay."

Bobby asks, "So how was it?"

Howie answers, "Best damn sex I ever had."

Danny asks, "Is she still getting married?"

Howie says, "I think so."

Bobby adds, "Oh well."

Howie stares at the worm in the bottom of the tequila bottle and says, "What I just told you about Catherine is part of our oath of silence. If we are to ever discuss what happened over these last two weeks then we meet in private and you know exactly what you have to do."

Bobby jokes, "I hope one of us wants to talk in private. I just want to see the look on their face, even if it kills me."

Chapter 11: The FBI

July 6th is a hot and muggy Monday in Washington, DC. At FBI headquarters the air-conditioning is broken. At 9:02 AM Bernie Fitzgibbon wipes the sweat from his forehead as he reviews the case with his team of fifty-six agents. He quietly walks around the outside of the large meeting room until all the agents are quiet. He stops, points at a series of pictures on the wall, and yells, "Let's go over everything we know for sure! At all three murder scenes we found the same size fourteen boot prints in the dirt. Boots are Alpinestars S-mx 2 Motorcycle Boots by Alpine. This might be a break because this is not a popular brand and they've only been on the market since Christmas."

Agent Bernie Fitzgibbon points at a picture of motorcycle tire tracks in the dirt and continues, "In Michigan we found Avon Cobra tire tracks. The Avon Cobra is the same replacement tire identified on the pictures in Gloucester. In Long Island no tire tracks were found. Although likely, don't assume 'The Antagonist' rode the Honda Gold Wing to the second murder site."

Walking in front of the north wall Bernie points at all the blow-up tourist pictures of the mysterious assassin taken in Gloucester. He yells, "South Carolina plates on the Honda Gold Wing match a motorcycle reported stolen in Greenville, South Carolina on June 23rd! We have confirmed the stolen motorcycle had Avon Cobra replacement tires. Lab analysis of the infamous red clay rubbed in "The Antagonist" carving of all six murder arrows identifies northern South Carolina or northern Georgia as the origin of this clay."

Agent Bernie Fitzgibbon steps back and studies the tourist pictures from Gloucester. He says, "We have a Daytona Shadow full-face gloss black motorcycle helmet. We have an extra-large armored padded motorcycle jacket by Xelement. We have loose fitting black leather pants by Xelement. From these pictures we don't even know if 'The Antagonist' is white, black, Arab, or Hispanic. All we know for sure is that he is between 6'1" and 6'6" and overweight."

Pointing at a blow-up picture of the compound bow he continues, "The compound bow 'The Antagonist' is holding is the latest in the IceMan series from Diamond. Model number is RH70. All six murder arrows are model Vapor Camo 500 from Gold Tip."

Agent Bernie Fitzgibbon looks intently at all fifty-six agents and says, "Build me a database of all people that have purchased these items in the last two years. I also want a study of all credit card activity between June 26th and July 5th. Look at gasoline purchases and motel stays. I want to know who was traveling between Michigan, Long Island, and Gloucester. Over the next week I want to individually review each possible lead. We've got a serial killer out there and my boss is breathing down my neck. I don't want a private detective solving this. This is what we get paid for. Start bringing me leads! Meeting adjourned."

Wednesday, July 8th, at 2:36 PM, Agent Jerry Cruncher carries a folder into his boss's office. Bernie Fitzgibbon looks at Agent Cruncher and says, "What do you have?"

"Three cousins, Howard Holden Roark, Daniel Crockett Roark, and Robert Edward Roark. Credit card records show they each purchased a model number RH70 compound bow either in September or October of last year."

"So did hundreds of other people. Why these three cousins? All evidence points to a lone serial killer."

"Credit card activity and cell phone activity indicate all three were camping in the Adirondack Mountains in Upstate New York during the time of all three murders. This is a good central location with respect to the murder sites."

"How old are they?"

Chapter 11: The FBI

"23, 20, and 20."

"How tall are they?"

"Medical records say six-four, five-ten, and five-nine."

"Who is six-four?"

"Howard Holden Roark."

"What do we know about his guy?"

"Turns out he has an FBI file."

"Really? Why?"

"He worked in China. All citizens that work in China automatically get a file."

"What's the file say?"

"Before graduating Cornell he was hired by the architecture firm Symanski and Nowicki. Worked in China for two months last summer before being laid-off. He is enrolled at Cornell this fall. He needs 20 more credits to graduate."

"Must be a smart guy if someone hired him before graduating. How much does this Howard weigh?"

"Medical record says 201."

"That's not very heavy for someone that is six-four. How old is the medical information?"

"Seventeen months."

"Do we have a recent picture?"

"I found this picture off the Internet from last month. Howard is the lead singer for some band by the name of *Ambivalent Swag*." Agent Jerry Cruncher hands the picture to his boss.

Bernie Fitzgibbon says, "He's definitely not fat."

"He could have stuffed a pillow in the leather jacket. Remember, Howard is a smart guy."

"What about the cell phone and credit card activity?"

"All three cousins made credit card purchases and calls in and around Saranac Lake and Lake George on the days of the murders."

"This Howard Holden Roark might be upset that he was laid off last year but he doesn't fit the mold of a serial killer. He's too young. He's going back to school. The whole damn multibillion-dollar cultural-entertainment complex largely caters to the taste of young boys. I doubt he was bored."

"I don't know sir. He may be some mentally-ill whiny guy stranded between adult things and childish pleasures."

"You're telling me we have some new breed of serial killer who murders just to find identity and meaning in his life."

"Maybe."

"I can't believe that. Besides, does he look like a guy that would ride a Honda Gold Wing? Kids from his generation wouldn't be caught dead on a Honda Gold Wing."

"Is that your psychological profile?"

"Yes."

"What should I do?"

"Did any of the cousins' purchase any of the items on the list other than the compound bows?"

"No credit card evidence."

"Evidence indicates Howard Holden Roark couldn't have been at the crime scenes. We already have over three hundred stronger leads. Toss this folder into the not very likely pile. Let's revisit this file once we get more evidence."

Chapter 12: The Money Seekers

When you reach your twenties life accelerates quickly. For Howie, Danny, and Bobby this is true more so than for most people.

On Saturday, July 11th, Catherine Halsey marries Peter Keating in a simple ceremony in Scranton, Pennsylvania. On Saturday, August 1, Dominique Francon marries Gail Wynand in an extravagant ceremony in Paris, France. On Monday, August 24th, Bobby attends his first class at Penn State University. He plans on majoring in accounting. On Thursday, August 27th, Howie attends his first class for the fall term. He dreads the fact that he will have to take two courses in the spring semester to graduate. On Friday, September 18th, Danny quits his job at the motorcycle repair shop and starts touring the Mid-Atlantic States with a band by the name of *Canadian Velcro with Salsa*.

For Howie and Bobby the classroom is a bore. Both find their professors' lectures lacking in real life experience and therefore meaningless. Howie pulls from his vast collection of Henry Cameron designs for his class projects. This gives him plenty of free time to surf the Internet and make contacts at the numerous networking sites for architects. Howie is somewhat discouraged with the downturn in the commercial real estate market. For most students the depressing blogs from out-of-work architects would make one cynical, but for Howie the online whining strengthens his resolve. He is willing to do anything to climb his way to the top in this winner-take-all economy.

Big Game CEO

Four weeks into his first semester Bobby finally figures out how to make money from the sugar daddies who use the website SeekingArrangement.com – blackmail. He informally hires two attractive coeds of questionable morals to hook-up with rich men. Bobby makes sure his targets are 'upstanding' men in the community who need to keep a clean reputation. With a hidden camera the young women video themselves having sex with their rich targets. Bobby then threatens to release the videos to the local media in the targets home town. In early November he makes his first score of $150,000.

This Thanksgiving is the first in what would become a yearly ritual for Howie. Already done with all his class projects for the fall semster Howie takes off the entire holiday week. First he visits Manhattan. On the Tuesday before Thanksgiving he meets Dominique Francon-Wynand. They catch-up on old times with small talk over lunch. Not wanting to be overheard they patiently wait to be alone before engaing in any serious conversation.

After lunch they adjourne to a private hotel room in Manhattan. Dominique says, "I bought you a present." Howie hesitates and looks warily at Dominique. She says, "Open it." He unwraps the small box and pulls out a gold money clip. She says, "Flip it open." Howie does. On the inside is an engraving – 'The Antagonist'. His jaw drops slightly.

Dominique walks over and opens the curtains. Looking over the Manhattan skyline she says, "A few minutes ago I was 90% confident you took out Boomer Mapple. Now I'm a 100% confident." Howie still doesn't say a word. Dominique continues, "You're a smart man Howard for keeping your mouth shut. This room could be bugged. You're probably wondering how I know you are 'The Antagonist'. It is because I could sense your presence in Gloucester."

Howie laughs and sarcastically says, "Really."

"Isn't it funny how public opinion is divided on whether 'The Antagonist' is a hero or a villian when in reality the murderer of those three CEOs was simply a brilliant manuever to accelerate your budding career."

"I have no idea what you are talking about."

Chapter 12: The Money Seekers

"Don't act stupid. Your cousins love hunting, love archery, and despise Manhattan types. You knew they were in search of a new sport where they could prove their manhood. So you used your cousins to secretly promote your agenda. Your biggest fear in life is becoming a middle-aged artist that has to beg rich people to fund your projects. To make your move into the big league you brilliantly selected CEOs who also sat on the board of numerous companies. Two of those men also sat on the board of my deceased father's old company. You didn't want to select three men that sat on the same board because that would have been too obvious. More importantly, you knew I was buying my time until I joined my mother on the board of Francon and McCoy."

"Your conspiracy theory is ridiculous. Why would I want you on the board of directors?"

"Because you're an architect and Francon and McCoy is the second largest hotel and gaming company in the world. You want an opportunity to win the design of our next resort."

"That's ridiculous."

"You're a damn genius. I love you more now than ever. I want to have your child."

"What's Gail Wynand think about this?"

"I'm not bringing the genes of that short, brutish man into the world. Luckily you and Gail have the same eyes. He'll never suspect a thing."

"Are you ovulating right now?"

"Don't be silly. There is no way I'm putting this body through nine months of hell. I'm hiring a surrogate mother to carry my fertilized egg."

"What the hell do you want from me?"

"I cut a secret deal with a doctor at Fallow Fertility Clinic. He'll switch the sperm samples. You have an appointment in thrity minutes." Dominque hands Howie a business card with the clinic's address on it.

"This kind of sucks."

"Sex does have a purpose. We breed ourselves for succes or failure. The fertility clinic is three blocks up the street. If you want to be the father of my child then you'd better go." Howie just smiles at

Dominique in silence, slowly shaking his head. Dominique then asks, "Any reservation about becoming a father?"

"I'm not becoming a father. I'm becoming a steed."

"Any reservation about becoming a steed?"

"Most men view life as a game. That is to procreate with as many beautiful women as possible."

"Are you like most men?"

"I don't know." Howie pauses to collect his thoughts, then asks, "So Dominique, do you love me?"

"I love you more than any man in world, but I don't love you as much as money. And I know you love me, but not as much as your career."

"Like you once told me, I love you because you're an honest bitch."

"We'll have our golden years together. We'll be masters of the universe. You'd better go. I don't want you to be late for your appointment."

Howie grabs his jacket. Grabbing the door handle he stops, looks at Dominique, and says, "How's business with your media company?"

"Our business roadmap predicts we will be profitable in five years."

"Those Hollywood boys and girls know the entertainment industry inside and out. They're hard to compete with."

Dominique replies, "I just need a few hit movies."

"Do you think you can get a few hits from a collection of misfit writers, directors, and actors?"

"Everyone in the entertainment industry is a misfit."

Howie responds, "Aren't we all." He pauses and acts like he is going to leave but turns and says, "Now that your on the board of Francon and McCoy, could you please work your magic and put me in the running for the design of your next resort. Target the month of March. I should be a partner at an architectural firm by then."

"I knew you would never settle for becoming a starving artist. Your soul is too strong for that. I love you now more than ever." With that Howie leaves the hotel room.

Chapter 12: The Money Seekers

Forty-five minutes later Howie is in a back room at the fertility clinic masturbating into a plastic cup. He asks himself, *"So is this what it means to be a man in the modern world?"*

Tuesday evening Howie, Danny, and Bobby meet-up at Bobby's father's lodge in Lords Valley. Wednesday morning they bow hunt. Danny kills a ten-point buck, Bobby kills a wild turkey, and not wanting to return empty-handed Howie kills a Canandian goose late in the morning. For Thanksgiving the three cousins and their three fathers eat smoked wild turkey. Topics of conversation include hunting, the economy, and women.

On Black Friday the cousins go car shopping. Bobby buys a new Porsche Boxster. Howie asks where he got the money. Bobby says not to worry about it.

On Friday night the three cousins go out in Manhattan. Bobby pays for all the cover charges and drinks. On Saturday night they go out in Scranton.

Howie meets Catherine Keating for a secret lunch on Sunday. She is five months pregnant. Howie asks about married life and Peter Keating. Catherine says she is happy. She spends most of their secret rendezvous talking about her sisters and asking Howie about his family. Howie looks at the buldge in her stomach and asks if he is the father. Catherine says she doesn't know. Sunday evening Howie drives back to Cornell for the last three weeks of classes for the fall semester.

On December 30th Bobby drives Howie in his red Porsche Boxster to Florida. Danny's new band, *Canadian Velcro with Salsa*, is playing an outdoor concert in Miami on New Year's Eve. During the concert Bobby and Howie reluctantly admit that Danny's new band is better than *Ambivalent Swag*.

On New Year's Day the three cousins have lunch. All three could care less about the college football bowl games playing on the numerous screens in the restaurant. Howie asks Bobby how he can afford a five-star hotel. Bobby says not to worry about it. By the look on Danny's face it is clear to Howie that he knows what is going on. Howie asks Danny how Bobby can afford the five-star hotel. Danny just plays dumb. Bobby changes the topic of conversation to deep sea fishing.

Big Game CEO

They agree to rent a charter boat the next day. Bobby says he'll pay for it. None of the cousins make New Year's resolutions that day.

On January 4th, Bobby and Howie drive from the 80-degree weather in Florida to the 30-degree weather in State College, Pennsylvania in 14 hours. With the help of his radar detector Bobby manages not to get a ticket. Howie then drives the remaining two and half hours in a rental car. When he arrives Ithaca it is 19-degrees.

For the spring semester Howie could care less about the remaining two classes that he needs to graduate. He spends most of his time making contacts, looking for a job, and planning his career. Jobs are scarce with the downturn in the commercial real estate market. But for Howie the downturn presents an opportunity, he just needs to play his cards right.

On Monday, February 22nd, Howie meets with Austen Heller and Roger Enright in Manhattan, the owners and original founders of the Heller and Enright Architectural Firm. For Howie, Heller and Enright is the perfect hand. Both Austen Heller and Roger Enright are in their late fifties. Their firm has international reach. More importantly, the firm is about to go bankrupt.

Howie sits down across the table from Austen and Roger. Austen says, "Henry Cameron talked about you. Best young architect he'd ever seen. But with the downturn we can't afford to nurture some young hot shot."

"I didn't request this interview looking for a job. I requested this interview looking to become partner."

Roger asks, "What the hell are you talking about?"

"I know your hurting for business. You've already gone through two series of lay-offs. By my calculations you'll have to file for bankruptcy this summer. The most likely scenario is that the bankruptcy judge is going to shut down your entire operation to pay-off the creditors."

Roger asks, "Then why do you want to become partner?"

"I can save the company."

Roger asks, "How in the world are you going to do that?"

"I have connections. I have original designs. I can win the Francon and McCoy contract for their new resort in Aruba."

Roger asks, "Then why the hell do you need us?"

Chapter 12: The Money Seekers

Instead Austen answers. He looks at Roger and says, "Can't you see this kid is a genius? He needs the backing of an established firm to win the Aruba deal. We are one of the few small commercial design companies with building connections in the Carribean. And he knows we are financially in trouble." Austen then looks into Howie's eyes and says, "Well played young man."

Roger asks, "Who's your inside contact at Francon and McCoy?"

"I know someone on the board of directors."

Austen says, "If you land the Aruba contract we'll pay-off your student loans and make you head architect."

Howie scoffs, "$340,000 is chump change. I don't want a meaningless title."

Austen replies, "You're only 23 years old. You know how long it took us to build this company?"

"All that hard work and your company is about to go under. Ashes to ashes, dust to dust."

Roger asks, "What do you really want?"

"Henry Cameron told me not to waste time reinventing the wheel. I have modified Cameron's collection of designs. They shall be the designs of the 21st Century. But those designs are just sitting on my computer, waiting to die a digital death. I want to buy your firm."

Roger asks, "You're a student. Where in the world are you going to come up with the money to buy our firm?"

"How much is your firm worth right now? Negative ten million?"

Roger answers, "We're not going to give you the company."

Austen adds, "Look Howie, I like you. In a few years when we retire I'd rather sell the company to you or someone like you instead of to an investment bank."

Howie says, "You know an investment bank is just going to destroy the company."

Austen agrees, "I know."

Howie says, "You are going to provide me with the collateral for the loan to buy your company."

Roger says, "And how are we going to do that?"

"You'll get a bridge loan for a few million and give it to me under the table. After I get the big loan I'll pay you back."

"You know that's illegal."

"It's not illegal if you know how to work the system. Besides, it's how investment bankers destroy other people's hard work."

Austen says, "I like you, but I'm not a fool. We're not going to sell you the company for less than what we can sell it to an investment bank."

"In good economic times how much is this company worth?"

"A hundred and ten million."

"It's not worth that much. Fifty million maximum."

"It's worth over hundred million."

Howie smiles and says, "I want a contract that says that you must sell your company sometime within the next ten years. I can execute my buy offer at any time before then. If I can match the offer then you have to sell the company to me. More importantly, the maximum price you can sell the company to me for is sixty million."

Roger says, "Winning the Aruba resort isn't worth your demands."

"As partner, I'll bring in more business than just the Aruba resort. I've spent the last eight months establishing other connections. There is a lot of penned up demand just waiting for the economy to recover."

Austen says, "I like you kid but your asking too much."

"It has been a pleasure meeting you. If you change your mind my cell number is on my resume."

As Howie is about to exit the Manhattan office building his cell phone rings. Austen says, "Get back up here. We'll accept your sixty million dollar buyout clause. But we need to negotiate the terms of you becoming managing partner."

Howie calmly says, "You made the right decision."

"Everything is contigent on you winning the Aruba contract."

"I know."

On Tuesday, March 16th, Howie, Austen Heller, and Roger Enright march the board of directors and the CEO of Francon and McCoy out of board room and down the hall to a small show room. On the way to the showroom Howie stops in the bathroom to check his appearance and to take a Dexedrine to help focus. For the last two weeks he's been working 18-plus hour days preparing for this moment.

Chapter 12: The Money Seekers

In three of the corners of the show room are displays with nine monitors each. The displays are playing Hollywood production quality videos of three resort options. Standing next to Howie's favorite design is the best looking female architect who works for Heller and Enright. Wanting his favorite design to get the most attention, Howie has purposely placed her in that corner.

The board and the CEO gaze in awe at the three designs. Howie gives everyone a few minutes to digest the form, flow, and function of his 21st century creations. Howie walks over and stands next to the boards newest member, Dominique. The two look like freak show oddities in a room filled with decision makers in their fifties, sixties, and seventies. Howie can tell Dominique is a little jealous because on this day he is the center of attention.

Dominique says, "You did the right thing calling Stephan for fashion advice. You look very modern yet professional without the tie."

"Thanks."

"Nervous?"

"Doesn't matter whether I'm nervous or not, it's showtime. My goal today is to out-do your Tasmanian Producers Festival performance."

"Break a leg."

Howie walks to the middle of the room and loudly says, "Thank you for this opportunity." The room quiets. Howie continues, "Just like the hotel and gaming industry is becoming more and more competitive, so is the business of architectural design. In today's world, a successful design must be space efficient, energy efficient, and inexpensive to maintain." Howie holds up a small folder, "In this report is the breakdown of the yearly energy bill and maintenance bill for each of these three resorts. I guarentee you on a per room cost no resort that you own comes close to these numbers."

Board members start whispering back and forth. Howie raises his voice slightly so that he can be heard above the discussion, "But turning a profit in this competitive world requires more than providing a guest a quality room at a low cost. Advertising costs money. And the cost of meaningful advertising goes up every year. That's why it is important to have a resort that sells itself. All three of these designs are

Big Game CEO

inspirational. Anyone who visits will tell their family and friends about the experience."

Howie walks over to his favorite design and stands next to the attractive female architect. Howie smiles, glances at Dominique, and continues, "To win in today's new world of hotel and gaming means being ahead of the game. People are sick and tired of theme park resorts. In this day and age theme park resorts are everywhere. These three designs say tranquility and balance – a place to rejuvenate your soul. Notice how the lines flow upward from the beach and blend in with the nearby hills. Note the subtle use of color – how the blue glass, blue steel, and blue concrete blend with the copper glass, copper steel, and copper concrete. These three resorts are like the Golden Gate Bridge – they compliment the natural beauty of the surroundings instead of competing with nature for our attention."

The CEO of Francon and McCoy says, "I see the size of the hotel rooms and size of the balcony are twice the size of a typical hotel."

"This is to help rejuvenate the souls of your guests."

"But what about costs?"

"Per room building costs are broken down in the last two pages of the report. Space and beauty are not expensive with good structural design and smart use of building materials."

"What about a hurricane?"

"Storm surge is not an issue. The lobby is forty feet above sea level. All balconies come with slide out steel shutters. A category five hurricane is not a problem."

"What else have you thought of?"

"Three helicopter pads are on the roof for your corporate clients. I read your internal report on maximizing profits through optimizing pedestrian traffic flow. The layout of the casino, pool, and lobby, and the positioning of the bars and resturants have all been adjusted accordingly."

"Is there anything that you missed?"

Howie glances at Dominique and says, "To win in today's world requires perfect execution." Dominique smiles at the moment Howie says execution. Howie concludes, "I think I've said enough. Look, study, enjoy. Don't hesitate to ask if you have any questions. That's why the team from Heller and Enright is here."

Chapter 12: The Money Seekers

Howie walks by Dominique and immediately starts talking with the CEO of Francon and McCoy. For the next forty minutes they discuss architecture and the companies five year roadmap for building new resorts.

That evening Howie and Dominique go out to dinner. After dinner they see the musical *In the Heights*. After the show Dominique jokes that tonight is the wedding reception of Howie's career. He laughs. After the musical they share a hotel room at the Mandarin Oriental Hotel. Their premier suite overlooks Central Park.

On Friday, March 19th, Catherine Keating gives birth to a seven pound fourteen ounce baby girl at Mercy Hospital in Scranton, Pennsylvania. On that same day Francon and McCoy informs the architectural firm of Heller and Enright that they have won the Aruba contract. Of Howie's three designs, his favorite is the one selected by the CEO. Two days later Catherine heads home from the hospital. That night while feeding the baby, Catherine looks down at Pammy, runs her figures through her Pammy's golden curls, and whispers, "You're perfect, just like your father."

On Monday, April 12th, Howie departs for Aruba to supervise the groundbreaking and construction of his first design win. He fails both of his spring semester classes and never graduates Cornell.

That same spring semester Bobby gets Bs in all his accounting classes at Penn State. By the end of finals week he has blackmailed his fifth rich target who uses the website SeekingArrangement.com. After paying his two attractive cohorts, his total profit for the year is $650,000. As an accounting major Bobby understands that the best part of the $650,000 is that it is all tax-free. That summer Bobby decides he has learned all he needs to learn about accounting. He drops out of Penn State, moves back to Port Jervis, and buys a restaurant. He renames the restaurant *Zen Barbeque*.

That same summer *Canadian Velcro with Salsa* cuts their first album. Their single, *Velvet Dancer*, climbs to 24 on the pop music charts. Danny spends most of the summer touring the Midwest, sleeping in cheap motels with uncomfortable beds, and eating fast food.

On Wednesday, September 1st, Dominique's surrogate mother gives birth to twins, a boy and a girl. Gaspard and Celeste both have curly blond hair. When the nannies ask Dominique who in the family has curly blond hair, Dominique just smiles and says, "Must be Gail's side of the family."

The week before Thanksgiving Howie returns to the United States for the first time since April. Besides supervising construction of the Aruba resort, Howie's been traveling to the resort area of Goa, India, scouting the area, talking with local construction companies, and preparing for his next design bid with Francon and McCoy. Just like the year before, on the Tuesday before Thanksgiving Howie and Dominique have lunch in Manhattan. Tuesday evening Howie, Danny, and Bobby meet-up at lodge in Lords Valley. Wednesday morning the three cousins bow hunt. For Thanksgiving the three cousins and their three fathers eat smoked wild turkey. On Sunday Howie meets Catherine Keating for a secret lunch.

Howie asks Catherine about Pammy and her sisters. Catherine asks Howie about his career, Aruba, and Goa, India. During dessert Catherine tells Howie she wants another child. Late that afternoon they get a hotel room. The next morning Howie catches a flight back to Aruba.

Over the following year Danny continues touring with *Canadian Velcro with Salsa*. In the spring the band tours the Southern United States and in the summer the West Coast.

Bobby hires a Henry Lamb to manage *Zen Barbeque*. Under Henry's management the restaurant loses $75,000 during its first year of operation. Bobby makes up for the loss and then some by blackmailing three more wealthy targets from the website SeekingArrangement.com.

Howie continues to supervise construction of the Aruba resort. In late spring he supervises the groundbreaking of his second design win in Goa, India. Over the summer, while flying between Aruba and Goa, he stops off at Macau, Monte Carlo, and the Western Cape of South Africa, scouting these other resort areas for future design wins with Francon and McCoy.

Chapter 12: The Money Seekers

On Sunday, August 28th, Catherine Keating gives birth to a eight pound two ounce baby boy at Mercy Hospital in Scranton, Pennsylvania. His name is Michaelis.

The week before Thanksgiving Howie again returns to the United States. Just like the two previous years, on the Tuesday before Thanksgiving Howie and Dominique have lunch in Manhattan. Tuesday evening Howie, Danny, and Bobby meet-up at the lodge in Lords Valley with their fathers. On Sunday, Howie meets Catherine Keating for a secret lunch. Catherine tells Howie it is good living close to her family. Her mother and sister are a blessing, helping to take care of Pammy and Michaelis.

Over the following year *Canadian Velcro with Salsa* cut their second album. Their single, *Crooked Arrow*, climbs to 11 on the pop music charts. Bobby's restaurant starts turning a slight profit. He decides to open a second *Zen Barbeque* ten miles away in Middletown.

After nearly two years of construction, the Aruba resort is complete. As a favor to Howie, Dominique subtly persuades the board of Francon and McCoy to name the new resort *Blue Sunset*. The bands *Radiohead*, *Death Cab for Cutie*, and *Canadian Velcro with Salsa* perform during grand opening weekend. That year *Blue Sunset* wins nearly every architectural award imaginable. Developers from around the world are now beating on Howie's door. Howie chooses to take on the two largest projects available that year – a building in the new finacial district in Hong Kong and a new soccer stadium in Berlin.

For the fourth year in a row, Howie has lunch with Dominique in Manhattan on the Tuesday before Thanksgiving. Howie congratulates Dominique that her media company has finally turned a profit. Dominique congratulates Howie on all his awards for *Blue Sunset*. She also tells Howie that Gail Wynand is in ill health.

That evening Howie, Danny, and Bobby meet-up at the lodge in Lords Valley with their fathers. On Sunday Howie meets Catherine Keating for a secret lunch.

Big Game CEO

In Febraury of the following year the lead signer of *Canadian Velcro with Salsa* quits the band. With a new singer they tour Europe in the spring and the United States over the summer. Reviewers say the new lead singer is not as good as their original lead singer.

Both of Bobby's restaurants turn a slight profit. To supplement his income he blackmails two targets from the website SeekingArrangement.com.

Early that fall Howie exercises his sixty million dollar buyout clause for Heller and Enright. When the financial community hears about the sixty million dollar buyout clause the investement banks quickly realize Howie has the upper hand. No bank decides to bid for Heller and Enright. Austen Heller and Roger Enright refuse to float Howie the collateral for a sixty million dollar loan. Austen tells Howie, "It is just business." Without collateral Howie is unable to secure the loan. Howie is mad but not out. Years ago he foresaw this possibility happening and moves to his Plan B.

Howie cuts a deal with an investment bank to bid on Heller and Enright. If he undercuts their bid with his sixty million dollar buyout clause he guarentees to pay the investment bank four million dollars. With nothing to lose and an easy four million dollars to gain the investment bank bids ninety-five million for the company. Howie uses the ninety-five million dollar offer and the fact that Heller and Enright have to accept his offer as collateral for a sixty-four million dollar loan. Heller and Enright aren't happy being forced to take the lower offer. At their retirement party Austen Heller and Roger Enright tell Howie he is a bastard-genius. Howie says, "You can cry yourselves to the bank, it's just business." The next day Howie changes the name of the company to Roark Design.

For the fifth year in a row Howie has lunch with Dominique Francon-Wynand in Manhattan on the Tuesday before Thanksgiving. That evening Howie, Danny, and Bobby meet-up at the lodge in Lords Valley with their fathers. On Sunday, Howie meets with Catherine Keating for a secret lunch.

The following year Howie expands Roark Design. He takes out an additional forty million dollar loan and sets up international offices

Chapter 12: The Money Seekers

in Paris and Tokyo. Like always, Howie works 18-plus hour days and takes Dexedrine like it is candy.

In contrast to Howie, things are not going well for Danny. *Canadian Velcro with Salsa* is playing smaller and smaller venues. Royalties from their two albums barely pay the bills. In August, the band's manager tells the band the only gig he can find is the Seneca County Fair. The next day Danny quits the band. A week later he moves back in with his mother and half-brother, Frederic, and takes a job with a motorcycle repair shop in Port Jervis.

That summer and fall Bobby blackmails two targets from the website SeekingArrangement.com. On Friday, October 10th, Bobby is found dead in his red Porsche Boxster behind his restaurant in Middleton – a single bullet to the back of the head.

Chapter 13: The Revenge of Ellsworth Toohey

Thursday, October 16th is an unusually cold day in Port Jervis. A steady 20 mph wind out of the north reminds everyone that winter will be coming soon. Following a black hearse, Danny rides with Howie in Howie's rental car. Firmly grasping the steering wheel with both hands Howie looks into the rearview mirror. He studies the long line of cars with their lights on. He says, "Even in death everyone loves Bobby. When I die there will most likely be only two dozen people at my funeral." Danny doesn't say a word.

Over four hundred people attend Bobby's funeral at Glenwood Cemetery in Port Jervis. Howie and Danny are pallbearers. After Bobby's casket is laid into the dirt hole, Danny lays Bobby's electric guitar and his Iceman crossbow on top of the casket.

After the funeral Howie, Danny, and the three fathers head back to Joe's lodge in Lords Valley. With Danny holding a bottle of tequila, he and Howie take a long, quiet walk. They walk past the old target practice area and Bobby's favorite dirt bike track. Finally they return to the west side of Beaver Lake where Danny shot the wild turkey with his Iceman compound bow six years earlier. On the east side of Beaver Lake a new subdivision is going up. Danny looks at a row of half built houses and says, "I guess lady progress doesn't stop for anything."

Howie sarcastically says, "To bad she's dog ugly. At a minimum I'd have to drink a case of beer to sleep in that house. "

Chapter 13: The Revenge of Ellsworth Toohey

Danny laughs at the snide remark. Howie finally breaks his silence about Bobby's murder and loudly asks, "What the hell is going on?"

"I promised Bobby I wouldn't tell anyone."

"Bobby's dead. That promise is null and void."

Danny hesitates. He's never seen Howie mad like this before. Danny looks down and kicks the dirt a few times as if he is digging another grave. He finally says, "Bobby told me that if anything ever happened to him I was to beat the police to his apartment and take his laptop. He didn't want his mother or father to find out about his career."

"Running two restaurants?"

"Blackmailing wealthy men who use SeekingArrangement.com."

"That's so Bobby."

"Bobby was always jealous of you. That's why he never told you about how he was making his money."

"Are you jealous of me?"

"Not really, but I wouldn't mind having your money. Look at you. You look terrible. How many hours a day do you work?"

"A lot."

"Still taking speed."

"I never took speed."

"Don't lie to me. When we lived together, your speed habit was a worse kept secret than Michael Jackson wasn't the father of his supposed children. Bobby and I used to joke about it all the time."

"It's not speed, it's Dexedrine."

"I don't care if it's approved by the FDA and made by a large corporation based in Jersey. It's still speed."

"Do I really look terrible?"

"You look thin and haggard. Plus for someone who spends a lot of time in the tropics your skin is all pale and dry."

"Enough about me, who killed Bobby?"

"I've narrowed the list to four likely suspects. There's Henry Lamb, the manager of Bobby's two restaurants. The two wealthy men Bobby was currently blackmailing. And there is Shelly Thomas, one of the girls who worked for Bobby."

"Why do you suspect Shelly Thomas?"

"She wears brown lipstick. Brown lipstick was found on Bobby's collar at the time of the murder."

"Bobby was probably sleeping with her."

"That's the first thought that crossed my mind."

"So who were the two men Bobby was currently blackmailing?"

"Don Issachar and Ellsworth Toohey."

"This is a such a small world. I know Ellsworth Toohey."

"I thought you'd be interested in Toohey. I remembered you talking about him last Thanksgiving. Do you think Bobby went after him as a favor to you?"

"I doubt it. Bobby's an opportunist. Most likely he saw Toohey's name at SeekingArrangement.com and said what the hell."

"We could take them all out."

"Don't be silly."

"It's not like you're adverse to killing rich hypocrites!"

"We took an oath never to speak of that again."

Danny dumps most of the tequila on the ground then finishes the last few shots, worm and all. He yells, "Permission to speak!" He then bends over holding his stomach and moans, "Jesus, that worm was nasty."

Howie laughs then says, "You remember when Bobby said 'I hope one of us wants to talk in private. I just want to see the look on their face, even if it kills me.' I bet he's looking down at us right now laughing his head off."

"Think Bobby is in heaven or hell?"

Howie answers, "Probably racing back and forth on his Kawasaki Ninja ZX-6R between both places hitting on every woman available. Who in the afterworld is going to stop him? The Devil or Saint Peter? I don't think so."

"Look, I doubt Henry Lamb or the brown lipstick chic did it. Why don't we just take out Issachar and Toohey and be done with it."

"There's nothing to gain killing Issachar and Toohey."

With an annoyed look on his face, Danny responds, "Like there was something to gain when we killed those three CEOs. Bobby's blood."

"We're not a couple of hillbillies."

"Even though you are spoiled, gifted, and arrogant, Bobby always stuck up for you. And he stuck up for you because he was your cousin."

Chapter 13: The Revenge of Ellsworth Toohey

A seasick look comes over Howie's face. He says, "I don't feel so good." He walks behind a tree, puts his hands on his knees and pukes.

Danny asks, "Are you OK?"

"I must have caught something on the plane."

Danny looks down and says, "Jesus, there's blood. We've got to get you to the hospital."

"I'll be fine. Just get the laptop. Let's see if we can figure out who killed Bobby."

"I'm taking you to the hospital first."

A little over a month later, on the Tuesday before Thanksgiving, Dominique visits Howie in the apartment he is now renting in Manhattan. She is stunned when a nurse answers the door. In a weak voice Howie says, "Thank you Nurse Barkley, you can go now."

Nurse Barkley grabs her coat and leaves. Dominique walks in and slowly shuts the door. Howie is wearing a green robe and sitting in a black leather recliner. She studies his frail body, swollen face, and baldhead. She solemnly asks, "Why didn't you tell me you had cancer? You should see my doctor."

"I knew that's what you'd say. I've been seeing your doctor for the last month. Your doctor put me in contact with the best doctors at Sloan-Kettering."

"Is the chemo working?"

"No. It's in my pancreas. It's in my liver. I've got three to nine months."

Dominique starts to cry, "We were supposed to grow old together. We were going to be masters of the universe."

"You'll still be master of the universe. You know damn well there's more than one fish in the sea."

"But there are few sharks like you."

"I'm too weak to banter. I've learned to accept my coming death."

"You're not going to die."

"I'm going to miss seeing Gaspard and Celeste grow-up. Please show me their latest pictures."

Dominique pulls out her cell phone and shows Howie a few pictures. With a tear trickling down her left cheek she says, "You can beat this."

"My final chapter is upon me."

"Don't talk like that."

"I called you here for reason. None of my designs have ever been built in America. I want the White Plains Renaissance Project. I need you to argue my case before the Development Board."

"You should win easily. Your staff should be able to handle it. Why do you need me?"

"I'm going up against Ellsworth Toohey. That bastard stole the New Jersey Financial Complex from me last year." Howie points out the window and across the Hudson River towards New Jersey and a nearly finished sixty-story office complex.

"I remember. That building is a spiritual void. Your design was a thousand times better."

"My problem is the politicians in New Jersey don't care if their constituents live in a hell-hole. All they care about is getting their kickback."

"Too bad Toohey owns all the development boards around Manhattan. I bet he owns the one in White Plains too."

"Can you do anything about that?"

"Manhattan is my turf. I have zero contacts in White Plains."

"See what you can do. The hearing is Monday, December 8th."

"I'll see what I can do." Howie doesn't respond. He is asleep in the recliner. For the next hour Dominique sits next to Howie simply holding his hand, looking at the pictures of her children she keeps in her cell phone, and staring out the window at the skyline of Manhattan, the Hudson River, and New Jersey.

On December 8th the first snow of the season gently falls over White Plains. Nurse Barkley helps Howie from the rental van into a wheel chair. As they head into City Hall, Howie says, "Stop." He looks up and down Main Street studying every line on every building. He looks up at Nurse Barkley and says, "What demons designed these buildings? Just looking at them increases my anxiety level. I'd hate to work here."

Nurse Barkley replies, "I'm sure the politicians are used to it by now."

Chapter 13: The Revenge of Ellsworth Toohey

Outside the board room Howie sees Dominique and Stephan talking to one of the local politicians. Howie points at the trio. Nurse Barkley wheels Howie over. The local politician sees Howie coming and quickly walks away. Howie asks, "What was that about?"

"He doesn't want to be seen with you. He loves your design and will vote for it, but only if we can get a majority."

"If we include him, 4-3 against with 2 undecided."

"Think you can sway the undecided?"

"Your design should easily sway the undecided. It all depends if they are on Toohey's pay-roll."

"Two can play at that game. Pay what you have to. How long can they lock me up for bribery?"

Dominique looks at Stephan and says, "See what you can do."

Stephan replies, "Yes boss."

Just then Ellsworth Toohey and his entourage enter the large atrium outside the hearing room. His entourage looks more like a group of union leaders, lobbyists, and crime bosses than architects and city planners. Among the entourage is Peter Keating, Catherine's husband. Howie watches with disgust as Ellsworth twirls his handlebar mustache as he proudly stomps across the hall like an alpha-male elephant. Ellsworth doesn't even acknowledge Howie's presence as he marches into the hearing room.

One person at the back of the entourage doesn't enter the hearing room. It is Catherine Keating. She looks at Howie. Her jaw drops. She runs over and says, "You didn't call me over Thanksgiving."

"I didn't want you to see me like this."

"Are you going to be OK?"

Howie looks into his lap and doesn't say a word. Catherine looks at the floor. She notices Dominique's designer Burberry brown leather boots. As Catherine's eyes move upwards, Dominique's eyes move downwards, first staring at Catherine's twenty-dollar haircut. Catherine takes in Dominique's copper Santana knit skirt and black and copper Parisian knit jacket. Dominique eyes Catherine's slightly worn single-breasted trench coat from J.C. Penney. Catherine looks in awe at Dominique's six hundred-dollar hairdo. Dominique looks in disgust at Catherine's classic leather flats she bought on sale for thirty dollars from Kohl's.

Catherine looks Dominique in the eye and firmly says, "Is there anything I can do?"

Dominique resolutely replies, "He's getting the best care money can buy."

Catherine strongly says, "Apparently it isn't good enough."

Before Dominique can speak, Howie says, "Catherine, we should get together. I'll call."

Catherine looks down at Howie and replies, "That will be good."

Before Catherine turns to walk away Howie asks, "I didn't know Peter was working for Ellsworth Toohey."

"For the last three years."

"Funny that you never mentioned it."

"Funny that you never asked." Catherine walks away and enters the hearing room.

Howie looks at Nurse Barkley, then Dominique, and says, "That was awkward."

Dominique replies, "I agree."

Howie asks, "Are you ready?"

"There's no doubt in my mind that I'm going to win."

Five minutes later the nine members of the Development Board, six women and three men, enter the hearing room. Dominique, Howie, and a few members of Howie's staff are seated to the board's left. Ellsworth Toohey, Peter Keating, and few lawyers are seated to the board's right.

Maria Ruskin, chairperson of the Development Board, with her brightly dyed red hair nods to Dominique and says, "You may begin."

A member of Howie's staff turns on a seventy-inch monitor. It displays a Hollywood production quality video of Howie's best design yet. After a fashionable pause, Dominique stands and addresses the board, "Our surroundings define us. If all you know are grass huts with dirt floors, do you think about building rockets and traveling to the moon or stars? If you live in the rundown inner-city, do you dream about being a doctor or do you dream about being a drug dealer?"

Dominique looks out the window. She stares intently at a large concrete and steel building of utilitarian design from the 1960s across the street. She continues, "Look at the large housing projects like

Chapter 13: The Revenge of Ellsworth Toohey

Cabrini-Green and Pruitt-Igoe. Those institutional buildings, cold and gray, sucked the individualism out of their tenants. Distraught, the inhabitants turned to drugs. And for the last fifty years the remnants of inner-city culture has been trying to rediscover manhood, with their warped displays of large gold chains, guns, and rap songs about shoving penises in front of women's faces."

She turns and looks at the gallery. She stares directly at Catherine Keating. Catherine mockingly smiles. Dominique glares back and continues, "Don't believe for a moment that the pointy-headed bureaucrats in DC give a damn about climate change or gas mileage or how much you pay for a mortgage or your child's education. Politicians have a dream, and that dream is to inspire mediocrity. Their tax-breaks and handouts are nothing more than meaningless grade school participation trophies. These trinkets make you feel good about yourself for a few moments but by the next day you feel empty and used. And where do the participation trophies end up? The trash."

Dominique glares directly at Ellsworth Toohey and proclaims, "The biggest lie is that the people who control the system want us to celebrate diversity! What they really want is a sick and twisted world of conformity – a conformity where the idea of manhood is squashed by bureaucrats and their regulations. A world where we mindlessly go to work in cubical farms, happily pay our taxes, and happily pay homage to the crushing social institutions that suck the last drop of individualism from our bones. Where there is no individualism there is no responsibility. And where there is no responsibility there is no morality."

Finally Dominique turns and looks at the nine-member board. She smiles at Maria Ruskin and says, "The decision that is made here today will echo for more than a hundred years. It is clear which design will inspire men and women of future generations to build a better life for themselves – a world where they take responsibility for their own actions. It is your choice to make the responsible decision. It will be the end of the community when we no longer acknowledge the best."

An eerie hush fills the hearing room. Dominique walks back to her seat, sits down with perfect posture, folds her hands and places them in her lap.

Maria Ruskin smiles and nods to Ellsworth Toohey. He stands, runs his fingers through his mustache, looks out the window, takes two steps forward, turns to the gallery, and says, "In the grand scheme of life, define best. Who is the best individual? Who has the best children? The best clothes? The best car? The best house? Who lives in the best community? Strong communities are not defined by best. Communities are organic creatures. They live and die just like we do. But unlike we humans, the lifespan of a healthy community is forever. And for a community to make that great walk into the distant future, it must grow strong by growing slow! How many monuments have been built that at the time of their creation were to signal a new age, and stand the test of a thousand years, only to find empty halls with the coming of a new generation? Today the pyramids in Egypt, the Parthenon in Greece, and the Coliseum in Rome are nothing more than hollow echoes from egos of long ago. And those are the few buildings that have lasted. Most castles that have been built by the ancients have now crumbled to the ground."

Ellsworth looks at Catherine Keating, then Peter Keating, and smiles. He continues, "What's stood the test of time is the family, and the never ending chain of generation after generation who define the human spirit. Families are the rocks upon which we build communities, and communities are the rocks upon which we build the best nations. And the purpose of our hard work, blood, sweat, and tears is not to stroke the ego of some flash in the pan genius that wants us to pay homage to his latest work of art. In the mind of a 'so called' genius, it is the greatest piece of art ever created. But is it? The purpose of our hard work, blood, sweat, and tears should be to build something that will make families and communities of the next generation stronger. Our nation will rise higher only if the families and communities that build the skyward stairway to the future become stronger with each generation."

Ellsworth stares out the window. Like Dominique he looks at the large concrete and steel building of utilitarian design from the 1960s. He points at the gray building and pronounces, "Only fifty-five years ago that building was the promise of some young aspiring architect to bring White Plains a better future. But today if you walk through White Plains, and the other decaying cities in America, you see deserted

Chapter 13: The Revenge of Ellsworth Toohey

shopping malls, empty factories, and abandoned neighborhoods. Not long ago these buildings were the promise of a new life, sold to the American public as a better future, planned and designed by the best and brightest our school system had to offer. But today as we walk through our cities, we are confused, wondering what happened to our investment. Wondering what happened to our hard work, blood, sweat, and tears that were supposed to build a better future. Were we misguided? Were we lied to? Were we naïve? Were we fools?"

Ellsworth looks at Howie in his wheel chair, and then at Peter Keating, "What our design team has to offer is not a monument to the ego of a self-proclaimed genius; it is a monument to the families of White Plains and the White Plains community. We are not going to suck the local tax base dry."

Dominique yells, "That's a lie!"

Maria Ruskin bangs her gavel three times and says, "Please, no outbursts."

Ellsworth smiles for he knows Dominique is rattled. He confidently continues, "We are not going to suck the local tax base dry. We will use Federal-matching funds to help create this stairway to the future. We will build this project in ten stages over a period of ten years. This way there isn't a boom or bust construction cycle that wreaks havoc on the construction workers lives. This is because meaningful and steady work is the best cure for the insanity that results when people get jerked around by the system. At the end of each stage we will convene a review board, listen to local input, and make design adjustments based on the new needs of the budding neighborhood. Our design is a holistic plan created to nurture community growth."

Dominique shouts out, "Don't drink from the Buzzword Kool-Aid! Holistic! Nurturing! What the hell is that?" She points at the display from Ellsworth's design team and continues to yell, "He's just using those feel good buzz words because he is trying to sell you an inferior design."

Maria Ruskin bangs her gavel six times and yells, "Another outburst and you will be escorted from the chamber!"

Ellsworth casually strolls over and stands ten feet in front of Dominique. He looks at her pricey hairstyle and expensive designer clothes in disgust. Stepping forward he looks Dominique in the eye, smiles, winks, and says, "The world is tired of building trendy empires of nothingness." He turns, looks at the board, and proclaims, "Today's latest design will be tomorrow's eyesore. Don't fall for the sleek images and fancy presentations. There's more to a building than steel, glass, and concrete. Think of the people that will live and work there. Think of the community. Thank you, that is all."

With a confident look on his face Ellsworth Toohey sits down and leans back in his chair. Dominique looks worried. Maria Ruskin simply says, "We have a difficult decision to make. We'll meet back here after lunch."

For the next four hours Dominique and Stephan work their contacts, trying to find out what is going on behind closed doors. Dominique tells Howie that Maria Ruskin is one of the swing votes. She's learned that for several years Maria Ruskin and Ellsworth Toohey have been having an on-again and off-again affair. Dominique then looks at the ceiling and says, "Too bad we don't have some dirt on Toohey."

Howie begins to speak but then hesitates. He simply says, "Too bad we don't have any dirt on Toohey." Howie's mind starts racing a mile a minute, reviewing his plans for secret revenge against Ellsworth Toohey in case he loses the contract.

Nurse Barkley wheels Howie over to a coffee shop inside City Hall. She talks to her elderly mother on her cell phone while Howie sits in his wheel chair, writing poetry on a small note pad.

Ellsworth Toohey and his posse walk across the street to The Melting Pot restaurant. At the top of every hour Ellsworth steps outside, lights up a cigar, looks across the street at the window where the Development Board is discussing their decision, and blows what appears to be smoke signals. Catherine Keating starts to go window-shopping in downtown White Plains. Alone and afraid of the neighborhood, she catches a train into Manhattan. She visits a few upscale stores and admires some of the overpriced items before catching a train back to White Plains.

At 1:30 PM everyone reconvenes in the hearing room. The nine members of the Development Board sit down. Maria Ruskin patiently waits until everyone is quiet. She then says, "After careful deliberation we have decided that we need to assess more information before making

Chapter 13: The Revenge of Ellsworth Toohey

the correct decision. Instructions will be mailed to both parties after the first of the year. We will reconvene here on Monday, March 23rd."

Dominique, knowing Howie will most likely be dead by March 23rd, yells out, "You're cowards! You're depriving a dying man his legacy!"

Ellsworth just smiles, looks at Dominique, and calmly says, "And you're trying to deprive the White Plains community of a better future." Dominique glares at Ellsworth then turns to the gallery and glares at Catherine Keating.

Howie finds the strength to look up. He gives Ellsworth Toohey a long, cold stare. Clearly, if Howie had the strength he would stand up, walk over, and punch Ellsworth in the face. Howie looks at Dominique and says, "The decision is now in God's hands, and the hands of the people living in God's country."

For the two weeks before Christmas the visitors to Howie's apartment include his mother, his father, his executive secretary, his head architect, his sister, Catherine Keating, and Danny. His conversation with his mother is short. Daisy primarily wants to know if she is in Howie's will. His conversation with his father lasts for three hours. As part of Howie's master plan, he gets his dad, Archie, to retell all the stories about how he hid money from his mother and Meyer Wolfsheim overseas in secret bank accounts.

Howie meets with his executive secretary every workday. They discuss office morale and plan for the transition after his death. Howie tells his head architect to stop work on the two ongoing projects. Howie then gives his head architect a new set of nearly finished plans and says he wants the team to identify the best construction companies, calculate costs, and have the plans ready for construction by Friday, January 9th.

Like his conversation with his mother, Howie's conversation with his sister is also short. That is because Phoebe is no longer his chief confident who understands the inner workings of his psyche. That position now belongs to his soul mate, Catherine Keating. On the day Catherine visits they talk for over six hours. They discuss what it means to be a man in the modern world. They discuss what it means to be a

Big Game CEO

woman in the modern world. They discuss a poem Howie wrote on the day of the hearing in White Plains.

Empires come and empires crumble
Wise men leap and then they stumble
The rest of us are oh so humble
As we dance in the winds of their blind ambition

Howie and Catherine then discuss the hearing and Ellsworth Toohey. Howie asks if Peter Keating is a good man. Howie then tells Catherine that he wants to leave most of his money to their children, Pammy and Michaelis, but he doesn't want to ruin her marriage. Together they set up a secret overseas bank account. Catherine then shows Howie a picture of Pammy and Michaelis. By the look in Howie's eyes, Catherine can sense a strong fear of death.

Fearing death, during the last hour of their conversation Howie confesses all his deepest and darkest secrets: how he lost his virginity; that Dominique's two children are his; and that he and his two cousins are 'The Antagonist'. Just after discovering that Howie is 'The Antagonist', Catherine excuses herself to the bathroom. She looks at a picture of her two children, then herself in the mirror, and vomits in the sink.

After returning from the bathroom they discuss in depth the multiple reasons Howie decided to become 'The Antagonist'. Catherine's attitude changes from disgust to acceptance. She now understands Howie's point of view – that some powerful individuals are above the law, and in some situations justice must navigate around the law. They discuss the moral dilemma of Howie's career and his advancement by killing three immoral men.

For the last thirty minutes of their conversation they discuss the topic, 'What is morality?' They discuss the morality of sex and having children. They discuss the morality of raising children and what is best for the community. They discuss the morality of Ayn Rand and self-interests, and how it applies to the gifted members of society. They discuss the morality of Christianity and community interests, and how it applies to the average members of society. In the end they both agree that life is complex, and simple ideologies are good for guidance for specific groups of individuals, but simple ideologies can't provide a

Chapter 13: The Revenge of Ellsworth Toohey

moral foundation strong enough to guide all members of a complex society. At the end of the confession a change in Howie's eyes signals a weight has been lifted from his soul. He is now ready for death.

During Danny's visit the two simply talk business. Danny doesn't even ask about Howie's health. The first words out of his mouth are, "A Raymond Sintes killed Bobby."

"How'd you find out?"

"I did some poking around. My dad's old friend, Nick Caraway, told me it was a Hell's Angel. I investigated. Cost me $500, but I eventually tracked him down. Sintes is a member of the Newark branch of the Hell's Angels."

"Good work. What did Sintes have against Bobby?"

"Nothing. A rich building tycoon paid Sintes to whack him."

"Had to have been Ellsworth Toohey. He must not have taken kindly to being blackmailed by Bobby."

"My thoughts exactly. What do you want me to do?"

"What do you think we should do?"

"Kill Toohey."

"Why not Sintes?"

"He's just a pawn. If not Sintes, Toohey would have hired somebody else."

"So Danny, how should we kill Toohey?"

"I thought you'd have that all figured out."

"I do. But were not going to kill him. We are going to destroy him. There are fates worse than death."

"And how are we going to destroy him?"

"Roll me to the west window." Danny pushes Howie's wheel chair over to the window and opens the curtains. The brisk west wind is blowing most of the pollution over the Atlantic, providing a clear view of the New Jersey shore. Howie says, "The New Jersey Financial Complex is almost finished. Do you know why Ellsworth Toohey was able to underbid me on that project?"

"No."

"He self-insures all his projects."

"I think I see where this is going."

"I also want to make sure we turn more than fifty million on this. There's one final project I want built after I die."

"I thought you were worth fifty million."

"I only have three million in liquid assets. All my wealth is in the company. I still owe the bank eighty million in loans. I've done some preliminary asking. Without me the company is only worth sixty million. I can't even pay off the loans if I sell. My plan is to give the company to my employees. There are a couple good guys working for me. Hopefully they can make a run of it."

"Bankers, they get everything don't they?"

"I know."

"So is Ellsworth Toohey a bad man?"

"He just chose to sell his soul to the system. Funny isn't it. During the last 2,500 years the Spartans, Romans, Christians, serfs, and Blacks all fought to be free. Now that the whole world is free most people choose to sell their soul for money and to the system."

"What about us?"

"I don't know. Seems like today any man of accomplishment sells a part of his soul with each decision he makes."

"When are we going to do this?"

"Saturday, December 27th. You'll be out of the country. I don't think anything will go wrong. If it does then I'll take all the blame. What are they going to do, execute me? Here's a list of what I want you to do. Memorize it then destroy it. Just like last time only pay cash."

"No problem." Howie hands Danny an envelope with $50,000 in it. Danny looks out the window again and studies the nearly finished New Jersey Financial Complex. He then studies Howie's baldhead, haggard check bones, and swollen forehead from all the chemotherapy. He asks, "You rented this apartment because it had a view of the New Jersey Financial Complex. That means you knew you were going to lose the White Plains Renaissance Project."

Howie smiles and says, "You're getting smarter in your old age. I never wanted to win the White Plains Renaissance Project. That was my Plan B. What I want to leave to the world is my Plan A. That's why I need the fifty million."

"You're always two steps ahead of the game, aren't you?"

"You're on to me."

"But I'm still not as smart as you."

"You will be when I'm pushing up daisy."

Chapter 13: The Revenge of Ellsworth Toohey

"Don't talk like that."

"Relax, I'm the one dying. Remember that summer when we started hanging out together, working on Uncle Joe's lodge? Both of us wanted to be Bobby's best friend. That's because everybody loved Bobby. As I look back on my life I have to say you are definitely my best friend. Life is never what you expect. But it's been a fun ride."

"I'm going to miss you. I might even cry at your funeral."

"Don't do that. Modern men don't cry. Death is just part of doing business."

The following week Danny buys two cell phones using a false name and steals four hundred pounds of plastic explosives from a demolition company in Memphis, Tennessee. Christmas Eve night Danny enters the nearly finished New Jersey Financial Complex through a storm sewer and places explosives at the twenty-two key support points Howie has mapped out. On Christmas Day, Danny catches a plane for the Cayman Islands. On Friday, December 26th, using one of Howie's secret overseas bank accounts, Danny places a $2,000,000 options order to sell short on Ellsworth Toohey's construction company. Danny places the options order with a dark pool, this way no one will be able to track the buyer.

Saturday, December 27th, at 9:05 PM, Howie rolls his wheelchair over to the west window in his Manhattan apartment and opens the curtain. Emotionless, he studies the lights of the New Jersey skyline and how they reflect on the Hudson River. He looks up and dials the detonation cell phone with the other cell phone that Danny has purchased. He then dials the detonation sequence 9 – 7 – 5 – 3 – 1. Moments later the New Jersey Financial Complex implodes. A fine cloud of cement dust rolls over the Hudson River. The glimmering lights on the water of the New Jersey skyline fade to black. Howie then rolls his wheelchair over to the bathroom and flushes the cell phone down the toilet.

Monday, December 29th, at 10:05 AM, Danny uses a dark pool to sell the short options on Ellsworth Toohey' construction company for $57,000,000. He then moves $50,000,000 into Catherine Keaton's secret trust and the other $7,000,000 into another secret trust that Howie has set-up just for Danny.

Chapter 14: The Power of Love?

Destiny is a strange thing. By the middle of January the cancer has spread to two more vital organs in Howie's body. Knowing the fight is now pointless, the doctors agree to stop the chemotherapy. No longer sick from the chemotherapy Howie asks Uncle Joe if he can live out his final days at the lodge in Lords Valley. Uncle Joe says of course.

Friday, January 23rd is one of Howie's good days. He asks Danny to drive him to the Bass Pro Shop in Harrisburg. Howie wants to buy Danny a going away present. Due to popular demand, Diamond has come out with a new Iceman series compound bow called 'The Antagonist'. This offering by Diamond is very controversial and has received a lot of press coverage. But as everyone knows the one thing more powerful than public opinion is the almighty dollar. 'The Antagonist' is Diamond's top seller.

Danny asks Howie on the way to Harrisburg, "Do you think we did the right thing killing those three CEOs?"

"Public opinion is still split down the middle."

"I could care less about public opinion. What do you believe?"

"We did the right thing. There is no such thing as moral hazard. Some people think life is a game and morality is simply the rational for justifying your own actions. Real men understand that life is war. When someone is above the law then you have to do what you have to do."

"I guess that's what war is all about."

Chapter 14: The Power of Love?

"That is what war is all about."

"So what's your biggest regret right now?"

"That I can't be a real Dad to any of my children."

"That has to be tough."

"You have no idea."

Danny says, "If we were women then we'd probably discuss this for hours and hours."

Howie responds, "Bottom-line: It sucks."

"Bottom-line."

To repeat, destiny is a strange thing. Agent Jerry Cruncher from the FBI is planning a fishing trip to Florida in February. The Bass Pro Shop in Harrisburg is a ninety minute drive from his house north of Washington DC. Agent Cruncher has decided to take the afternoon off so he can buy a few new fishing poles for the trip. And as destiny would have it Agent Cruncher is standing in the check out line behind Howie and Danny.

Agent Cruncher is visibly annoyed that Howie and Danny are purchasing 'The Antagonist' compound bow. Then it happens. Howie says, "Danny, I told you this is my treat." Howie reaches into his pocket, pulls out a big wad of bills held together with a gold money clip, flips open the clip, and hands the cashier eleven hundred dollars. Agent Cruncher notices the inscription on the inside of the clip – 'The Antagonist'. He mumbles under his breath, "This can't be him."

Agent Cruncher steps forward and says to the cashier, "Damn it, I left my billfold in the car. Can I set these two fishing poles to the side? I'll be right back."

The cashier replies, "Sure."

Agent Cruncher follows Danny and Howie to their truck. He then quickly walks over to his car and follows Danny and Howie as they drive towards Interstate 81. Cruncher calls his partner at the FBI, Agent Martin. He says, "Can you give me the information on a New York plate DNB 14R6?"

Agent Martin casually replies, "I thought you took the afternoon off."

"I did. I'm just following up on a wild hunch."

"We'll let's see if you hit the lottery. You should be following a black 2005 Ford King Ranch F-150 Super Crew Pickup Truck owned by a Daniel Crocket Roark."

"Holy shit! I remember looking at his file several times when working on 'The Antagonist' case. What else do you have?"

"Interesting. The truck was originally owned by his cousin Robert Edward Roark. Robert is now deceased."

"How'd he die?"

"Bullet to the back of the head. Case is marked as unsolved."

"Can you pull up my Roark file from 'The Antagonist' case?"

"Already ahead of you. The third cousin's name is Howard Holden Roark."

"Can you check his medical records? The guy with this Daniel Crocket looked really ill. Like he had cancer or something. I bet you that's our Howard."

"Bingo. Howard Holden Roark has been treated for cancer the last three months at the Sloan-Kettering Institute."

"Sloan-Kettering? This guy must have money."

"He owns an international architecture firm."

"How old is this Howard?"

"Twenty-eight."

"Kind of young to own your own international architecture firm."

"Kind of young to have cancer."

"Agree."

"Maybe he also blew up the Jersey Financial Complex since he is an architect."

"Maybe."

"Amazing no one died in that explosion."

"Luckily the building wasn't finished yet."

"So how should we proceed?"

"Where are you right now?"

"Heading north on I-81 just outside of Harrisburg."

"They have to be headed towards Scranton. How much gas do you have?"

"Half a tank."

"Good. I'm looking at the map. Let's pull them over just before Wilkes-Barre. There's the perfect place where I-81 splits and makes a

Chapter 14: The Power of Love?

long right. They won't see the roadblock and they won't be able to turn around."

"How long till we get there?"

"Fifty minutes."

"What if they change course?"

"They won't change course. The only thing they might do is pull over for gas. Just follow them and keep talking to me."

Three highway patrol cars and two FBI cars are waiting a mile beyond the bend just outside of Wilkes-Barre. Two other highway patrol cars are hiding behind a grove of trees just waiting to trap Danny and Howie from behind. At 3:21 PM Danny and Howie approach the bend. The state police cars form a roadblock and slowly waive cars by in only the right lane. Danny and Howie round the bend. They see a line of twenty cars and the police roadblock. Danny slows down and gets in line. He looks in his rearview mirror and sees two police cars behind him. He looks at Howie and says, "Shit."

Howie looks in the sideview mirror, sees the two highway patrol cars behind them, and says, "We have to figure out how to get you out of here."

"Maybe they are after somebody else."

"I don't think so. Even if I take the blame they'll hang you for being an accomplice. It's my fault. I should have never bought you that damn compound bow."

"What are we going to do?"

"I'm going to die soon anyway. Luckily the dirt bike is in the back. But how to get you out of here."

"I've got an idea. See that service trail up the mountain to that cell phone tower?"

"Yeah."

"It's below freezing. The ground is hard. The truck will be able to make it across the ditch. I'll need to gun it to make the upslope and break through that fence."

"Then what?"

"I remember my survivalist training. I can live in the woods in the winter."

"Where do you want to get off?"

"At the top of the mountain. I'll turn the truck around. You'll barricade the road and turn yourself in while I get away."

"Better than any plan I can think of. See, you're already smarter than me and I'm not even pushing up daisies."

"You're not going to turn yourself in, are you?"

"I'm going to die anyway. I might as well die like a man."

"Any last words?"

"Not really. Just here's all my money. And here's the key to my secret post office box in the Cayman Islands. As we already discussed, pick-up my mail and complete my will."

"No problem." Danny rests his head on the steering wheel as if to pray. He then says, "Tell Bobby hi for me."

"I will."

"And when you get there, find a nice plot of land with a beautiful view of both heaven and hell. When I get there we'll build ourselves an even better lodge than our fathers. And of course, you will design it."

"Sounds good. Bobby and I will be waiting for you with a bottle of tequila."

Danny looks up and says, "Let's do this. Hold on. It's going to be rough at the bottom of the ditch." Danny waits a moment for the car in front of him to pull forward. He then hits the gas, turns right, crosses the shoulder, and then accelerates down a thirty-foot slope. At the bottom of the ditch the truck slams into the upward slope. Howie hits his forehead into the dash. Danny keeps his foot on the gas. The truck struggles on the ice covered upslope. It starts to lose velocity. Danny keeps his foot on the gas. The truck just manages to break through the fence. The front tires reach the service road and gain traction. Danny doesn't hesitate. He straightens out the truck and speeds up the dirt service road as fast as he can.

The highway patrol and FBI agents are caught completely off guard. The two highway patrol cars behind Danny and Howie drive the wrong way on the shoulder of I-81 for two miles until they reach a place where they can easily get onto the dirt service road. By now Danny and Howie are at the top of the mountain. Next to the cell phone tower is a wide spot in the road. Danny turns the truck around. He quickly unloads the dirt bike and grabs the brand new compound bow. Howie says, "Good luck."

Chapter 14: The Power of Love?

Danny replies, "Good luck to you too and give the Devil hell." With that Danny takes off into the woods.

Howie slides into the drivers seat and looks at himself in the rearview mirror. He sees a weak and frail shell of his former self. He looks at the cut on his forehead and wipes the blood with his sleeve. He closes his eyes and imagines himself five years earlier, hunting with his cousins – strong, healthy, and master of the outdoors. He pulls the truck forward fifty feet to a narrow place in the road. He watches as the two highway patrol cars struggle up the icy dirt road. The highway patrol cars stop fifty feet in front of the truck not knowing what to do. Soon the other eight other law enforcement cars are behind them. Howie cranks the radio to mask the sound of Danny riding away.

Some of the highway patrol officers and FBI agents pull their guns, get out of their cars, and surround Howie, taking positions behind trees. Howie doesn't do a thing other than pretend he is talking to Danny who is laying in the backseat. Howie just sits there, stalling, occasionally turning around, all in an effort to give Danny more time to slip away. One of the highway patrol officers yells, "Come out with your hands up!" Howie just ignores him.

Howie then overhears another officer say, "I'm not killing a guy dying of cancer. That's just wrong. I'm sick and tired of people using the police as a means for suicide."

The law enforcement officers and Howie sit there for more than ten minutes. Finally, one of the highway patrol officers says to his partner, "Wasn't there a dirt bike in the back of the truck?"

Howie says to himself, "If Danny is going to get away then he's most likely gotten away by now." But let's give him a little more time. Just then the 4 Non Blondes song *What's Up* starts playing on the radio. Howie thinks back to the karaoke night when they formed the band *Ambivalent Swag*. With his now much weaker voice Howie sings along, "Twenty-eight years and my life is still, trying to get up that great big hill of hope, for a destination..."

He keeps singing. His voice can no longer hit the high notes when he reaches the line, "And I pray, oh my God do I pray, I pray every single day, for revolution." It's at that moment he starts the truck and drives up on the hood of the first highway patrol car blocking the road, crushing the engine into the front suspension. He backs up and drives on top of the hood again. One of the highway patrol officers opens fire. Howie just laughs. He backs the black 2005 Ford King Ranch F-150 Super Crew Pickup Truck off the front of the car. He maneuvers to the wide part in the trail by the cell phone tower and turns the truck around, as if he is going to make a run for it. The police officers shoot out all four of his tires.

Howie grabs Danny's rifle from the gun rack in the back window. He opens the door, steps out, and points the gun at the FBI agents. He fires one bullet into the ground by an agent's feet. A second later Howie is dead from multiple gunshot wounds.

Danny manages to escape to a cave north of Scranton that he's known about since he was a kid. In one of the largest manhunts in Pennsylvania history Danny somehow manages to avoid being caught. On the second night he kills a deer with his new compound bow and lives off the meat for the next week.

The revelation that Howie is 'The Antagonist' is a gold mine for the cable news networks and the blogosphere. For the psychology experts 'The Antagonist' makes no sense. Why would a successful Ivy League graduate kill three CEOs? They offer a smorgasbord of pop-psychology answers that fall into the standard preconceived narrative of the cable news networks. These answers include too many violent video games, America's consumer culture, a mental disorder, the lack of God in young people's lives, too much stress in our school system, and the ultimate narcistic answer that 'The Antagonist' is the result of a culture saturated with pop-psychology. All these answers have little to do with Howie and everything to do with the experts' favorite topics. None of those psychologists even come close to understanding why Howie did the things that he did. They never even considered the power of love as a motivation.

For over a week 'The Antagonist' is the lead topic on every cable talk show and Internet bulletin board. 'Is 'The Antagonist' a hero or villain?' is every pundit's favorite question that week. Every viewer and every blogger has an opinion and all want to be heard. But there is little progress in the way of understanding among all the loud opinions from the various chattering classes.

Chapter 14: The Power of Love?

There is a lot of speculation on the cable talk shows and blogosphere that Howie is responsible for the destruction of the New Jersey Financial Complex. There is a long FBI investigation, but with no evidence the case is still classified as unsolved. In civil court, Ellsworth Toohey sues for damages, and for ownership of Howie's architectural firm. With the case unsolved, Ellsworth Toohey loses the civil trial. Years later the civil suit is still under appeal.

Danny is one of the 50,000 people that line the route of Howie's funeral procession. As the black hearse passes by where Danny is standing, he looks over the massive crowd and mumbles to himself, "With death the golden boy managed to accomplish the one thing that eluded him his entire life. He is now more loved than Bobby."

Two cars behind the black hearse Danny notices Howie's father, Archie, sitting next to his own dad, Charlie. Archie's eyes are red and tears trickle down his cheeks. It is the first time Danny has ever seen the alpha-male Archie show any sign of emotional weakness. Danny wants to witness the lowering of Howie's casket but with all the FBI agents at the funeral he figures better not to press his luck.

After the funeral Danny catches a bus to Miami. From there he catches a boat to the Cayman Islands. There is only one package in Howie's post office box. Danny opens the box and reads the will. Knowing that the FBI is looking for him Danny decides to lay low for almost a year before heading back to the states. For the next ten months he lives in a small bungalow and slowly but surely withdraws all $7,000,000 from his secret bank account.

On Wednesday, December 23rd, a man with a beard walks into the Borders Bookstore in Scranton and hands a women working the information desk a list of books he would like to purchase. These books include *Bonfire of the Vanities, The Great Gatsby, The Art of War, Roughing It, Hamlet, The Fountainhead, Shane, A Farewell to Arms, A Tale of Two Cities, Moby-Dick, Catcher in the Rye, The Scarlet Letter, Thus Spoke Zarathustra,* and *The Stranger.* Catherine Keating looks up and recognizes Danny. He says, "We need to talk."

Catherine takes an early lunch. They walk to the Applebee's at the Viewmont Mall. After they order Danny hands Catherine a letter. He then gets up and says he is going to the bathroom. Catherine reads the letter.

My Dearest Catherine,

    You taught me that a man is not defined by how he lives or dies but by what he leaves behind. My only regret in life is that I didn't pursue your love more strongly. For my buildings are just empty shells unless there are women like you walking their halls. Only then are they magnificent works of art.
    I'm writing this letter just after our six-hour long conversation just before Christmas. I spilled my heart to you on that day. Thank you for listening. There is nothing more for me to add.
    As my farewell present I leave you the following gift. Using the secret trust I have purchased an old farm seven miles west of Scranton. I have left you the blue prints for a futuristic community development. There are blue prints for the roads and infrastructure. There are blue prints for each house. I've included directions on which construction teams to hire, and a detailed list on what building materials to use. This community is beyond state of the art so make sure you use the construction teams on the list.
    May Pammy, Michaelis, Peter, your sisters, and the rest of your family have a wonderful life.

My Love Burns Eternal,

Howie

    I remember staring at the letter and not knowing what to make of it. I didn't cry. I didn't get angry. I just sat there with an empty feeling. That's why I wrote this book – to clear my head and to figure out what to do next.
    To gain a better understanding into Howie's head I decided to write this book from his point of view, and the point of view of his two cousins. I knew if I wrote the book from my point of view Howie would come off as a selfish, self-absorbed rich kid from Manhattan. I'm still mad at him from the day he told me, "… women have a hard time writing anything original for the same reason they make lousy stand-up comics and scientists. Women have a hard time objectively observing people from an outsiders' point of view. Women always want to write about themselves and how they feel. You know how boring that is." But now I know Howie said that because he loved me and wanted me

Chapter 14: The Power of Love?

to become a better writer. And I did become a better writer. He was my mentor and I never knew it until I wrote this book. And that's what I loved most about Howie. He expected perfection from himself, and he expected everyone around him to push himself or herself to a higher level. The problem with that philosophy is Howie never really understood just how exceptional of an individual he really was. Few men can climb to his intellectual level.

Which leaves me with the question, 'What to do next?' I've been looking at Howie's design for the community of the future. I never cared much about architecture, but I have to admit that his design is amazing. All the roads are underground. You can let your kids run wild on all the hiking and biking trails and never worry about them getting hit by a car. The houses are an ultra-futuristic design where the roofs are grass. Each house has many big glass windows, a deck in the back for family get togethers, and a courtyard and porch in the front so you can hang out front and connect with your neighbors. Each house is so well designed you can't tell where the house stops and nature begins – the indoors and the outdoors seamlessly blend together. Heating is geothermal and there are groups of windmills at two locations in the development that provide for almost all the electricity needs. Bottom line is that the utility bills are almost zero.

But I keep asking myself, "Is Howie just too far ahead of the curve? Why did he ask someone like me to manage the construction of his most amazing design? Why didn't he choose his head architect at his design firm?" I'm still not sure if I'm going to build it. I'm still not sure what I'm going to do with the $50,000,000.

You are probably also wondering what happened to Danny. Here's what I know. After I finish reading Howie's letter Danny returns to our table at Applebee's carrying a small box of notebooks and external computer hard drives. He tells me, "Here's golden boys most amazing design yet."

After we eat Danny walks me back to Borders Bookstore. At the front of the store Danny says, "Good-bye."

Before he can turn around I ask, "Where are you headed?"

Danny looks deep into my eyes and says, "I know I can trust you. I plan to see my mom and half-brother Frederic on Christmas Eve and give them a part of my inheritance. From there I think I'll visit

Argentina. I need some time to think. I'm not a very good student. I'm a little slow so I want to take my time and figure out what it means to be a man in the modern world."

"So you're looking for El Dorado?"

"What does El Dorado have to do with Argentina?"

I fumble through my pocket and pull out the reading list Danny handed me earlier. I read over the list and say, "I thought you missed a book." I lead Danny into the store. We walk over to the classics section. I pull *Candide* from the shelf, hand it to him, and say, "Read this."

Danny smiles and says, "Thanks."

In the classics section I collect the remaining books from Danny's reading list. I smile and say, "Good-bye."

Danny says, "Good luck. Hopefully are paths will cross again once I'm a man."